STOLEN HEIRESS

Joanna Makepeace

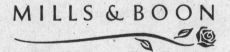

MILLS & BOON

*MILLS & BOON and MILLS & BOON with the Rose Device
are registered trademarks of the publisher.*

*First published in Great Britain 1996
Harlequin Mills & Boon Limited,
Eton House, 18–24 Paradise Road, Richmond, Surrey TW9 1SR*

© Joanna Makepeace 1996

ISBN 0 263 80009 1

*Set in 10 on 11½ pt Linotron Times
04-9701-86419*

*Printed and bound in Great Britain
by BPC Paperbacks Limited, Aylesbury*

CHAPTER ONE

CLARE HOYLAND stood near the glazed window of the solar, looking out over the herb plot. It had snowed three days ago, but there had been a partial thaw and most of the snow had melted. However, last night there had been a hard frost and the remainder had iced over so the brown earth was iron hard. It would be difficult going for the men on this foray.

Clare shrugged her squirrel-lined cloak round her shoulders for it was still cold within the solar, despite the logs burning brightly in the hearth and an extra brazier near the side window. She had put on the cloak for extra warmth, yet perhaps it was her misgiving for this venture which caused her to shiver so violently. In this winter of 1461, who could know what the future would hold?

Certainly the hopes of the Duke of York had foundered at Sandal only weeks ago. Her uncle, Sir Gilbert Hoyland, and her brother, Peter, had crowed over the Lancastrian victory which had given Queen Margaret the day and allowed her the vindictive pleasure of having the unfortunate Duke's head placed high on Micklegate Bar in York and topped with a crude paper crown some wag in her train had made for her. In such a fashion was the Yorkist victory of St Albans overturned and, to Sir Gilbert's and Peter's joy, the death of her father avenged.

Clare could not be glad of these tidings. The wars had continued for so many months now and so many unfortunates slain both in the several battles and skirmishes and also within the constant armed sallies of

5

companies on both sides. She had mourned her father deeply, of course, but nothing could bring him back to them. This useless quarrel with their neighbours, the Devanes, in her estimation, could do no good whatever.

She sighed as she returned to her chair by the fire and leaned forward to warm her chilled hands at the blaze. This latest feud had started in so senseless a fashion: a sucking pig stolen from one of their sties, meant for the final feast of Twelfth Night. Their steward had investigated and determined that one of the men-at-arms from the Devane manor had been responsible.

Certainly there were tales that a roasted pig had been enjoyed by the Devane retainers on the last but one night of the Christmas festivities. A man-at-arms had boasted of the plunder to some village wench and a skirmish had broken out between armed men from both manors. A Hoyland sergeant had died and Sir Gilbert had declared his intention of demanding satisfaction and compensation.

Sir Humphrey Devane had sent back an insulting reply and, early this morning, a company of Hoyland men-at-arms had sallied out, breathing threats of fire and slaughter against their habitual rivals. It was all so pointless. Clare prayed that no other soul paid with his life for such senseless folly, nor any man be badly wounded as a result of this ceaseless wrangling between the manor lords.

She could not believe the Devanes in any way responsible for her father's death at St Albans. The Devanes were declared Yorkists. It was said that the younger son, Robert, served in the train of the Earl of Warwick, cousin to great York. Sir Humphrey and his son, Walter, had fought at St Albans on the Yorkist side but many men had done so. The death of her own father couldn't be laid at their door. But the feuding had continued.

Now, since the Yorkists had been driven from their stronghold of Ludlow Castle by Queen Margaret's force and York's widow, Proud Cecily, taken prisoner with her two youngest sons, the fortunes of the Yorkists had declined and, with the death of York at Sandal near Wakefield, were at their lowest ebb.

Clare could not dismiss the thought that it was this very notion that had prompted her uncle to risk an unprovoked attack upon his neighbour. Sir Humphrey was unlikely to complain to the King's justices, whatever the outcome, as many Yorkists had been proscribed and their estates and property seized by the vengeful Queen.

Throughout Clare's eighteen years of life she had had to listen to her father's, her brother's, and now her uncle's constant carping complaints about their neighbours. She sighed again. Since the death of her mother, almost five years ago, she had been forced to gradually take into her own hands the management of the manor. She knew, well enough, her father had been wealthy enough to harbour no feeling of envy towards the Devanes, whose prosperity could never match their own.

Now Peter, at twenty-one, had inherited and she wondered how soon it would be before he brought a bride home, to oust Clare from her position of authority within the household. It was a moment she both dreaded and welcomed. She would be glad to be rid of the responsibility, for her endeavours were rarely praised by her brother. Since childhood he had bullied and despised his younger sister, resenting the love their father had had for her, and now he made no secret of the fact that he considered her a decided encumbrance.

'Sweet Virgin,' he had declared only last night at supper, 'what is to be done with a plain creature like you? I don't know. With the country in such a state of disarray it will be even more difficult to find a suitable husband for you, and God knows I'm disinclined to provide a dowry for you to become a Bride of Christ.'

Clare had been heartily thankful for that decision. She had no vocation to take the veil, but neither had she any desire to remain on the manor, a poor relation, the butt of Peter's unkindness and either ignored or resented by a new mistress of Peter's choosing.

So far he had made no attempt to seek a wife. The Court had moved from place to place, constantly on the move under the fretful rule of the warlike Queen Margaret and neither she or the saintlike and feeble-minded King Henry showed any inclination to arrange Court alliances.

Peter aimed high, since his wealth entitled him to the hand of some lady from an influential family who could assist him into the counsels of the nobility. For so long as he was prepared to wait, Clare would be expected to manage Hoyland Manor for him competently and without complaint.

Aware that she was not beautiful, not even remotely pretty, Clare seldom bothered to press for elaborate gowns or jewellery and infrequently looked at her reflection in the small ornamental mirror of Italian glass presented to her by her father on her tenth birthday.

In it she had seen that her features were, indeed, unremarkable. Her hair was brown, almost mousey, she thought ruefully, her face oval, but her brows were too dark and heavy and dominated her olive-tinted face. She would have preferred to have had a pink and white complexion like her uncle's daughter, Isabel, whose golden locks and large blue eyes had been greatly admired. Clare's eyes were large and her father had fondly declared them luminous, but were an undistinguished grey.

Peter's dark good looks were attractive to the manor wenches, Clare had noticed, but her own, by comparison, were simply acceptable, though she was not ugly. She possessed some good features; her mouth was wide and generous but she determined her nose too large and not enhanced by the slightest tendency to tilt up at the end. To add to all this, she was over-tall for a woman and gawky, her clumsiness increased by being continually under the critical gaze of her older brother.

Clare stayed huddled near the fire, glad to be alone for a while. She had been busy inspecting the kitchen, buttery and dairy. Soon she must go into the hall and make sure the trestles were being put up in readiness for the evening meal. She hoped the corner she had curtained off would not be required to house any wounded men her uncle brought back with him. She leaned her head back against the padded head-rest of her chair and closed her eyes.

It was good to be here, quiet without the fussy attentions of Bridget, the kitchen wench she had tried to train as a personal maid. The girl was willing but talked incessantly and found it hard to retain instruction from one day to the next.

It was growing dark in the room already and someone would be up shortly to seek her permission to light candles and prickets. She had insisted that the use of them be curtailed somewhat. Recently they had been left burning too long and supplies of mutton fat and tallow were dwindling.

She thought she heard a lone horseman ride into the courtyard, but did not stir. She would know by the number of horsemen and the noise of arrival, the shouts and demands for service, when the raiding party returned. She was more than a little irritated when she heard feet ascending the stairs and Bridget's over-shrill voice calling for leave to enter the solar.

'Mistress Clare, oh, please, Mistress Clare, you must come at once. . .'

Bridget was always easily excited and Clare rose reluctantly. Obviously some domestic crisis demanded her attention. Possibly one of the maids had scalded herself or cut herself in the kitchen.

'What is it, Bridget?' Already she was on her feet and turning towards the door.

It flew open and a panting and tearful Bridget erupted into the room. Behind her, grim-faced and equally short of breath from the hasty climb up the stair, was one of Sir Gilbert's men. The fellow had come with her uncle from his own manor in Northamptonshire and so was not well known to Clare. He stopped in the doorway and hastily ducked his head in an embarrassed gesture of respect.

'Mistress. . .'

She stood stock-still and faced him, as if, already, she knew he brought ill tidings.

'What is it, man? Clearly you have been sent back to me in great haste. Is Sir Gilbert hurt? I have already made preparations in case. . .'

His wide-spaced eyes regarded her steadily, then, meeting her anxious gaze, awkwardly drew away to look well beyond her.

'It's—it's Sir Peter, mistress, he's—' frantically the messenger drew a hard breath '—he's—he's dead, mistress, took an arrow in the gorget. He—he lived only moments. There was nothing anyone could do.'

He waited while the shock of his news registered fully, then he added, 'Sir Gilbert sent me ahead to warn you— let you prepare. There are one or two men slightly wounded and there are—prisoners.' She remained very still, hands clasped tightly before her and he rushed on, 'The raid was successful, mistress. Sir Gilbert bade me tell you the Devanes paid hardly for—for Sir Peter's death.'

She moved at last very slowly towards him. Bridget was sobbing hysterically and Clare said curtly, 'Stop crying, girl. There is much to be done and I shall need you.' Her legs were trembling and resolutely she tightened her back muscles. She must not collapse weakly into her chair. Her uncle would need her to organise the household. There would be time later to grieve.

'Bridget, send one of the grooms for Father Crispin. Go now, quickly, then go into the hall and halt preparations for supper there. A—a trestle must be put up ready—to receive Sir Peter—when—when they bring him home. We shall need two wax candles and the large candlesticks to place at the head and the foot of the trestle and—' Her eyes were blurring with sudden tears and her mind dulling with reaction. She could not think beyond the need to receive her brother's body.

Sweet Virgin, they had all gone out in such haste, on a drunken whim—had he been in a state of grace? He had been so confident that he could wreak havoc at the Devane manor and return with loot—her mind shied from all the ugly realities of the attack. There would be burning and pillage—the Hoylands had been victorious her uncle's messenger had informed her. What did that mean? Had they fired the Devane manorhouse? Had women been subjected to—and Peter dead in the midst of all this wickedness and all unprepared—?

She brushed away tears with the back of her hand as the man turned awkwardly, as if uncertain how to proceed now that his errand was done. Bridget cast her another frightened, startled glance and then scrambled in an undignified rush down the stairs to summon the village priest.

Clare hastily crossed herself and murmured a prayer to the Virgin for the well-being of her brother's soul, then hurried down to the hall. Servants were gabbling excitedly as she entered and then hushed abruptly. She signalled them to continue with their work, then called to Bridget again.

'Has someone gone for Father Crispin?'

'Yes, mistress.'

'Then go into the kitchen and prepare a ewer of warm water, basin and towels.' She blinked back tears again. 'We shall need to wash—Sir Peter, and I shall need fresh clothing for him. See to it.'

The girl sped off again as if relieved to be out of her mistress's presence. A trestle was made ready in the oriel embrasure and covered with an embroidered bed-covering from Sir Peter's chamber. There was no private chapel at the manor—the household used the parish church in the nearby village. Peter would need to remain here, until final preparations could be made to receive his body into the chancel tomb in the church to which her family had made considerable contributions of coin for the last century or more.

They would need to summon a craftsman to create a brass- or an image-maker from Bristol. Her father's tomb on one side of the chancel was still waiting for the completion of his image. Clare knew her mind was grappling with these future problems rather than coping with the immediate feelings she was trying to repress.

Noise came from the courtyard now and she knew the van of the little company was riding in. She nodded to the two serving-men near the prepared trestle as the tall candlesticks were being placed in position, then moved to the screen doors and took up her place at the top of the steps over the undercroft, leading to the hall.

Sir Gilbert Hoyland rode into the courtyard, dismounted and walked stiffly towards her. He was a shorter man than either her father or Peter had been, but formidable looking for all that. He was dark like most of the Hoylands, with craggy features roughened by the wind for he was a soldier and spent much of his time out of doors. He mounted the steps, briskly drawing off his mailed gloves.

'They are bringing him on a horse litter.' He bent to touch her hand and she nodded acknowledgement. He swallowed hard as if uncertain how to say more, then cleared his throat. 'I wish I could have done something, but it was too late for a physician. He—he died very quickly. I think he felt little. . .'

'So your man informed me.' Clare's voice was a little hoarse. 'I—I have sent for the priest. All is prepared. The men will have to eat elsewhere than in the hall tonight. Later, we can arrange for them to bed down—'

'I'll see to all that,' he agreed. 'You're a sensible wench, Clare, thank the Lord. I think,' he added heavily, 'that Peter did not always appreciate that.'

He turned from her to let his gaze dwell on the gathering in the yard below as men came in, some on foot, trailing pikes and bills. Most appeared to be whole, Clare noted, mechanically, though one was being supported by a companion and several were clutching oozing wounds on arms and lower limbs.

The older serving-women she could trust would be able to deal with these minor wounds and refer anything more serious to her later. She had herb lore from her mother and would be competent to deal with most problems. Anything that threatened life or the continued use of the sword arm, or became infected, might have to be left to an apothecary in Leicester she had used on occasions. Her duty now was to tend Peter's body.

At last she saw the horse litter being drawn into the yard from the gatehouse arch and her lips trembled slightly. She could see the outline of the still form covered with a frieze cloak and supported on each side by two men on foot so that it did not slide from the hastily constructed litter of wattle, probably torn from some sheepfold.

Her attention passed briefly from the sombre sight to a pitiful group of prisoners, pushed unceremoniously along from the rear, prodded by the Hoyland men wielding daggers and broadswords. All were staggering, their garments mudstained; one who towered over the rest was walking proudly though obviously inconvenienced by a wound near the thigh, judging from his blood-drenched woollen hose.

He was the tallest man Clare had ever seen, and she was no small woman herself. He was no mere man-at-arms, that was clear, for he carried himself like a king and with a swagger to match. He stumbled and almost fell as a sudden prod from behind jerked him forward close to the litter bearing the dead man. Clare saw him right himself and stand, head high, staring back at the two on the steps.

He had bright hair, she thought, almost red gold. From this distance she could not discern his features clearly, but the very carriage of the head and the haughty movement to stand erect, despite his injury, and the fact that his hands were pinioned behind him, told her that he was used to admiration, probably from other men as well as women.

She drew her gaze from him and moved slightly forward as her brother's body on the wattle hurdle was unhitched from the horse traces and two men moved into position to convey it towards the foot of the hall stair. They managed the awkward passage of stairs with difficulty and, shoulder high, conveyed their lord into the hall through the screen doors.

Clare moved quietly beside the litter while Sir Gilbert went ahead of her, to instruct the men as to the disposition of their burden. He gave thought briefly to his prisoners still waiting below.

'Keep them all securely guarded in the stable,' he snapped. 'As to the red-headed fellow, I'll have the hide of any man who allows him to escape.'

An elderly serving-maid and the frightened Bridget were waiting with the required water and cleaning cloths. Clare motioned away the two men-at-arms who were still hovering over her brother's body. She looked down at him after she had drawn back the covering cloak. At this moment she could not be sure of her own feelings for Peter. There was grief, certainly, and a numbed awareness, an overwhelming pity for the loss of the satisfying life which had stretched before him.

He had had everything to live for, the promise of love and children, a fulfilled life managing the manor and estates. All this had been snatched from him by the dispatch of a single lethal arrow. She could see the broken-off haft still protruding from the gap between his breastplate and gorget. Dispassionately she thought, I shall need a man's strong hand to help me withdraw that before I can begin to lay him out decently.

She could not dismiss the thought that he had deliberately sought this violence which had destroyed him and she shied from the thought that she had not truly loved him. Peter had not been an affectionate brother. Now he was gone and she could not begin yet to worry about what would happen to her now.

Her uncle moved closer to her side and placed a hand upon her arm. She was not sure if this was a clumsy attempt to comfort her, but she turned and acknowledged the gesture with a half-smile.

He said, abruptly, 'Summon your steward and between us we'll get him out of his armour and clothing before you start to prepare the body. Don't concern yourself. I'll deal with the arrow.'

She nodded and the older woman set down her basin of water and hastened off to fetch Master Clements, their steward. He came hastily, ushering in Father Crispin, who was clearly shocked and looked hurriedly around the hall for Clare to give him instructions.

Clare abandoned her brother to the care of her uncle and Master Clements and went to the elderly, frail priest. He listened, wide-eyed, while she explained what she knew of the raid, and nodded with lithe bird-like movements of his head when she told him their needs. Once the body had been laid out he would immediately say the prescribed prayers for the repose of Sir Peter's soul and eventually make the necessary arrangements for burial in the church chancel.

She went about her task of washing and laying out her brother's body with a calm sense of acceptance. She had dismissed Bridget, whose hands were shaking so badly that she had threatened to spill water over all of them. The older woman helped Clare and together, competently, they completed their work, dressing the still form in a clean linen shirt. Then Clare knelt beside her uncle as Father Crispin began to intone the offices for the dead.

Later she went to see that the work of caring for the wounded in the curtained-off section of the hall was proceeding smoothly and efficiently. She was satisfied;

her mother had taught Clare herself and the women of the household well.

They had had ample opportunity to perfect their skills, Clare thought wearily, over the last years when they had needed to deal not only with the minor accidents which occurred about the manor but with the injured men who continually returned to them from the various skirmishes and battles brought about in this jockeying for power between the weak King Henry and his cousin the mighty Plantagenet Duke of York.

York was dead now but his son, Edward of March, would succeed him, backed by the powerful Neville lord, Richard Earl of Warwick, and the struggle would be continued with renewed hatred on both sides.

She was about to withdraw from the hall when her uncle signalled to her.

'There is a special prisoner I would like you to tend personally, or, at least, see to it that he is fit to travel tomorrow or soon after. I intend to send him to Coventry to the King's court there. I've no authority, more's the pity, to deal with the fellow here.'

Clare looked at him curiously and he explained.

'He's Sir Humphrey Devane's younger son, Robert. We took him prisoner after a bitter struggle, but his leg is injured. He could walk well enough but he was losing blood and I don't want him to collapse on me before he reaches Coventry.'

'You intend to demand ransom?' Clare was puzzled. Surely there would be more likelihood of that if the King were not informed. She was only too aware that this private quarrel and the attack on the Devanes could be regarded as unlawful and her uncle could place himself in the wrong by submitting this prisoner for the King's justice. The man might well plead his cause and come from the court the victor.

'No,' her uncle growled and a wolfish expression curled back his upper lip and revealed sharp, predatory white teeth. 'Robert Devane is one of Warwick's whelps, served him as squire. It was unfortunate for him he was present at his father's manor today.

'The fellow is an out-and-out pirate. Since Warwick fled from England with other Yorkist curs and took refuge in Calais with his tail between his legs, he and that scum he calls his followers have been preying on shipping from their stronghold at the port of Calais. I've no doubt Queen Margaret will be delighted to get her hands on this Devane dog and will, doubtless, hang him out of hand.'

Clare moved back, a trifle repelled by the note of vengeful spite she heard in her uncle's tone. She felt slightly sick. She was being requested to see to the tending of this man so that he might recover, only to end his life ignominiously kicking upon the gallows. Nevertheless, it was incumbent upon her to see that their prisoner did not suffer unduly while he remained in their charge.

'Where is he?' she asked curtly, 'I'll see to it myself.'

'Locked in the barn. I'll get my sergeant to show you and remain close to see you protected from insult.' He laughed harshly. 'He cannot harm you, he's too closely watched.'

Clare swallowed. She did not relish her task and her senses were still shocked by Peter's death. She called to her elderly maid. Bridget would be of no use whatever, half-frightened out of her wits by the sight of the Devane prisoners.

Sir Gilbert's sergeant accompanied her to the guarded barn. They had no dungeons at Hoyland. Indeed, the manor was not crenellated, had never received a licence from the King. For almost two centuries, the snug, well-built house of warm yellowed brick had lain protected within the small vale carved out from a stream, a tributary of the River Nene.

The Hoylands had been granted the land by the Conqueror and the house had replaced a wooden one and been gradually added to over the years. Even the violent tumultuous times following the death of King Henry I had not touched the peace of this land lying upon the boundary of Leicester and Northampton shires, until the bitter spirit of envious greed for power and fortune had come with this recent struggle for the Crown.

Clare's father's prisoners, more usually men who had poached unlawfully or been guilty of some wanton, drunken behaviour which had offended their neighbours had been confined briefly within barn or byre to be judged at the manor court. Now, their more noble prisoner had been kept here to await his fate from a more vengeful soul than her father or even Peter would ever have proved.

Even here, at this secluded manor, Clare had heard of the awe and dread in which the Angevin Queen was held, even by her own followers. Henry might be merciful but Margaret held sway in the Lancastrian Court and if this son of the Devanes was held to be guilty of piracy upon the high seas then he would, undoubtedly, receive short shrift and hang.

Two stalwart men-at-arms guarded the barn door. Sir Gilbert's sergeant barked out a quick command and one unlatched it and the two stood back to allow Clare to enter with her escort. The place was gloomy, for the wintry sun, already leaving the darkened sky, had not reached into the interior so Clare advanced cautiously, unable, at first, to see where the prisoner was.

'I shall need some light, ' she told the sergeant. 'Can one of your men fetch me a brand?'

Again an order was barked out and the taller of the two men set out in search of a lighted pitch brand which could be fixed into a sconce on the barn wall.

There was a slight stir and movement of soft hay still strewing the floor, then Clare saw the vague outline of a man rise from a seated position near the wall and push himself upright to face his visitors.

A pleasant, slightly husky voice said, 'Ah, some show of hospitality, at last. I hope Sir Gilbert hasn't the intention of starving his guests. It must be well nigh suppertime.'

The sergeant snapped, 'You, be silent. You'll get fed when and if we feel inclined to do so and certainly not if you're insolent with the mistress of the house who has come to tend your wound.'

'Indeed?' The pleasant voice sounded vaguely curious and Clare thought the man inclined his head towards them as if to view her. Neither could see the other at this stage until the man-at-arms came running and thrust the lighted brand into the hands of his sergeant who turned to fix it into the iron sconce behind him.

Immediately the dim place flared with golden light and Clare saw that her patient was, as she had suspected, the tall red-headed man she had seen limp in earlier behind her brother's bier. He was leaning for support against the wall and, seeing her clearly now for the first time, he gave her a mocking bow. The action cost him dear, for he winced sharply and almost fell forward, losing, momentarily, the support of the roughened stone of the wall behind him.

Clare thought either the wound was more serious than she had first thought and he had lost a great deal of blood, or he had stiffened during his awkward, half-crouched stay on the floor. It was icy cold in the barn and she shivered and pulled her cloak closer around her. Afterwards, she could not have said whether the movement was actually because she was cold or because she had no wish for this man to see her body more clearly.

She stepped nearer and saw the brand light up his face, haloed with flickering gold flares, and touch shimmering sparks from his flaming red hair. She had been unable to guess at the cast of his features when she had seen him first in the courtyard, only that he was tall and seemingly red-headed, now she saw he was incredibly handsome, in a bold, inviting way.

He was laughing, his long lips curling back from white, even teeth, despite the pain he must be feeling, and she felt sudden irritation for the manner of raillery in which he greeted her.

'An angel of mercy. By the sweet Virgin, you are welcome, mistress.'

'You had better sit down on the ground again and let me examine your leg,' she said curtly. 'By the look of you, you'll collapse very soon if you don't.'

The older serving wench who had come up behind them with her basin and ewer of water came into the barn now to join her mistress, impatiently pushing aside the importunate movements of the second, smaller manat-arms who had jostled her good-humouredly and much too familiarly for her liking.

'You,' she said, icily, 'can make yourself useful, which I think is rare. Idle fellows, all of you, unless you be killing and looting and bothering females who want no truck with you. We'll want a shirt to tear for bandaging, a clean one, mind. Get on with you. My mistress'll not want to be here all night.'

The sergeant nodded his approval of the errand and

the man, still grinning, despite the tongue lashing, sidled off to find what was wanted.

Clare had knelt beside the injured man and bent to look more closely at the blood-soaked hose. He lowered his head to follow her gaze and his hand brushed against hers as she touched experimentally the stiffening wool. She snatched her hand away almost instantly and his merry laugh rang out again.

'Faith, mistress, you've not hurt me yet. I can stand the touch of such fair hands.'

She gritted her teeth. 'I am in no mood for mockery, sir,' she reproved him. 'My brother lies dead in the great hall.'

'And mine and my father in the ruins of ours,' he responded quietly, and there was no glimmer of humour now in the grave tones.

She looked up at him sharply and his mouth tightened, the laughter lines quirking his lips, fading. She saw now that he was not, indeed, as classically handsome as she had first thought. The attractiveness of the countenance lay rather in the openness and pleasant joviality of demeanour.

His mouth was long and generous, though now held tightly as he considered the ruin of family and home. A very slight scar at one corner marred the beauty of form, though Clare thought, when he smiled, as she guessed he did often, that that slight deformity would quirk up those mobile lips becomingly.

His eyes glittered in the uncertain glow of the brand and were startlingly blue, flecked with greenish lights. Clare possessed a lump of turquoise her father had bought for her once at Leicester Fair, which he had had enclosed in gold for her and which now hung from the end of a favourite girdle. The colour of those eyes of his were like the changing hue of the stone, now glinting steely and hard, narrowed in considered grief for those he had lost.

His nose was dominating and the small bump on the bridge which spoilt its line spoke of some blow he had possibly received from an opponent in a bout of fisti-cuffs. He was square jawed, the chin deep split in a dimpled cleft. Yes, Clare thought, women would find this man overwhelmingly attractive and men, too, would admire the manly clean lines of that face and the rangy, hard-muscled strength of that tall form.

'I am sorry for your loss, sir, ' she said softly, and instantly he smiled again, though she thought it more wintry this time, less winning.

He gave the slightest of shrugs. 'Men have often said war is hell, ' he said briefly, 'though I would not describe this attack as war, merely an unprovoked raid which had unfortunate consequences for all concerned.'

She realised he was totally unarmed, dressed in a shirt of homespun linsey woolsey and a leathern jerkin over grey woollen hose. Clearly the Devane household had not expected an attack and had been seated comfortably by their own hearths when the alarm had been sounded by their watchman on the gatehouse. Probably this man, Robert Devane, had only recently returned from a ride or inspection of the manor land, for he was wearing riding boots. Her own brother and uncle had been well armoured and prepared, in breastplates and gorgets over padded gambesons.

She gave the faintest of sighs and felt Sir Gilbert's sergeant move restlessly behind her. The man was clearly impatient for her to complete her task so that he might lock up his valuable prisoner for the night, confident of his safe keeping until the morning. Sir Gilbert, she knew, was not the man to overlook any negligence in his subordinates. The man her maid had despatched had come back now with a patched but clean shirt of homespun and the woman hastily snatched it from his grasp.

Clare turned to the sergeant behind her. 'We shall be quite safe with this man, since I know you will keep a close guard outside. I shall need more room for my work. Leave us, please.'

The man was obviously unwilling. He pursed his lips uncertainly, having received careful instructions from Sir Gilbert to keep a careful watch on his niece but her hard stare was insistent that he obey her and she could come to no harm surely with his men so near, ready to be summoned instantly, should she have need of them. He grimaced in disapproval but made her a respectful nod and withdrew.

The turquoise eyes of the prisoner danced in amusement. 'You appear to have a way with underlings, mistress. Did you, perhaps, wish to be alone with me?'

She darted him a glance of withering scorn. 'I cannot imagine, sir, why you should think I might have such a purpose. I never enjoy the company of piratical scum, for such I hear you are. As I explained to my sergeant, I need room for my task. Now, let us get on with it without delay.'

He had slid back into a sitting position against the wall now and was regarding her coolly.

'So you have received instructions to patch me up fairly, so Sir Gilbert can hang me tomorrow in full view of his men, without fear of being accused of having his men forced to half carry me to the gallows.'

She said evenly, 'I understand you are to be conveyed to Coventry when you are fit to travel, sir. There will be no unlawful trial here. The King himself will decide your fate after a fair hearing.'

'And that she-wolf Margaret will determine the way

of it.' His blue eyes had narrowed again. She noted he had long curling lashes tipped with gold like a maid's.

With the maid's help she withdrew his left riding boot.

She was bending close now over the injured limb, seated upon the ground before him, her box of unguents and medical requirements opened before her, and her maid was pouring water into the basin.

Clare took the small pair of scissors that hung at her belt and were used normally for her embroidery, to cut open the bloodstained wool of his hose and reveal the gaping wound, long and deep, clearly made by a sword thrust. It ran from the knee slantwise almost to the ankle and she made a little moue of concern at the sight of it.

'I'm afraid this will hurt, but I think it should be stitched.'

Again he gave that half-rueful shrug which she took to be permission to proceed and she motioned her servant forward. He made no sound while she washed and cleansed the wound, nor did he comment when she took her sharpest and finest steel needle and finest linen thread and made ready to draw the puckered edges together. First she had cleansed the wound thoroughly with a herbal infusion and rubbed in tansy ointment.

His lips tightened as he leaned back against the wall and she glanced mutely up at him to signal that she intended to begin the painful process of stitching the wound. He nodded, his lips parting in a faint smile, but she read apprehension in his eyes. She had watched her mother perform this service several times and had heard the cries and seen the struggles of men held down by companions who had needed such treatment.

She wondered briefly if she could call the sergeant from outside to steady her patient but she caught his expression and the almost imperceptible nod of his chin and she bent to her task. He made little fuss, with only one or two faint catches of breath, but she knew she had pained him. When it was over and she had padded the wound and bound the improvised bandage into place, she saw him lean back again, his body sagging a little as relief had its way.

'Dorcas, go to the buttery and fetch me some brandy wine and also a bottle of burgundy. This man has lost a deal of blood and needs to make it up. Keep the bottles beneath your cloak. I do not wish the men outside to see what you bring.'

Dorcas nodded and bustled out with the basin and jug of now-bloodied water.

Blue green eyes regarded Clare steadily. 'I see you intend to ensure that I am fit to travel tomorrow,' he said mockingly.

'You will not want to faint in the saddle, I'm sure, sir,' she retorted.

'But you are cossetting me. I hardly think your uncle would approve of your providing me with good wine. Bread and water is all I'm like to receive from the guards out there. Is it that you think I should enjoy some last comforts before I die?'

'I think,' she said quietly, 'that you should consider seriously your crimes and what has brought us all to this, especially your dead kin and mine.'

The green blue eyes flashed dangerously. 'You think I do not grieve because I do not weep?' he demanded harshly. 'As for the cause of all this, don't you think the price was over-high for the value of one small sucking pig?'

She sucked in breath. He had put into words too closely her own view of the matter and she could find no words with which to answer him. Then she recovered somewhat and said stiffly, 'My uncle says you are indeed guilty of piracy. Is that true? Did you prey upon shipping and harm women and innocent travellers?'

Amusement lit up his features again and she knew instinctively that he used this show of raillery to hide the true depths of his grief. 'Women rarely complain of my treatment of them.'

She coloured hotly. He had a way of making her acutely embarrassed yet he was her prisoner.

'Nevertheless. . .'

'Nevertheless, this quarrel between princes is no fault of mine. I serve my master, my lord Earl of Warwick, as your father and brother—and your uncle—served the King. The Yorkist lords were forced to flee to Calais after treachery brought down the castle at Ludlow. Calais is in the control of my lord Earl but hunger and shortage of supplies could well have forced him out. We attacked Lancastrian shipping merely to survive.'

'I doubt if the King will see it that way,' she said drily and he lifted his shoulders and let them fall again as if in acceptance of the inevitable.

She said uncomfortably, 'This struggle for power between the royal houses gives us all cause for grief.'

'And makes many rich and yet more powerful.'

'Is that what you wanted, riches, land?'

His eyes opened very wide. 'I am—was—' he corrected himself '—a younger son. I needed to make my own way. That was not a problem for your brother, as the only son.'

Her lips trembled. 'He has naught now but a final resting place, as have your kin—and is it worth it all?' The last few words were bitterly spoken.

He sighed. 'It seems I shall have little time to repine. Naturally I would have liked to win my spurs but, as you say, in the end it matters little.'

'But why should you support York? The King is God's anointed.'

His expression became serious. 'The Duke of York has, surely, the better claim. Remember the House of Lancaster acquired the throne by the usurpation of King Harry IV and the murder of the anointed King, Richard II. The Duke of York's grandmother, Anne, was daughter of an older son than Henry of Lancaster, old Gaunt, Lionel of Clarence.'

He held up a hand to check her outburst. 'I know that is all long past, and York would have accepted that, I believe, had he been treated fairly. He was not supported in the French Wars. The Queen has ever gainsaid him in council and the King, God bless him, as we all know, is often unfit to rule. Last year's Act of Accord settled in October allowed the right to rule to the end of his life for the King but gave the succession to York and his heirs. Was that not a fair enough settlement after years of discord?'

'But the Queen was not going to stand by and allow her son to be disinherited,' Clare rejoined hotly. 'Would any mother agree to such a settlement?'

He smiled again. 'I see you would prove a veritable vixen of a mother and stand by your cubs to the death.'

She went white to the lips. Peter's often declared taunts that she would be unlikely to wed and have children rang in her memory and she turned away. Wearily she stood up, after packing away her pots of unguents and the implements used in treatment into the small box she kept for the purpose.

'What I would do is of no matter, it is what the King will decide about you. I am sorry for your predicament and even sorrier that a foolish brawl in the village should have brought us all to this but you are my uncle's prisoner, sir, and I can but do my best to ease your pain and—' she hesitated as Dorcas hastened in with the two skin bottles of wine, which she withdrew from the cover of her frieze cloak '—and I promise I will pray for the repose of the souls of all who died today—and for you.'

Gratefully he took from Dorcas's hand a wooden drinking cup of brandy-wine and drained it, for there was a whitish line about his lips which spoke to Clare eloquently of the suffering he would not openly acknowledge.

'Thank you, mistress, and I will pray for you.' He raised the cup as if in a toast and angrily she turned and hastened out of the barn into the cold darkling gloom of the courtyard. She was conscious that her eyes pricked with tears, whether of irritation for that final act of bravado or for distress at his danger—for he was a young man, as Peter had been, on the threshhold of life, and doomed so soon to die—she could not be sure.

Clare took a hasty supper in the solar, wishing to return very quickly to her vigil by her brother's body, so she was somewhat annoyed when her uncle joined her there and brusquely ordered food to be brought for him too. She did not wish to talk to him. She was too confused, her emotions disturbed. Peter's death had been too violent and too sudden for her to have come to terms with it yet and there was the question of Robert Devane, languishing under guard in the barn.

Sir Gilbert said without preamble, 'I wanted to ask you what you thought of young Devane's condition. Will he be fit to travel tomorrow under guard?'

She hesitated. 'The wound is deep and he has lost a considerable amount of blood. I should see him again in the morning before I decide how to answer that question.'

He grunted and carved a slice of meat for himself

nodding to one of the kitchen boys who waited to pour wine for him. 'You can go, boy. I can manage.'

Clare pushed her own plate away impatiently. She had no appetite and had had to force herself to eat. She made to stand up but he reached across the table, taking her hand to prevent her and indicating she should be seated again.

'There's no haste for you to dash back to the bier. Father Crispin can manage alone for a while and there will be a constant watch made, I promise you. You'll need to take some rest. All this has been a great shock to you.'

She sank down again reluctantly. 'I have faced such blows before, uncle. There will be a great deal of arrangements. . .'

'I've seen to most of them. The men have been fed and bedded down for the night. I'll dispatch a small company to Coventry tomorrow with the prisoner. That will take some of the men off our hands for a while. The rest will be occupied in tidying up at the Devane manor.'

'I have been meaning to talk to you about that. I wish the Devane father and son to be decently laid to rest within the churchyard and masses said for the repose of their souls. It is our responsibility,' she said firmly, 'since Robert Devane will not be able to see to it himself.'

Sir Gilbert grunted again and waved a hand testily. 'Very well, I'll speak to Father Crispin about the matter and send over some woman to lay out the bodies and men to arrange for their safe bestowal. The bodies of the men-at-arms have been already gathered and. . .' He broke off and avoided her gaze. 'You will not have to worry yourself about any of them.'

She nodded. Her throat was very tight from unshed tears and she was finding it difficult to frame words, but as he rose to leave her she said, 'Is it necessary to send

Robert Devane to Coventry? Surely there can be no more trouble from that quarter now that his father is dead? The King will decide the disposal of the manor, since Yorkist lands have been proscribed. Out of Christian charity, Uncle, can we not let the man go?'

'And allow him to return and threaten our peace? Nay, niece, you do not understand the way of these things. The Devanes have been thorns in our flesh for two or three decades. Now we have the means of scotching their hopes once and for all, we would be fools to lose the opportunity. Besides, have you thought that your future must be secured? I cannot be with you constantly. My place will be near his grace the King. Hoyland is yours now and its safety must be assured.'

She had not considered that. She made to protest but he was already striding out of the room and she heard the ring of his spurs on the stone steps outside.

He was right. She was tired, her reserves drained totally. She had done her best for the prisoner, pleaded his cause, but she knew her will was not strong enough to withstand her uncle's. Doubtless the King would appoint him her legal guardian and she must be guided by him, as she had been by Peter. She sighed. He had mentioned her future. It might be very grim indeed.

Peter would never bring a bride here, as she had feared, but what prospects were there for Clare? While the war continued, the King and Queen would be far too occupied to concern themselves with her problems. She must depend on her uncle's goodwill and—just now, it would be unwise to antagonise him further as to the fate of Robert Devane, pity the man though she did.

Robert Devane half lay, half sat against the back wall of the barn. He moved his aching leg restlessly and cursed beneath his breath. The woman had certainly made a fair job of her stitchery but the wound still pained him like the fires of hell. The wine had strengthened him. He no longer felt likely to faint, a condition which had unnerved him.

Sir Gilbert's men had brought him stale rye bread and water as he had expected and he had laughed silently in the darkness, thinking of the bottle of good wine hidden beneath the straw on the barn floor. The girl had been shrewish—what would you expect of that cursed Hoyland blood?—but she'd been charitable enough to see his need.

He grunted as he eased himself into a more comfortable posture and reviewed his situation. This was a pretty coil indeed. He'd been taken unprepared with hardly time to seize a weapon and the manor had fallen with scarcely a fight. If the girl was correct, his chances of extricating himself from this threatened fate were slim indeed. And yet—

He stiffened as he heard the stealthy rustling outside. The silence had been profound out there for a good hour or so. He knew the barn door was securely latched and two men left on guard. The rest of Sir Gilbert's men, apparently, were already bedded down in the surrounding outhouses. He had heard them carousing and boasting of their conquests for several hours before that. He shuffled up into a sitting position and waited, all his senses upon the alert.

A hoarse whisper came from the slim line of light as the door was cautiously pushed partially open.

'Messire Rob, are you in there?'

Rob smothered a half-laugh and shuffled himself upright, standing awkwardly on his good leg.

'Come in, come in, Piers. I wondered just how long it would take you to find me.'

His visitor advanced softly with all the grace of a cat

into the darkness of the barn. Behind him, Rob could glimpse a fire in the courtyard where the men had caroused earlier flickering only faintly, already dying down.

The man said in that curious harsh voice, accented as only one to whom English was not his native tongue would use, 'We've disposed of the two guards, Messire Rob. *Sacré nom*, but we cannot take on the accursed company. Silas waits near the gatehouse. I sent him back and told him to stay well hidden.' He bent and looked at the leg Rob held awkwardly. 'Is it that you are wounded? Can you walk. . .?'

'I'll walk,' Rob promised grimly. 'Get me out of here as soon as you can.'

The other put a supporting arm round his shoulder. He panted as the two moved cautiously out of the barn, '*Messire*, we arrived at the manor too late to. . .'

'I know that, old friend. I cannot linger now to do what is right for my father and brother. If we stay, we shall all of us be taken and pay the price of serving the wrong master.' He laughed grimly and softly. 'Give me a dagger, Piers. If need be, I'll defend myself, at least.'

The other muttered beneath his breath, 'The two here will give no trouble, *messire*, and the rest sound too besotted with wine to rouse. We must climb the wall, dare not go by the gatehouse, but. . .'

'I'll manage.' Robert limped forward in grim determination after bestowing the dagger Piers gave him safely under his belt. He turned to give one final glimpse at the dark bulk of the manor house. 'I will be back, mistress,' he murmured softly. 'The Devanes do not give up so easily that which they have held for centuries—and, by the Virgin, there must be a reckoning.'

CHAPTER TWO

CLARE returned from the church with Bridget the day following her brother's funeral to find her uncle waiting for her in the hall. He turned from the hearth as she entered and she saw that he was frowning slightly, as if in deep thought.

'Is something wrong?' she asked as she came quickly to join him, holding out her chilled hands to the blaze. 'You look worried.'

'I've had a courier arrive from London and feel I should leave early tomorrow. There are matters decided in Council which might need my attention.'

She seated herself in the chair and leaned forward, staring into the cheerful flames which sent the shadows in the hall dancing, for the day was again a grey one and there was little light in the place. She felt chilled to the bone, for she had spent over an hour kneeling on the cold stone before the altar praying for her brother's soul and those others who had died in the attack on the Devane manor.

Sir Gilbert turned to dismiss Bridget, who hovered in the doorway waiting for orders, and moved about a trifle fretfully until the girl had gone. He rubbed his hands together distractedly and Clare could see he still had something disturbing him.

'You must go,' she said mildly. 'It is your duty. I shall be safe here. As you said, any reprisal would be slow in coming since the defending force at the Devane Manor has been decimated. It will take time for Robert Devane to muster any household sufficient even to repair the damage, let alone lead a force against us. In any case, the man is on the run and unlikely to be able to complain about the summary justice meted out to his family'.

She recalled again her uncle's fury directed against the two guards left on duty outside the barn when he discovered his important prisoner had escaped.

'I'll hang the pair of them,' he'd stormed. 'Aye, and the drunken sots in the stables who, apparently, were so gone in ale that they heard nothing. God's teeth, how could it have been managed? Devane *had* to have help. The two guards were struck down. His friends must have climbed the wall and got him clean away. That couldn't have been easy if the fellow's wound was as bad as you said. It was sheer negligence, the result of over-indulgence following their too-easy victory. I should hang and thrash a few to encourage the rest to remember their duties in future.'

Clare had patiently pleaded for the injured guards. Both were nursing sore heads. One had been very dazed indeed—she had wondered if he had suffered some permanent damage to the brain from the severe blow to the back of his head that he had taken from the rescuers, whoever they had been. Neither man could be blamed. Their attackers had obviously come silently and stealthily. They had accomplished their purpose and fled immediately into the night with the prisoner and Clare, for one, had been thankful.

There had been more than enough violence and death over the last few days to wish not to add to the score the Devanes would have cause to settle. Privately she had been thankful that the cheery red-headed prisoner had escaped the rope. Her uncle, though still seething, had calmed down after a while and granted the two threatened men clemency.

But he had made his anger known pithily and the

sergeant had seen to it that no one in the household repeated the offence of negligence and the manor had been restored to a seeming normality—if it could ever be again when its young master lay coffined, awaiting burial.

There had been so much to be done over the past days that she had not allowed herself to think about the time when she would be left alone on the manor, unprotected. Now the moment had come upon her all too soon.

Her uncle was still restlessly prowling the room. Abruptly he stopped and faced her, his thumbs thrust into his sword belt.

'You realise, Clare, that your position here has changed dramatically. You are now a very wealthy heiress and your prospects considerably improved, as, also, your possible danger.'

She stared at him incredulously. 'I had not thought...'

'There are men who will now covet your fortune, men who would stoop to take advantage of your vulnerability. It would be impracticable to leave you here, even with a garrison of my own choosing.'

She waited for his decision, a little breathless with dread. Did he wish her to go to his own manor in Northamptonshire? If so, her role would not be much changed from the one she had envisaged as poor relation to Peter and his wife. Sir Gilbert's lady, her aunt, would not welcome her, especially since she was now to be sought after in marriage and Sir Gilbert's own daughters, her two cousins, whom she rarely met, would feel likely to be in competition with her for suitors.

No. She straightened her shoulders determinedly. She would not go. Life there would be insupportable and she would not have it thrust upon her.

'I have decided to place you under the protection of

the Queen,' he announced. 'Margaret will welcome you as an attendant, and at Court you will have opportunity to see and be seen by suitable suitors. In arranging a marriage for you, the Queen would find some advantage as she could, in this way, cement the loyalty of the successful candidate for your hand, to say nothing of other suitors who would be anxious to secure her goodwill.

'We cannot leave you now without royal protection. The country is in such disarray that it would be unwise to trust to even a loyal garrison here. Fortunately Margaret has established Court at Coventry so your journey there in this inclement weather will not be too difficult. I can escort you part of the way south when I leave tomorrow.'

'You expect me to leave tomorrow?' Clare rose in her chair in alarm. 'But, Uncle, I am all unprepared and there are still arrangements to be made concerning Peter's tomb and. . .'

He waved a hand, dismissing her argument. 'All that can wait. Times are out of joint, Clare. We must take decisions hurriedly and act on them. You can take that girl Bridget and necessities can be packed tonight. Later, your clothing chests can be sent on to you. At present you will require only your mourning gowns.'

'But don't you see, Uncle, that my very state of mourning makes this journey and the possibilities you speak of quite out of the question? I should remain here quietly until I feel more settled and. . .'

He came towards her and she saw his mouth harden into an obstinate line. 'I have already explained, Clare, that we must act quickly. In better times there would have been a need for longer reflection but these are not better times. Once my business in London is completed I shall return to my own household to see to their defences. You must do what I say. I'll not accept any argument. Now go up, there's a good wench, and see to your packing. You've always had practical common sense and I know I can rely on you to see the need for haste.'

She turned back to the fire, avoiding his dominating stare. She wanted to protest vehemently. She was bemused, shocked, as she had pleaded, she felt the need for a period of quiet contemplation here, but her change of circumstance had come so suddenly and at such a difficult time that she had to admit that what he was saying made sense.

She sighed, and rose reluctantly. Would Queen Margaret prove as unpleasant and demanding a guardian as Peter had often proved himself? Fervently she prayed that this would not prove the case.

Bridget chattered excitedly all through their hurried preparations. She had heard the rumour that her mistress was to be presented at Court and her head was quite turned by the prospect of the grandeur this evoked. Clare, who would much rather the girl had not been informed about the purpose of the journey, or, at least, not yet, was irritated beyond reason. Several times she was tempted to slap the girl, who would not concentrate on the task in hand and, repeatedly, tried to press Clare to take some more colourful gowns.

'Bridget,' she snapped finally. 'Will you be silent! You are making my head ache. Of course we cannot appear in such gawdy clothing, when Sir Peter has only just, yesterday, been placed in his tomb. Now hurry up. Pack exactly what I say and nothing else. See you have everything you will need for a protracted stay, for we cannot return for anything once we begin the journey.'

She would have much rather relied on the services of one of the more sensible elder women, but they were all married and she could not insist that they leave husbands and family to follow her so many miles from their homes.

Once the novelty of the idea wore off and Bridget discovered that living at Court was most likely much more uncomfortable and cramped than living at Hoyland, she would probably calm down. There was no help for it. Bridget was the only serving maid who could be spared and Clare would have to try to lick her into shape. At least she was a reasonable needlewoman, which ran in her favour.

She dismissed Bridget at last and sat down for a welcome moment of peace. Since Christmas there had been nothing but alarums in this house and very soon she would be leaving it. She had never been farther afield than Leicester Town and those visits had been rare.

She loved the old manor house and wondered, sadly, how long it would be before she would be able to return to it. Possibly, never. Only too well she knew it likely that the Queen would choose for her some Court official who would most likely not wish to live in the wilds of Leicester shire.

She peered at her features in her mirror. Fortunately it was portable. She would need it at Court. Her reflection swam mistily back at her. Her mourning gown certainly did not enhance her appearance, for black did nothing for her rather olive-tinted complexion or bring out the luminosity of her grey eyes. Sorrow had etched lines of tension round her nose and mouth and there were purple shadows round her eyes.

She looked much older than her eighteen years, she decided. She made a wry gesture of distaste. It was not a comforting thought that now she would be sought in marriage for the value of her lands and dower chests—

and yet—it could not be denied that the prospect of marriage and children, a household of her own, was preferable to the dull fate she had seen in store for her only days ago.

She had no wish to be embroiled in Court intrigue. She had taxed Robert Devane with disloyalty to his sovereign in his championship of the late Duke of York and his son, the Earl of March, who must now, she thought, be accepted as the new Duke now that his father was dead following the battle of Sandal. Robert had assured her that his loyalty was to his own master, the Earl of Warwick, and he had made a convincing enough case for the succession of the Duke of York to the throne.

Even her own father, a firm supporter of the House of Lancaster, had been driven to exclaim at the inept rule of the kind but erratic King Henry.

Bouts of withdrawal from reality bordering on madness had made him more than once unfit to reign and Clare knew that her uncle's strategy in placing her in the control of his consort, the warlike Queen Margaret, was the correct one.

Henry could not be relied upon to protect Clare's interests as the Queen would do. Margaret would recognise the advantages to be gained by such a guardianship. Clare bit her lip thoughtfully. She also knew Margaret was arrogant and merciless. The cruel treatment meted out to the survivors of Sandal had revealed the ruthless streak in her nature. Warwick's father, Salisbury, had been executed after the battle.

Once Clare's father's natural caution in gossiping about the nobility had lapsed and he had let it slip that many folk at Court believed Margaret's son, young Edward, was not indeed the true son of the King. Since Henry was known to be unworldly and, in true saintlike fashion, frequently absented himself from his wife's bed, it was likely enough that such scurrilous gossip would readily be accepted. Clare could not imagine herself enjoying her stay at the Lancastrian Court.

She slept uneasily, her thoughts strangely haunted by the face of Robert Devane and pictures of the ruined house and the bodies of the two slain men. She had seen to it that her uncle had kept his word. Sir Humphrey and his elder son, Walter, had been reverently interred within the village churchyard. The surviving prisoners whom Sir Gilbert had brought to Hoyland had been released and allowed to disperse. Only a skeleton household remained now at the Devane manor and it would be left to the King to decide whether the property should now be sequestered.

The morning dawned fair but still very cold and frosty. Clare breakfasted early within her own chamber and then stood, warmly cloaked and hooded, by her uncle's side at the top of the house steps, watching the sumpter mules being loaded. Later, mounted upon her palfrey, she turned once to gaze back at the house as, with her escort of Hoyland men, she rode out under the gatehouse.

Sir Gilbert seemed wrapped in his own thoughts as he rode beside her and was uncommunicative. Clare wondered if he had received bad news from the London courier but she did not press him for information about that or for details of the Queen's coterie. She considered, wryly, that she did not really want to know. When she arrived and was established at Coventry would be quite soon enough.

Bridget rode pillion behind one of Sir Gilbert's men and, even from her place at the rear of the cavalcade, Clare could hear her chattering away excitedly.

At Lutterworth, Sir Gilbert took his leave of his niece, taking the old Roman Watling Street south to London, while Clare's now smaller escort of six men-at-arms was to proceed on towards the village of Brinklow and finally Coventry. Sir Gilbert embraced her warmly on parting, but Clare could see his thoughts were still elsewhere. He assured her she had only to send a message to his manor if she had need of his help or advice. Then without further delay, he rode off with the rest of his men.

Clare felt bereft as she hesitatingly gave her hastily promoted sergeant the order to set off again. She had seen little of her father's younger brother, but when they had met he had always been kind and, once or twice, had supported her when her brother had been deliberately cruel in his verbal attacks on her.

She felt very alone and glanced briefly at the still-chattering Bridget, then sighed. She could expect little help from that quarter. How she longed for the brusque kindness of her old wetnurse, who had unfortunately died only last Martinmas.

These were not her own men and had been given instructions to report to Sir Gilbert when they had seen her safely to Coventry. She was thankful that a messenger had been sent ahead to announce her coming—at least she would not arrive unexpectedly, which would have proved a distinct embarrassment. As she rode, she found herself trying to imagine just how the Queen would greet her. Somehow, she could not dismiss the notion that she would be unwelcome.

Queen Margaret had too much to concern her in dealing with the Yorkist lords—in particular the youthful Edward, Earl of March, the Rose of Rouen, as he had been aptly named, both for his birthplace and his exceptional physical beauty—to want to bother with a new lady in waiting who was recently bereaved and in need of eligible suitors, who would have to be persuaded to offer for her hand in marriage, however wealthy her inheritance.

'The wound's clean, Master Robert, and closing nicely. Mistress Hoyland did a fair job.'

Margery Lightbody got up from her kneeling position by his stool and bent to collect the basin and the pot of salve she had been using to dress Robert Devane's leg.

She stretched, putting a hand to her aching back.

'You should be well enough to begin the ride to London tomorrow, but heed my words, take it easy. The stitching was well done, but you could still burst them by riding hard. We don't want the wound to start oozing pus, do we?'

'No, we don't,' Robert mimicked her domineering tone and grinned back at her.

Margery was a good soul, but beauty and charm had eluded her when the good God had created her. She was one of his father's most loyal servants, having been born to service at Devane Manor, and Robert valued her as had all the members of his family. Margery had been a younger nursemaid who had chased after him when he had toddled and his wetnurse had been too fat and wheezy to do so.

He had seen little of her lately since his stay in Calais, had not known of her marriage to Will Lightbody, but he was always glad to see her. Now that Will was gone — cut down in the attack on the manor—and though concerned for her safety, Rob had protested when she had joined the little knot of retainers determined to follow him in his flight from the district, but he had given way at last. Margery was not to be gainsaid.

She was a big, raw-boned woman, solemn of features

and surly of tongue, but he knew her to be worth her solid weight in gold. She pushed impatiently at straggles of dark hair which had escaped from her cap and gazed moodily out of the unglazed window.

It had been Margery who had suggested the weary little band should rest up here in the old foresters' hut where her grandfather had once lived. Not far from Lutterworth, the place, deserted for years since the old man's death, was well hidden by forest scrub. It was a convenient hiding place for the needed respite, close to the London road that Rob was determined to take the moment he was recovered enough to ride.

The two were alone together in the dark and cold little hut, the other members of the band out looking for game for the pot. Margery had managed to get a sulky fire of sorts going beneath the one smoke hole, but the air in the hut was fouled by the smoke that remained in the place and it was still deadly cold. At least it had prevented them all from freezing to death throughout the three nights that they had stayed here.

Rob grinned at Margery as she moved to stir the small hanging pot over the fire. What in the Virgin's name she had in it, he dared not think, probably herbs and roots sufficient to keep them alive and warmed. Her scolding tongue had hustled out the hunting party to search for a hare or pigeon. She'd had the forethought to bring the pot and other necessities like her herbs and salves in her flight from her home.

His grin faded as he thought how her practicality might well have deserted her. She had remained grim-lipped and uncommunicative about what had befallen her after the attack, but he had drawn his own conclusions. He turned from her now to draw up his hose and tie his points. Margery might not be as gentle in touch as Mistress Hoyland nor as skilful, but at least she wasn't determined to hand him over to those who would see him swing at a rope's end. No, he could not refuse her protection.

The men had been warned, on peril of their lives, to leave her unmolested; Rob grinned inwardly as he considered any man brave indeed who would even accost her. They had watched her warily as she had stolidly tramped the frost-hardened fields and rutted roads with them, grunted with relish at her culinary skills and kept their distance.

Even Piers Martine, that swarthy rapscallion who'd accompanied Rob from Calais and come timely to his rescue at Hoyland, had not dared to challenge Margery and Piers constantly boasted that all women were fair game to him.

Rob looked up sharply as his straining ears caught the sounds of approach through the undergrowth near the hut. Margery nodded imperceptibly and moved near to the door.

Sym and Diggory Fletcher knocked cautiously on the old warped door and, as warily, pushed their way in. Neither appeared to be carrying food for the pot. Margery sighed, then clucked her tongue in disapproval.

The two were brothers, men-at-arms who had served his father loyally and they had joined Piers Martine and Silas Whitcome, expressing their determination to join Rob and eventually see retribution exacted on those Hoyland men who had killed their master and damaged their home manor.

Sym crouched by Rob's stool and his brother sauntered over to the pot and sniffed at its contents.

'We heard some news we thought might interest you, Master Rob, and came straight back to tell you.'

'Without so much as a pigeon for the pot,' Margery sniffed.

Sym ignored her while Diggory simply grinned.

'Sir Gilbert Hoyland set out this morning with an escort of about twenty men. He was making for the London road, I reckon, and though he's got a sizeable company and won't be expecting trouble, I think as 'ow we could give 'im some, 'specially as we could ambush the party from the scrubland. We 'eard it from a woodcutter who'd recognised the device on the men's jacks. Most of the folk 'ereabout 'ave 'eard of our trouble and see 'ow we'd like to get even.

'We managed to skirt the road and saw the party. I counted the men-at-arms and there seem to be fewer than was mentioned. P'raps he sent some of his men off to 'is own manor, anyway 'e'd be an easy target for us now.' He grinned wolfishly. 'There's five of us and me and Diggory's expert archers. What does you say, Master Rob?'

'I say the master's got enough to do in his state to see himself safely to London and on his way to Calais,' snapped Margery. 'There's time enough when he's got more support from the Earl to think about getting even with them Hoylands.'

Rob's lips parted in a slow smile. 'Do you know where Piers is, Sym?'

''E's near enough for one of us to find him. Diggory's a good tracker.'

Rob pushed himself up. 'We could do with some horses,' he said thoughtfully and Margery snorted again. They had had some difficulty in releasing one from the Devane stables under the noses of the Hoyland guards left there. One was needed for Rob's progress to London since walking had been difficult as his wound had pained him, but the rest could manage easily enough without. She considered this proposed attack madness but, catching her Rob's eyes, saw it would do her no good at all to say so. His blue eyes were already shining with enthusiasm for the venture.

Diggory was dispatched and, sooner than expected, returned with the Frenchman and Silas Whitcome. Piers cheerfully brandished a brace of pigeons and the company sat on the earth floor near the fire near Rob's stool while Margery plucked and prepared the pigeons for the cooking pot. Rob spelt out his proposed ambush and Piers Martine reflectively fingered a gold hoop which dangled from one torn ear.

''Ow many men do you think there now are?' he questioned Sym. The lanky shock-haired man-at-arms shook his head, pursed his lips, looked to his brother for confirmation and ventured an opinion.

'I'd say no more 'n ten, possibly fewer.'

'With Sir Gilbert, who is presumably a skilled fighting man, that is almost two to one, *mon ami*.'

Rob nodded in agreement, 'But an unexpected ambush—' His eyes narrowed. 'I owe this to my father's memory and to Walter. If I could take Sir Gilbert and hold him for ransom, I could recoup some of our losses.'

'I'd do more'n 'old 'im for ransom,' growled Sym.

'I agree entirely,' Rob said smoothly, 'but in these matters you have to do what is best. We need ready gold and Sir Gilbert could provide it.'

'And for how long do you intend to lie about here, waiting to be caught?' demanded Margery sourly. She made no bones about arguing with Master Rob.

Rob smiled again in her direction. 'There is a risk, certainly,' he acknowledged evenly, 'but I consider it worth the taking. We can demand that Sir Gilbert send to his own manor, which is not too far away, while we hold him and any of his men who survive the attack. He can hardly inform on us and this hiding place has served us well up to now. How fast was he travelling?' he asked

Sym. 'Can we cut through the woods to get ahead of him?'

'Aye, Master Rob. The company was travelling slow, loaded down with two sumpters and one maid or p'raps a wounded man riding pillion, I didn't stop to look too closely.'

Rob rose to his feet. 'Then the sooner we are on his track, the better.'

Piers eyed him thoughtfully, '*Mon ami*, should you not...?'

His voice trailed off as he met the full scornful gaze of those blue-green eyes. He shrugged philosphically. 'So be it, *messire*. We 'ave nevaire been afraid of taking the risks before, *n'est ce pas*?'

Despite her protests, Margery was left behind to tend their dinner and the little party set off led by Diggory, who, true to his brother's word, was a fine woodsman and knew his way. Rob cursed his bad leg for the first half-mile—it had stiffened over the last few days due to enforced inactivity—but as they continued he found himself walking and even running over difficult ground more easily and well able to keep up with his men.

Diggory, ahead, stopped, keeping his head lowered, and signalled that they were now getting close to the road. Rob turned and cautioned his men with a gesture to silence and warily and quietly approached to squat behind Diggory.

They were now able to see clearly from cover the road to Brinklow Village. Diggory turned slightly as both of them heard the sound of a considerable number of horsemen approaching. Rob turned and signalled again to his men. Silently, without the need for further instruction, they rose from their crouched positions and began to position themselves for ambush.

Sym and Diggory Fletcher, both fine archers, began to

look to their long bows. Silas Whitcome and Piers Martine had both been with Rob for some time in service, both in London and Calais. Each was preparing himself for combat in his own way. Silas was easing his sword in its scabbard as Rob was his own weapon.

The Frenchmen had already found himself a suitable tree and sat astride a branch, giving him an excellent view of the road while still affording him some measure of bare branches for cover. His own deadly crossbow was ready for action.

The company of horsemen came steadily on. Rob could hear one female voice chattering on and judged Sym had been right in assuming it was a maidservant who was riding pillion. His whole body was tensed now, ready for action and, deliberately, he quietened his breathing. It was essential that each man of his company performed now to the best of his ability and experience.

He trusted all of them. The Frenchman was a fighting machine in his own right and Silas was steady and careful, not one to rush into danger without conscious thought. The Fletchers he had not seen in action recently, but knew they were experienced men-at-arms of his father's company; he relied on them to do well in this coming engagement.

The first two men of the advancing escort were in sight now and Rob saw Diggory rise and nock his first arrow. He did not wait for orders. He knew well enough it was necessary for the company to come further into range before dispatching his fatal feathered missile.

Rob was waiting, half-stooped, his back hand ready to signal a message to Sym and Silas behind him. Piers, he knew, had a very clear view and, like Diggory, would take his own time.

The Hoyland escort came on, riding two by two. He could see the cold winter light glinting on their metal salets and the devices on their leather jacks were easily recognisable. He breathed a sigh of relief. It would not do to attack some other poor unsuspecting wight on the road going innocently about his business.

Behind the first two came one of the sumpter mules Diggory had spoken of and a single man-at-arms, with a woman clutching anxiously at his waist riding pillion. Rob cursed under his breath as he saw her. He would have preferred the wench to have been riding at the rear of the escort with the other mule he could see. He had no wish to see her fall victim to an arrow but, already, Diggory had loosed off his first shot.

The leading man, presumably the sergeant, gave a half-cry and fell foward over his horse's head. The beast rose, forelegs in the air, whinnying in sudden panic, and reared across the path of the fellow who rode beside him.

The man bellowed a warning shout to those of his company behind and inexpertly tried to extricate his own mount from the oncoming hoofs of his erstwhile partner's mount.

Pandemonium broke out in an instant. Arrows flew from cover and two other men screamed and fell. The road was now blocked by a company of plunging mounts and the noise of panicked bellows from those still in the saddle. It took only moments for Rob to establish control of the situation. He had only to emerge from cover, dash into the road and seize the reins of one of the plunging, frenzied horses, pulling the beast to a standstill.

He called a crisp, decisive command to the remaining men-at-arms to surrender.

'Throw down your arms and dismount. You are my prisoners. My men have you all well in their sights.'

All of his men but Piers, who remained at his vantage

point in the tree, emerged from cover and stood, bows full-stretched, threateningly. Silas had already dashed up to another of the men who gave signs of giving further trouble and neatly held his sword too close to the fellow's throat.

A woman's voice broke across the confused chaos. 'Desist. There is no point in dooming yourselves. This outlaw robber has the upper hand. I'd have no more blood spilt on my behalf in a vain attempt to protect me.'

Rob looked up, startled to see that the palfrey which was bucking under his hand on the reins was carrying Mistress Clare Hoyland.

She leaned down to try and soothe her frightened mount with a reassuring pat and, recognising Rob immediately, said coldly, 'I see you have so far escaped the King's justice, Master Devane. Very fortunate for you, less lucky for my escort.'

The horse quietened as she spoke to it soothingly and Rob relaxed his tight grip on the rein and gave her a mocking half-bow. Behind them the men of her escort were sullenly obeying him and dismounting. Silas was efficiently collecting up their discarded weapons. Three men still lay on the ground, one very still and two others groaning and cursing from the pain of arrow wounds.

The woman mounted pillion was screaming shrilly and hysterically beating away the hands of the soldier behind whom she'd been riding as he vainly attempted to lift her down from the saddle.

'Bridget, be quiet,' Mistress Hoyland snapped. 'You cannot be hurt badly, if at all, to be able to scream like that.'

She herself remained mounted, proudly looking down at her attacker.

Silas sidled up to Rob, carrying his toll of weapons, swords and daggers.

'There's no sign of Sir Gilbert Hoyland,' he murmured hoarsely. 'It looks like he isn't in the company.'

Rob cursed beneath his breath and turned to the girl, seemingly unafraid, who managed her palfrey skilfully despite its continued nervous sidling. She was dressed in mourning in a black fur-lined frieze cloak, suitable for travelling, and her black hood, drawn up against the winter chill, covered her simple white linen coif.

He said, his ill temper mounting at the unexpected turn of events, hardening his tone, 'Where is your uncle, mistress?'

Her shoulders rose and fell only slightly. 'He is on his way to London, sir, though why his whereabouts should concern you, I have no idea.'

His blue eyes were staring at her accusingly. 'He left you to travel without his protection?'

Her chin lifted a trifle. 'He accompanied me as far as Lutterworth and then took the Watling Street road to London.' She hesitated for a fraction of a moment then, feeling she needed to make some excuse for her uncle's conduct, added, 'I understand he had urgent business at Westminster.'

'Here's a pretty pickle,' Silas murmured at Rob's ear. 'What do we do now? Do you want me to deal with the rest of the escort? Master Rob, we should be moving off the road.'

Rob nodded in irritation. His gaze passed to the little knot of defeated Hoyland men-at-arms who had gathered defensively close together and were clearly concerned about their own fate. As yet they had made no attempt to go to the help of their injured comrades.

Rob waved a hand towards Diggory and Sym who were still mounting guard over the prisoners.

'Get them into the wood. Is that fellow dead?' He looked dispassionately at the still figure of the sergeant in the roadway.

'Aye, Master Rob, it would seem so.' Sym's voice revealed no hint of sympathy for the victim. There had been too many dead men left to rot at the Devane manor.

'Well, get the body into the wood and bury it. I know the ground is hard but do your best, cover it with brushwood if necessary. Secure the horses and pinion the wrists of those prisoners on their feet, but first let them tend to their wounded.'

His hand was still holding the palfrey's leading rein and he made to draw the horse under the cover of the trees.

Clare addressed him coldly. 'I trust, sir, that you don't intend to butcher my unarmed men or me?'

He swung to face her and she saw that his expression was granite set.

'If my men did so, mistress, I could not find it in my heart to blame them. Men died in plenty at my manor, aye, and women too, some most unpleasantly.'

He saw her grey eyes widen and a shadow of fear crossed her proud face. The maid, now on foot and gripping tightly to the panier on one of the sumpters, gave another shrill scream which was instantly halted as her mistress turned her imperious gaze upon her once more.

Clare did not resist as he led her horse under cover some quarter of a mile into the wood where woodsmen had fashioned a clearing.

He held up his arms commandingly to lift her down. For the length of a heartbeat he thought she would refuse to obey, then she allowed herself to be lowered to the ground and moved a fraction from him. Diggory had brought up the struggling maid who, once he released her, ran, panting and sobbing, to her mistress's side and clutched desperately at her cloak.

'Mistress Clare,' she gulped. 'Oh, Mistress Clare, whatever is to become of us?'

'I do not know,' Clare replied woodenly, 'but I do know it will not improve our prospects for you to continue to give trouble and cry like that.'

The wounded had been conveyed into the clearing by the survivors and laid down upon the grass. Without seeking permission from Rob, Clare went instantly to them and knelt by them. She made a perfunctory examination, then said quietly, 'They do not appear to be too gravely hurt. None of the arrows have damaged vital organs, but they should not be left long in this bitter cold without help. I ask you again, sir, what are you going to do with us? I understand, from your question earlier, it was my uncle you sought.'

'It was indeed, mistress. He and your brother were responsible for the raid on my manor and, since Sir Peter is dead and cannot be called to account, Sir Gilbert alone must answer to me for his actions.'

'Then you will let us proceed on our way to Coventry?'

'Coventry?' He raised one eyebrow in surprise. 'You go to join the Court at Coventry? Was that in hope of seeing me hang, Mistress Hoyland?'

'It certainly was not, sir. I was already well aware of your escape and I thanked God for it. As you have said, too many men died in that fruitless attack on your home and I would not have had your name added to the list, whatever your crimes against the King's Grace.'

He was leaning against a tree bole, watching her as she still knelt by the wounded men. He was silent for a moment then he said, 'You are right when you say too many men have died, but there is still a debt to be paid. You understand that?'

She rose to her feet and calmly dusted herself down. 'These injured men are hardly responsible, Master Devane. They did but obey orders even if these men, personally, were involved in the raid.'

'Naturally. I hold the Hoylands responsible.'

He saw her wince at the implication but still she showed no fear.

Rob turned to Piers who had come up, soft-footed as a cat, as usual.

'We shall not want to be hampered by these men. If we take the horses as planned I think we can allow them to remain here.'

'Pinioned?'

Rob hesitated. 'Mistress Hoyland warns me of the danger to them of leaving them tied here in these bitter conditions, particularly the wounded men. When we have left, they can seek help for their injured companions in Brinklow. They will be on foot and unable to pursue us.' He turned and whispered so that Mistress Hoyland could not overhear him. 'They cannot know of our hiding place.'

'And the women, *mon ami*? Since Sir Gilbert is not here—the *demoiselle* would bring a considerable ransom in his stead, *n'est ce pas*?'

Rob turned and regarded her slowly. He could tell by the very rigidity of her stance that she was struggling to maintain a semblance of courage. She lifted one hand to push back a lock of brown hair, which had come loose from its pins when she had stooped to see the wounded men. He rubbed one side of his nose thoughtfully.

'We'll take her to the hut,' he said at last, 'and consider, later, what is best to be done.'

'Did I hear the *demoiselle* say she was bound for the Court of *le roi* in Coventry?'

'You did.'

'Then, *mon ami, naturellement*, a courier will have been sent in advance to announce her arrival. She will be sought for—assiduously—is that not how you say it?'

Rob grimaced ruefully. 'Doubtless she will, especially when the men have reported her disappearance, that is.' He gave a slow smile. 'I think, Piers, these men will not be anxious to return to their service. Sir Gilbert Hoyland is no man to cross, I am sure, and will deal harshly with any he deems to be inefficient or to lack courage. These fellows will know well enough they will be blamed. I think I can guarantee they will disappear into the countryside. I can only hope they take their injured companions with them. This will give us a breathing space.'

Piers shrugged and looked towards the tethered horses. Left to his own devices, he would have made very sure there was no pursuit, but Messire Robert Devane was often unpredictable and prone to unfortunate scruples.

He moved off to see that the prisoners were informed what was to happen to them. They were all young, the dead sergeant being, apparently, the only experienced man in the company. Piers Martine considered Sir Gilbert Hoyland a fool to have trusted his niece to such an undisciplined rabble.

Clare Hoyland drew a hard breath and marched up to her captor. It had to be faced. She needed to know her fate—now.

'I demand to know, sir, when you will release me?'

He narrowed his eyes and she saw his lips tighten. His was such a normally genial countenance that she was chilled by the sight and stepped back a little.

'Certainly not yet, mistress,' he said brutally.

'But you said—it was my uncle you expected. . .'

'It was, but you, too, are a Hoyland.'

She gave a sharp exclamation. 'You intend to hold me prisoner?'

'You have guessed it, mistress.'

'You will hold me for ransom? But, my uncle. . .'

'Will pay it gladly,' he mocked her. 'I have not yet decided, mistress, but, for the present, you will come with us and without protest.' He glanced towards the band of prisoners. 'If you resist, it may rouse some core of chivalry in those youngsters there and I am sure you realise that could only end in their deaths.'

She inclined her chin and her single word was a trifle breathy. 'Yes.'

He turned from her. 'Then that is settled.'

She called back to him. 'Sir?'

'Madam?'

'You intend to let the men go free?'

'Yes.'

'Will you let my maid go? She will only hinder us and—and she will prove difficult to handle.'

His eyebrows rose again in some amusement.

'You would go with us unchaperoned?'

Colour flooded her face, now pale with suppressed fear.

'For her good—yes, and—' it came out in a rush '—if you mean me harm or—humiliation—I do not think her presence would deter you.'

He threw back his head and the laugh echoed in the little clearing.

'You read the situation correctly indeed, Mistress Hoyland.'

He looked towards the maid who was still hysterical

with fear. Certainly the girl would be of little use to her mistress in her present state.

'Yes, she may go, but I hope and trust she will fare better with those of your men than she would have cause to fear mine.'

'She will have to take that chance,' Clare said evenly.

He moved from her then to give orders for their departure and she went to the frightened girl.

'Bridget, you are to go with those men to the nearest inn at Brinklow. I do not think they will harm you. They fear Sir Gilbert's anger too much.' She drew a swift breath. 'At least I believe you will be safer with them. These ruffians cannot be trusted.'

'But you, mistress?' Bridget's lips rounded into an 'o' of shocked horror. 'I should not leave you.'

Clare forced a confident smile. 'I do not think I am in any real danger. Master Devane, for all his piratical ways, is a gentleman. We must hope and pray that that is the case. In all events it would do no good for both of us to be endangered and I can trust you to raise the alarm. I do not know where I am to be taken, but my uncle's men must be alerted and, doubtless, they will search these woods and the surrounding district so there is every chance I shall be found.'

The girl drew a quivering breath. 'Yes, mistress.'

Clare gave her a little push in the direction of the Hoyland prisoners and turned resolutely to Robert Devane, who was striding purposefully back towards her.

'You must mount up, now, mistress, we are ready to set off.'

The Frenchman, whose bold dark countenance and mocking grin she distrusted most, brought up her palfrey. Robert Devane prepared to lift her to her saddle and she flinched from the feel of his two strong

hands upon her waist, but knew it would be useless to
protest. Better Devane than his foreign henchman.

He settled her comfortably and handed her the reins.
She resisted the urge to kick her horse into a canter and
make for the road. It would be useless, she knew and
shuddered inwardly at the thought of an arrow between
her shoulder blades. She had seen how proficient these
men were with their weapons. They were ruthless. Her
uncle's conduct had made them desperate and she must
pay the price.

She waited docilely while the little troop mounted up
behind her then, with Robert Devane's masterful hand
upon her bridle rein, she allowed him to lead her along
the forest track.

CHAPTER THREE

CLARE struggled to keep her fears under control as her captor led her along the woodland paths. Already she was convinced she was totally lost even if she were able to evade her guards. Her heart was beating painfully as she realised that allowing Bridget to remain with the members of her wounded escort had left her completely compromised. She gave an inner laugh. Bridget's presence, as she had been at pains to point out to Robert Devane, would hardly have proved any real protection but, though the girl was feckless and often silly, Clare was missing her now sorely.

The men did not speak but pushed steadily on, sure-footed, the leader clearly knowing his way. Clare stole a glance at Robert Devane, who rode serenely beside her. She had noticed that he was still limping when he walked to her in the woodland glade and she wondered how well her treatment had progressed. She knew, only too well, that the very real danger of such a deep wound was the possibility of infection setting in. If that occurred, the patient either lost a limb—or his life.

The man in the lead paused and turned. Robert Devane shortened the leading rein of her palfrey and rode in close.

'We are very near to our destination now,' he informed her coldly. 'When we arrive I want your promise that you will make no attempt to escape, otherwise I must keep you pinioned.'

She looked back at him proudly. 'I shall give you no such promise, Master Devane,' she said icily. 'I am completely at your mercy and expect no soft treatment from you.'

'Nor will you get it, Mistress Hoyland,' he returned, but without rancour.

He was smiling and she had no way of knowing whether there was malice in the words or merely an amused rejoinder.

A hut loomed up before them suddenly, almost hidden by the dense foliage. It was a poor place of wattle and daub with a roughly constructed and warped door of split logs. Smoke was escaping from a hole in the ill-thatched roof.

The hut had obviously been used occasionally by some woodcutter or charcoal burner, Clare thought, for it was hardly substantially built enough for winter weather. She shivered inside her fur-lined cloak and was glad of its warmth and the protection it afforded her from Robert Devane's eyes observing how she was trembling.

One of the men slipped inside and, almost instantly, a woman emerged, big, raw-boned, unfriendly looking. She stood, arms akimbo, regarding Clare stonily as Robert Devane lifted her down from her palfrey.

He greeted the woman cheerily, 'Ah, Margery, as you see, we have a prisoner. This is Mistress Hoyland. I wish you to keep a very close watch on her.' He gave a brief bubble of laughter. 'Especially since she decided to dispense with the services of her maid. Didn't trust the lass to our menfolk.' He looked over at them jovially. 'A sentiment I can well understand. But now she is without chaperon and will need you to act as such.'

The woman addressed as Margery looked even more sourly from her master to his prisoner.

'And she is the prize, is she? What of her uncle, Sir Gilbert?'

'Had left her on the road to our mercy, gone on to London about his own concerns.'

'What you'd expect from a Hoyland,' the woman spat out vituperatively. 'Has no care for his own womenfolk nor any respect for others.'

Clare felt herself going even paler and, stiffened from her ride, almost fell as Robert Devane's supporting arm was withdrawn from round her waist.

The woman stood aside as the prisoner was marched through the hut doorway.

'So you intend to hold her for ransom instead of her uncle?'

Clare was sure that the woman was a servant yet her familiarity of expression showed she had been close to Robert Devane over a number of years. Clare's eyebrows rose as she stared at her. Was she his mistress? No, Clare decided, unlikely, the woman was now revealed as much older than her master and by no means comely. She was strong, though, and Clare doubted that, in any trial of strength with the woman, she would come off best. Margery, whoever she was in the Devane household, was trusted and her strengths well known.

Her hostility towards Clare probably proceeded from the attack on the manor. Had she lost some kin in that raid? If so, she would prove as formidable an opponent as any of the men, yet the sight of another female in this place was some small measure of comfort.

The fire gave little warmth but there was protection from the wind in the hut and Clare sank thankfully down on a pile of dried bracken that Robert Devane indicated. She made no effort to remove her cloak or put back her hood.

Robert Devane stood directly in front of her, his thumbs thrust deep into his sword belt as he grinned down at his captive. She waited anxiously for his answer to Margery's question.

'Ransom?' he said slowly, his eyes raking over Clare's huddled form. 'It is a possibility. At any rate I've forbidden any of my men to touch her until I've finally decided. I'll need you to guard her like a dragon, Margery, both from her own desire to escape and lose herself in this unfriendly wood and from the others—' his eyes twinkled merrily '—particulary from Piers.'

Clare controlled a shudder as she recalled the predatory gaze of the Frenchman. She looked up to meet Margery's cold brown eyes in direct appeal.

'Aye, I'll keep my eyes on her, you can be sure of that, Master Rob,' the older woman said with a disparaging glance at the prisoner.

There was a savoury smell issuing from the pot suspended from a roughly made iron support over the fire. Clare was made aware for the first time that she was actually hungry. Her escort had not paused on the journey to eat. Sir Gilbert had been anxious to press on and Clare had thought to stop at an inn in Brinklow. She looked away, flushing darkly, as she saw Robert Devane's amused glance follow hers to the pot.

'Don't worry, Mistress Hoyland, I have no intention of starving my prisoner. I have an excellent memory and was very grateful for your hospitality extended to me in your barn. Without that fine wine to give me strength, I might never have managed the escape when my men came for me.'

If he had expected her to make some spirited comment that she would have done better to have held her hand from such kindness, he received no reply. He turned his attention to arranging for adequate guard to take turns while the little company ate. A slight stir outside informed Clare that the rest of the group had returned. Soon they were all crowding into the small hut.

The Frenchman was eyeing her speculatively again and she turned from him stonily to look fixedly at the rough daubed wall.

Robert Devane placed two men outside to keep a close watch and he himself sat down very close to Clare while Margery began to deal out the stew into wooden bowls. Someone had come well prepared from the Devane manor, Clare thought. Robert Devane handed her a bowl and wooden spoon and gratefully she began to eat. The stew was good—rabbit or pigeon, she thought—seasoned with herbs from the wood.

The men ate steadily, again with little comment, and Margery sat down at last to consume her share of the stew, after taking rations to the two outside. The Frenchman Robert Devane had called Piers sat back idly after he had finished, swinging his wooden spoon loosely from the fingers of one hand and emitting a tuneless whistle which both irritated and alarmed Clare. In some subtle way he managed to raise her fears without one word or action of threatening behaviour.

She had the notion that he was no servant of Robert Devane, but a close companion, and any control Rob Devane had over the man lay in the friendship each had for the other. Were she to be separated from either Devane or Margery, she would become very frightened indeed.

The light in the hut was beginning to fade and Clare realised it would soon be full dark. The guard outside had been changed and Rob Devane had been discussing with his men his plans for the following day. She had been kept with Margery Lightbody—as she had discovered the woman's full name to be—at the other end of the hut and, strain her ears though she might, she could not hear what was said.

Margery took her outside at last so she might obey the call of nature and Clare was embarrassed to see not only that the woman kept her in sight all the time but they were shadowed by another of Rob Devane's men, though at a somewhat discreet distance. She was beginning to get more and more fearful about the sleeping arrangements, but kept trying to reassure herself with the thought that Robert Devane had declared his intention of holding her for ransom. Were she to be molested by him or any of his men, she would prove virtually worthless, so, surely he would see to it that she was kept safe throughout the dark hours.

He came to her side as she and Margery returned to the hut, still followed by their watchful guard.

'You will sleep in this corner of the hut.' He indicated the pile of bracken which had been drawn out into the shape of two rough beds. 'Margery will lie beside you and you will remove your shoes and hand them to me now.'

When she was about to protest he said, 'If your feet are cold in the night you must accept that as a consequence of your refusal to give me your word you would try no tricks. Wrap them up in your cloak. You are lucky I do not intend to carry out my threat and keep you tightly pinioned. That, I'm sure you realise, would prove acutely uncomfortable.'

Mutinously she lifted her gown and began to remove her shoes, conscious that covert glances were being cast at her from the far side of the hut. The Frenchman's regard was not in the slightest covert. He continued to smile as she withdrew both soft riding shoes and handed them to Robert Devane.

'Good,' he said tersely. 'You would find it extremely

painful to try to hobble through the wood without these, mistress, and, I warn you, there are predators out there, animal as well as human, so lie down now and do your best to sleep. We have quite a way to travel in the morning and will set off at first light.'

'How will you send to my uncle and demand ransom?' she asked. 'I trust you will do so very soon and allow me to be free of your hateful presence as quickly as humanly possible.'

He made her that little, mocking bow she found so annoying.

'I assure you, Mistress, I am as anxious as you are to see an improvement in my fortunes. Your brother's conduct has forced this hateful necessity upon me. I can only hope that your uncle is as willing to value your freedom as you hope he will be and makes no delay in meeting my demands.'

She turned from him angrily. She did not wish him to see her expression and was grateful for the dimness within the hut, the one horn lantern being furthest away from where she was to lie. She, too, had her doubts about her uncle's intentions. He had been in such a hurry to further his own interests that she feared he would take some time before he considered the welfare of his niece, who had been thrust so quickly as an unwelcome burden upon him.

Her thoughts sped to the Queen at her Court in Coventry. By now messengers would have been sent alerting her to Clare's arrival. Soon it would be recognised that she was overdue. Would the Queen consider herself at all responsible for her newest attendant—and one, at that, whom she had never seen—and send out a search party? Clare rather thought not.

Both the King and Queen had overmuch upon their minds during these uncertain times to worry themselves about the safety of some hapless and unimportant girl. Her only hope lay in being ransomed. If her uncle could not be contacted soon...or should he refuse to co-operate with Robert Devane—she thrust that fear aside as being too terrible to contemplate.

Margery Lightbody saw to it that the fire was safely banked down and eventually lay down beside her charge. Not once since she had first seen Clare had she addressed one word to her and Clare felt she could expect no help or mercy from that quarter. Margery was entirely devoted to her master and would obey his commands to the letter.

It was becoming bitterly cold and Clare lay huddled in the corner. The men had also settled themselves to sleep some distance from the two women. Robert Devane had gone outside to take his turn on watch. Clare lay sleepless, unwilling to turn or move and disturb Margery Lightbody. Her thoughts went over and over the events of the day and her fears for the future.

She wondered if Bridget had been able to alert someone at Brinklow who would return to the Hoyland manor or send word of her predicament. Surely Bridget would not be feckless enough to forget her duty and run off with some man from the escort. Sighing inwardly, she had to admit that, knowing Bridget as she did, that was quite within the realm of probability.

She had to face the bitter knowledge that she was helpless in Robert Devane's hands and unlikely to receive succour from any outside source—at least within the next two or three days.

Clare was roughly shaken awake at first light. Again she went outside with Margery and returned to the hut where the men were dividing up a quantity of dark rye bread and sharing ale. Robert Devane silently handed her a hunk of the bread and a wooden cup containing ale. He made no apologies for the poorness of fare and she made no complaints. It was still very cold, but the wind had dropped considerably and she had noticed a lightness, compared to the previous day's leaden sky, which heralded the possibility of a wintry sun showing itself later.

She saw the men making preparations for departure, packing their meagre supplies and checking their weapons. She became anxious to know if Margery Lightbody was to accompany the party. Hostile as the woman was, she represented Clare's one female supporter amongst this motley company of men.

Robert Devane soon disabused her of that fear.

'Margery is to go with us. Unfortunately, she cannot ride alone and must go pillion. Have I your word that you will be sensible? Otherwise, I must carry you face down upon my saddle bow.'

Clare grimaced. The very humiliating idea of the threat convinced her that, for the present, she must co-operate with her captor.

'I will agree to ride with you throughout this day only,' she rejoined coldly. 'Later, I will make no promises.'

He nodded and gave the signal for the little group to leave the hut and saddle up.

She was glad of her own palfrey, who whinnied with pleasure at sight of her. Margery watched stolidly while Robert Devane assisted Clare into the saddle. Then, somewhat apprehensively, she mounted behind Sym Fletcher, who made some ribald remark that made her snort as he insisted she tuck her arms firmly round his waist. Clare noticed that the Frenchman rode companionably close to Robert Devane and, though he said nothing, his black snapping eyes showed his amusement at her discomfiture.

The company rode as silently as they had traversed the wood the previous day, only the clopping of the horses' hooves and the faint snapping of an occasional twig marking their passing. She still had no idea where Robert Devane was taking her and was much too proud to enquire. They fell into single file as the woodland path grew narrow and Clare saw Silas Whitcome was bringing up the rear leading the sumpter mule.

She looked about her constantly and, at last, realised they were heading south, eventually taking a well-worn path, which she thought ran parallel to the Roman highway that ran to London and St Albans. While they were still comparatively close to Clare's own manor, Robert Devane was taking no chances of riding along the main highway, with the risk of Clare being recognised and the company challenged.

Some miles further south he issued an order. Apparently, he now thought it was safe enough to run onto the main Roman thoroughfare. Were they riding to London? Clare wondered. Perhaps Robert Devane was intending to join his master, the Earl of Warwick, whom she had heard had now left Calais and landed on English soil. If so, then the Yorkist lords were already beginning to once more gain ground and confidence after their defeat at Wakefield.

Robert Devane certainly felt confident enough of his prisoner's co-operation to lodge at an inn at Towcester, a poor place certainly, and not one where questions were likely to be asked of guests. Margery Lightbody and Clare slept in a common room upstairs, fortunately alone, for normally this common room was crowded, especially on market days, while the men slept downstairs in the ale room.

Clare made one brief step to the door, only to find Robert Devane lying across the threshold. He raised his head and grinned at her. She shook her own head angrily and went to lie down as far from him as possible near the draughty horn window.

The place stank and she thought, viciously, that she would find herself alive with vermin next day—the straw they lay on was filthy. At least they were out of the cold and wind and she wrapped herself up in her cloak, after consuming a poor supper of rye bread, pottage and salted pork, followed by a doughy apple tart. Though she lacked appetite, she forced herself to eat—she would need her strength for later.

Breakfast was taken before first light again, a similar frugal meal of bread and cold meats. She was glad to note that today Robert Devane had purchased bread and cheese and ale for the party on the road. Yesterday, they had gone hungry until reaching the inn at night.

Still Margery made no conversation with Clare and the ride progressed as on the previous day. Now the men were happier and exchanged badinage as they rode. Once or twice the Frenchman cast her mocking glances and chatted to Robert Devane in French.

Clare had some knowledge of the language, but he spoke so fast and with a strange accent so she was unable to catch the gist. She was convinced that he was making fun of her for, several times, Robert Devane looked back at her and then laughed out loud. Her cheeks flamed.

Towards evening he rode close to her while Piers Martine forged ahead to ride with Diggory Fletcher.

Robert Devane said smilingly, 'You must be very tired, mistress, having taken only the briefest of rests. We shall soon be at Fenny Stratford. Unless you give me your word to be sensible again, I cannot take the risk of lodging us at an inn and we must camp out in the fields. I think you would find that cold comfort for a show of open resistance.'

Clare compressed her lips tightly. 'I must agree, Master Devane, for if I refuse to comply with your demand, others will suffer also.'

He shrugged. 'The men are used to discomfort. Certainly they will complain, they always do, but they will manage. Margery is a different matter.'

'Is she one of your servants?'

'She was one of my nursemaids. She has lived all her life on our manor. This is her first journey of more than five miles from the nearest village.'

'Why did she come?' Clare blurted out, then was uncomfortably aware that she was being rudely curious. Had her first thought about the woman been correct? Was she more than a mere servant to Robert Devane? 'Surely she could have remained on your manor, though it was badly damaged. I know many servants remained, for I...'

'Yes?' There was a curious note to the one single question.

She coloured hotly. 'I—I went to see—if anyone needed my help. It was when—when arrangements were being made for your father's and brother's burial.'

She saw a little tic move at his temple. He was silent for a moment then he said stiffly, 'I find I must thank you for yet one more favour.'

'They lie in hallowed ground in the churchyard and masses were said for their souls. I could not, in common charity, do less.'

He made her a grave little bow from the saddle. 'And what did your uncle think of that?'

'He—he saw—he was swayed by my—'

'Determination?'

'Yes,' she answered unwillingly.

He nodded. 'I hope he will realise what a treasure he has lost,' he said lightly and rode from her again to join Diggory and the Frenchman in the lead. She realised he had still not answered her enquiry about Margery.

In the common chamber of this new inn, more salubrious than the last, Clare made an attempt to break the silence between Margery and herself.

'This is a better place, don't you think?'

'Yes,' Margery agreed grudgingly.

'You have undertaken a difficult and dangerous journey to be with Master Devane.'

The woman turned her dark eyes directly upon Clare. 'He was my nursling. He was hurt and needed my help.'

'I know. I saw the wound when—when he was first brought to Hoyland.'

'Aye. He might have lost the leg but for you.'

'I imagine he heals well. He—he looks in excellent condition. He keeps fit fighting and exercising, I suppose.'

'Aye, he does that. He's a fair warrior, Master Rob. Men need to be in these hard times. If'n there had been more warning of that raid and he'd bin there earlier, it might have bin a different tale, I'm thinking.'

'Did—did you lose someone in that fight, Margery? You probably know my brother was killed. . .'

'It seems to me he had only his self to blame. As parson says, "He that lives by the sword dies by the sword."'

'That could also apply to Master Rob.'

'Aye, it could, and this foolishness is likely to lead him near to his end, as I tell him.'

'Then you don't approve of my being held prisoner?'

'I don't, but don't go thinking I'm in favour of helping

you, 'cos I'm not. It's for me to do what Master Rob says.'

'Yes, of course. Then you left your manor because of him?'

'I left becos there wasn't nothing left for me there. My man had been killed.'

'I'm sorry.'

'Don't be, he was ever a brute to me, after my child died, so I don't know as I shall miss him that much, but he was my man. Now I follows Master Rob.'

So Margery was childless and now a widow. Clare could understand her bitterness against the Hoylands, but was still unaware of the lodestone which drew this dried-up, unhappy woman to her master to the extent that she would leave the relative comfort of her manor home in winter to hazard herself on some dangerous adventure likely to give her nothing but problems.

Clare had suffered some bite marks from vermin on the previous night but, thankfully, had been able to change her underwear and gown, after her baggage had been brought up to the chamber for her. This time she took the precaution of lying on the bare boards, well away from any dubious straw, and slept the better for it.

They pressed on steadily south and Clare was now convinced that Robert Devane was travelling towards London but when they turned off the highway just south of Dunstable she was slightly bewildered.

They were travelling quite openly now, as if Clare was a member of Robert Devane's household, and she was totally surprised when they approached a brick-built manor house set some two miles from the village of Kenswick. There was a small gatehouse where the company was challenged, then allowed to proceed further into a cobbled courtyard.

Clare was impressed by the dwelling house, newly built in brown brick, with an undercroft, as at Hoyland, and a small, defensive tower. Like both Hoyland and the Devane house, the building was not crenellated, but defended only by the gatehouse and company of armed men-at-arms.

Robert Devane rode up to her palfrey's side, dismounted and reached up to lift her down.

'We shall stay here some days. This is the house of my friend, Sir Reyner Astley.'

As if in answer to his name, a young man emerged onto the hall steps and ran quickly down them. He was comely enough, Clare thought, square built, not nearly as tall as Robert Devane, fair and elegantly clad in a fine wool doublet of the fashionable Yorkist colour, murrey.

As Robert faced him, holding Clare tightly by the arm, he hastened forward in smiling greeting.

'Welcome, Rob. I thought you would ride south to meet up with other members of my lord Earl's household. And this is?' He looked enquiringly from Clare into his friend's face.

'This is Mistress Clare Hoyland. She is my travelling companion. I have Margery Lightbody with me. Could you provide Mistress Hoyland with a chamber for the night. . .' he hesitated and looked meaningfully back at his friend '. . .one well protected from any unwelcome disturbance?'

The fair young man's eyebrows rose but he smiled faintly, bowed gallantly to Clare and nodded.

'You, too, are very welcome to my home, Mistress Hoyland. You must be verily saddle-sore and hungry. I'll have my wenches bring you up warmed water and prepare a bath and then you must come to the hall to take supper with us.'

Clare inclined her head graciously in thanks, feeling

Rob Devane's steely grip upon her arm, and she moved with the two men towards the manor entrance, Margery following close behind.

Rob faced his friend later that evening as they sat before the blazing fire in the hearth. At last they were alone. Clare had been accommodated in the tower room with Margery close by, and Piers had finally left them to roister with the other men of the company whom the Astley steward had bedded down in one of the outbuildings adjoining the bailey wall.

Clare had been very silent over supper though politely acknowledging the courtesies Reyner had afforded her. Rob was aware that his friend was intensely curious though he had, as yet, asked no direct questions. Now he leaned back in his chair, idly swirling his fine malmsey wine in his goblet, still refraining from looking at Rob.

Rob stirred uncomfortably and thrust his long legs out towards the hearth. He cleared his throat noisily.

'You will be wondering what I am doing, travelling with the Hoyland girl?'

'I assumed, perhaps erroneously, that she is your prisoner.'

'Yes.'

'Well, the tower room is not easy of access and that former nursemaid of yours is quite a dragon and capable of staving off any violent action on Mistress Hoyland's part, I'm thinking.'

'You have heard about the raid on my manor?'

Astley nodded gravely. 'News such as that quickly filters through. I did not know what to say about your father and brother—in front of the girl, I mean. You know you have my deepest condolences.'

Again Rob nodded and gazed into the fire.

'So you are now master of Devane manor.'

'Master of a ruined shell,' Rob rejoined bitterly and took a deep pull of his wine. 'I have no means of repairing the damage and at present cannot return there. The Earl has command of my services.' He hesitated. 'Gilbert Hoyland took me prisoner and determined to hand me over to Margaret for summary justice. Piers and Silas came to my rescue.'

He fell silent for a moment, brooding. 'We heard Hoyland was riding out, presumably for London, and determined to attack and hold him for ransom. Unfortunately, by the time we managed to ambush his company, he had already divided it and ridden off, leaving his niece to journey to Coventry with only a token escort.'

Astley whistled softly. 'So you took the girl instead?'

'Aye. As yet I have sent no demand for ransom to Gilbert's manor in Northamptonshire.' His lips curled in an ironic twist. 'He seemed so anxious to rid himself of the burden of his niece I doubt if he'd trouble himself to pay a ransom.'

Astley's eyes echoed his friend's cynical humour.

'I have heard the man is so eager for gold he would do most things to get it.'

'Well, he got little from our house. We have never been wealthy and the wars have impoverished all of us.' Rob turned to his friend, one eyebrow rising in sardonic amusement. 'The truth is I'm not sure what to do with the girl. She's a Hoyland, should pay for what was done, though she suffers too. Her brother, Peter, was killed in the engagement. She was destined for Margaret's court at Coventry.'

He gave a harsh laugh. 'I imagine Gilbert saw the opportunity of matching her with some influential member of Margaret's coterie. That would be to his advantage. Mistress Clare is a wealthy heiress now.

Margaret's arrangement of a suitable marriage, and her gain in gold and loyalty by it, would win Gilbert more influence in her service. If I free her. . .'

Astley's eyes widened as they met the blue ones of his friend. 'So she is a wealthy heiress, my friend,' he said slowly, 'and in your hands. A profitable marriage would go some way to compensate you for your ill fortune.'

Rob banged down his drinking goblet on the table by him and swore roundly. 'Such a rascally plan would never have occurred to me.'

Astley's eyes twinkled. 'Well, let it occur to you now, my friend. It will not be the first time it has been done to advance the fortunes of some poverty-stricken squire.'

'The marriage could be dissolved.'

'With difficulty,' agreed his friend, 'but were you to consummate it. . .?'

Rob growled again, but his protest was half-hearted now as the advantages of his friend's outrageous proposal became clear in his brain.

'The Earl might disapprove.'

'I doubt it.' Astley's lips spread wide in a grin. 'His own family have enriched themselves over the years with a plethora of advantageous marriages.'

Rob's breath was coming fast as he looked beyond Reyner into the distant shadows of the room.

'The girl will refuse and I've already seen evidence that she is stout hearted.'

Astley shrugged lightly. 'Under the circumstances she has little choice but to accede to your wishes. She is already compromised. Should you threaten. . .?' He broke off meaningfully.

Rob moodily chewed his nether lip. Wild thoughts seethed in his brain. He had often considered the possibility of mending his poor prospects by some advantageous marriage but had imagined that the plan

would be accomplished by his own charms, winning him
some willing maid. He misliked the notion of compulsion—and yet—the Hoylands were responsible for the
ruin of the Devane hopes. Why should not Clare
Hoyland pay the price?

The wine fumes were mounting to confuse his over-
wearied brain. His lips set mutinously. Astley was right.
He would be a fool to harbour scruples. The girl was
comely enough, not beautiful, but she had spirit. Had
they met in other circumstances, he would have come to
admire her.

Peter Hoyland had been a contemptible enemy,
niddling and carping about rights to land and privileges
he had no right to. He had attacked Rob's home
deliberately because he had believed the prize would
fall to him with little real opposition, being totally
unexpected, and so soon after the Holy Season of
Christmas, when all warlike men held their hands, for a
while, at least.

His sister was of different mettle. Rob thrust aside the
thought that she did not deserve to pay the price of her
brother's folly. He grinned hugely. Was it such a hard
price? He would not make such a bad husband. Once
the matter was concluded, and his rights to the Hoyland
estates agreed, he would leave her to her own devices.
She, on her part, could remain at her own manor,
possibly—the idea was hazy—in time she would give
him an heir. . . The plan boded well.

The light behind those intensely blue eyes blazed up.
'I think you have made an excellent suggestion, Reyner,'
he said suavely, 'and how soon could you find me a
priest to bind our betrothal?'

The tower room proved comfortable and the bed linen
wonderfully clean and comforting after the discomforts

of the journey, but Clare found herself surprisingly very restless in the night. Margery slept soundly beside her on a truckle bed. The woman had been her usual uncommunicative self and had watched very carefully every move Clare had made.

Now, in the darkness, her feet blessedly warmed by a wrapped brick, Clare stared up at the tester, her mind worrying at the events of the past and her growing alarm for her future. Sir Reyner Astley had been welcoming and solicitous for her comfort but she knew he, too, considered her a prisoner and would work with his friend to see that she remained carefully guarded.

During the journey she had had little time to grieve for Peter, being too concerned for the danger which faced her. Now she allowed herself to remember and the tears began to course down her cheeks. She had never been truly close to her brother, but she recognised all he would now miss in life and the futility of it all flooded over her. Father and brother killed in this senseless warring—it was all such a terrible waste.

What now of her prospects? Would Robert Devane, now that he had reached a house where he could remain safely, send to her uncle to demand ransom? If so, would it be paid? The frightening realisation struck her that her uncle would be considerably better off if she were to die, for he would inherit. He had made a life for himself and won land and influence by his own loyalty to the House of Lancaster but, as a younger son, he must often have resented the necessity.

Her father had inherited the Hoyland estates and Sir Gilbert had been forced to fend for himself. She had seen the two brothers together but rarely and could not guess how close in affection they had been. Now, brutally, she faced the possibility that she could be sacrificed for her uncle's ambition. He had sent her off to the Queen's Court, apparently concerned for her future prospects and safety, but now her abduction gave him opportunity to throw her to the wolves.

No one need ever know the ransom had been demanded. Sir Gilbert could simply allow her to die and then accuse her captor. He could say he had never received a demand for the price of her safety and all her lands and wealth could fall into his hands like ripe plums at harvest time.

Her heart began to pound rapidly at her increasing fear. Surely her uncle would never do that? He had always treated her with a rough show of affection, especially since the death of her father, yet child heirs and vulnerable heiresses died—sometimes in mysterious circumstances—and, in these difficult times, often no one was brought to account for these crimes.

Margery stirred and turned over. Clare lay very still, holding her breath. It seemed that the very darkness within the room was pressing down on her. If forced to, how would Robert Devane dispatch her? A pillow pressed hard down upon her face would be simple enough. She gave a hastily suppressed inarticulate cry and buried her face in the pillows.

Breakfast was brought up to her chamber and warmed water for washing but Margery remained with her and it was made clear to Clare that she would not be allowed to roam free in the manor house. She finished her meal and nodded to Margery who had eaten with her.

'You can go to the door now and summon a servant to carry away the dishes.'

Margery nodded dourly, as usual, and rose to obey her. She was prevented from doing so as the door was jerked open and Robert Devane strode in. He glanced at the remains of the repast on the table and noted how pale and strained his prisoner appeared in the cold, wintry sunlight which streamed through the horn window.

'You can go below with that tray, Margery. I'll call you when I need you.'

His former nursemaid looked at him sharply and her gaze passed impassively to Clare. She said nothing, but moved to pick up the tray and left the room as he ordered. Clare noted, with grim amusement, that Margery never made any effort to curtsy or make Robert Devane any gesture of obsequious respect.

She herself rose at his entrance and stood facing him, one hand grasping at the table edge.

'You have eaten?' His tone was gruff as if with embarrassment.

'Thank you, yes.'

'I trust you were comfortable in the night.'

She inclined her head gravely.

'I ask because you do not appear to have slept well.'

'Possibly the reason for that is that I still do not know my fate.'

'Fate?' He moved easily towards her, one hand gripping his dagger sheaf on his ornamental sword belt. 'A curious word. I hope it will not come to that.'

'Come, sir. Do not play games with me. Have you sent to my uncle?'

He seated himself on the stool Margery had vacated and thrust out his long legs , obstensibly at his ease.

'Tell me,' he said in a deceptively mild tone, 'who was it who suggested the raid upon my manor? Your brother, Sir Peter, or was it Sir Gilbert?'

'I do not know. . .' She checked and stared back at him suspiciously and remained standing. 'Why do you ask? Does it matter?'

'It matters to me.'

She drew a rasping breath. 'Yes, I imagine it would. I am not sure. I think it was my uncle, but. . .'

'Ah!' The single word expressed a world of understanding.

'Since my brother is dead it can make little difference. You can only, now, hold my uncle responsible for the deaths of your people.'

'Yes,' he agreed quietly and his blue eyes continued to gaze intently into hers. 'Then you, too, must hold him responsible for the death of your brother.'

'That would be ridiculous,' she burst out. 'Peter was killed by an unknown opponent in the. . .' Her voice trailed off miserably as she recalled her frightening suspicions of the night.

He was watching her closely and his eyes narrowed in thought. 'I see you have come to the same conclusion as I have.'

'I do not condone the raid,' she said hastily. 'I have always said this senseless feuding is wanton foolishness, but it was understandable that after the death of my uncle's sergeant he should seek. . .'

'Revenge? For a sergeant? I think that unlikely, Mistress Clare. Gilbert Hoyland took the first opportunity to hand to enrich himself and there is the outside chance that he thought. . .' He laughed a trifle harshly. 'But there, I should not alarm you further. I might remind you, mistress, that you were singularly ill guarded on that journey to Coventry. If you had died in some unforeseen attack. . .'

'Which I might well have done,' she snapped back at him.

'Which you might well have done, I would have been an opportune culprit to blame.'

'But he could not know you were in the district.' She

refused to accept the dawning horror of what his words implied.

'No, he did not,' he said suavely and he continued to play absentedly with the ornate hilt of his dagger. 'But then, I need not have been, need I—to blame, I mean? There could have been other attacks. In this uncertain age, such ambushes are frequent enough.'

She turned from him abruptly, tears spilling down her cheeks. How dared he imply—she would not believe Peter's death had been anything but an unfortunate consequence of war. . .

'You will see, Mistress Clare, that, under the circumstances, it would be unwise for me to demand ransom from that quarter. I have had time to consider and—' he paused for a moment until she turned again and he had her full attention '—I have come up with another plan, one which is likely to prove more profitable than my first intention.'

'I do not see how. . .?'

He smiled and her own eyes widened at the full splendour of that smile. He was so very handsome, even when he was being so cruel in his taunting of her.

'Oh, yes, Mistress Clare, a much more profitable conclusion and one which will ensure your safety. I will marry you, Mistress Clare, and then your fortunes will become mine. A simple and just solution, do you not agree?'

She stared at him incredulously. 'Are you quite mad?'

He continued to smile. 'Not at all. You are a wealthy heiress. I am a penniless squire who needs to repair his fortunes, those which have suffered unduly at the hands of your family. The proposal seems perfectly fair to me.'

'The King would never allow it.'

'Ah, but how long will poor mad Harry remain our King?'

'The Act of Accord. . .'

'Much has happened since the Act of Accord. The Battle of Wakefield happened. Our Duke's body was foully mocked at Micklegate Bar in York. My Earl's father, Salisbury, was executed and York's son, Edmund of Rutland, hardly more than a boy, was mercilessly cut down on Wakefield Bridge while appealing for sanctuary.'

He shook his head mockingly. 'Edward of March will not accept this reversal of fortune. With Warwick and other northern lords he will march on London. Queen Margaret is no favourite of the Londoners. They have heard too much about the depredations of her men on other towns and villages while moving south. London will open its gates for Warwick and Edward will drive eastwards from Wales. Once my master is established in a position of power—as he will be, I'm sure of that—he will see to it that the new King will make no opposition to my claims to my wife's holdings.'

She was gripping the table edge very tightly so that her knuckes gleamed whitely. 'I shall never consent to become your wife,' she said through clenched teeth. 'You cannot force me.'

'To become my wife? No, I could not force you to that,' he replied quietly.

His eyes had become very steely and she gulped uncertainly. 'Well, then. . .'

'Mistress Clare, may I remind you that you are in my power—totally within my power?'

Her facial muscles had suddenly become very stiff and her tongue clove to the roof of her mouth so that she could hardly frame her next question.

'I do not understand you, sir.'

'I think that you do, Mistress Clare,' he said very gently.

'You would not in honour. . .'

'What can a Lancastrian pirate know of honour?'

She was paler than ever and he saw that she stood tall and proud with determined effort, her spine rigidly held straight.

He leaned forward in his chair. 'Let me explain. You are already compromised. Were I to take you—by force if necessary—and no one to prevent me, you would be further so. Heiresses have been so constrained before. You know this. No one here will interfere with my wishes. You cannot look to anyone for help.

'Don't think of Margery. She was brutally raped by the very Hoyland men-at-arms who raided my manor. You did not know that?' He was smiling mockingly, 'I thought you might have guessed. She will have little sympathy for you, Mistress Clare.'

He rose as she moved to turn deliberately from him and, coming close, put an imperative arm round her waist and drew her close to him. His face was so very near to hers that she could smell the breakfast ale on his breath and other, manly scents: oil from the metal of his belt and dagger, leather, a clean, herbal soapy scent. The soft fanning of his breath on her cheek made her senses swim.

She tried to press backwards away from his dominating influence and the native fear he aroused in her, but he put out his free hand and tilted her chin, his other arm still holding her body rigidly close to his own.

'Now you will not be foolish and force me to compel obedience,' he prompted, still in that falsely gentle demanding tone. 'I am, despite your uncle's opinion of my services to my lord Earl, a gentleman. I have never found it necessary before to force a maid.

'I shall give you time to come to terms with your new position. All I ask is that you consent to go before a priest with me and plight our betrothal vows. You will then be bound to me until our marriage can be celebrated later. I shall not prove a bad husband.' His blue eyes sparked mischief. 'We shall deal well enough together. I shall not beat you unless you deserve it, of course.'

Her teeth were biting down so hard on her nether lip that she could taste blood. She would not allow herself to break down now and cry. She remained perfectly still and continued to stare back at him proudly and silently.

'Reyner will find me a priest. You have until tonight. After supper, shall we say?' He relaxed his grip on her waist and, stiffly, she drew away from him. 'Think it over, mistress. If you consent to our betrothal, I shall be perfectly prepared to wait. If not—then tonight we can anticipate our bridal. Give me your decision at supper. I shall be patient until then.'

She gave a little faint gasp and he bowed to her and moved to the door. She stood stock-still, this time with no support. He thought her luminous grey eyes appeared glassy with shock, but she made no reply. He bowed again and withdrew. She heard him speaking to Margery outside on the stair and knew the maid would enter immediately so she would have no private moment to give way to her terrible sense of horror and rank terror.

CHAPTER FOUR

CLARE ignored Margery when she entered the room and, though the woman cast her curious glances, refused to pass any comment. She sat on at the table, not even moving to the comfort of the hearth fire. Nothing could bring warmth to her numbed spirit. Margery occupied herself stitching at some man's shirt she had brought up with her. Clare did not know if it belonged to Robert Devane or some other member of the company.

Her thoughts were in turmoil—she could come to no conclusion. When dinner was brought up by an avidly curious young page whom Margery dismissed brusquely, Clare pushed the pewter plate away in disgust, having still not come to any decision.

The brutal truth finally hit her squarely. There was simply nothing she could do to avoid her fate. She shuddered in retrospect as she recalled the closeness of Robert Devane's body to hers when he had cruelly explained her position. There was no doubt whatever in her mind that, if she refused to accede to his wish and pledge herself to him, he would take her by force.

A betrothal was binding, certainly. She would need a dispensation to break it, but if he kept his word and refrained from forcing unwelcome attentions on her, she could, surely, later—when he was brought to book for this conduct, as surely he must be—appeal to Rome and be free of him.

Despite her fury, her thoughts also began to dwell on the possibility of marriage with Robert Devane. He was young, undeniably handsome and, though she had fought against his threatened domination, she had to confess to herself that she had been stirred by her close contact with him.

Would any man of the Queen's choice prove a better husband? He had teasingly sworn to treat her well, but could she trust him? Come to that, could she trust any man? Peter had cruelly averred no man would want her. Now she had lands and wealth that was no longer so, but even wed, with a household of her own, happiness could not necessarily be guaranteed.

Robert had talked of the possibility of the Earl of March ascending the throne. Though she was Lancastrian to the core, she could not dispel the notion that he might well be right.

The merchants and peasants were tired of the constant depredations caused by these senseless wars and, since Henry was weak and Margaret universally hated and feared, might turn eagerly to this youthful and handsome warrior for a more appropriate King. Backed by the powerful Warwick, he could achieve his object, mount the throne and revenge the death and humiliation of his father at the same time. If so, her chance of freeing herself from this forced marriage would be slight.

She shivered as she recalled Robert Devane's hints that her safety could not be assured under her uncle's guardianship. If she were to die before she was married, then Gilbert Hoyland would be very wealthy indeed. If, as Robert Devane had implied, her uncle had deliberately engineered the attack on the Devane manor and arranged for Peter to be killed. . .

Her mind shied from the ugliness of it—and yet—it had to be faced. Betrothed to Robert Devane might well prove safer for her. At the Queen's Court she certainly would have been safe, but first she must journey there and—her escort had been *very* small. . .

Abruptly she snapped, 'Margery, will you find your master and ask him to come to me?'

Margery nodded, grim-lipped, rose to her feet and left the room immediately.

He lost no time in answering her summons. Deliberately she stood, waiting for him to dismiss the maid. He nodded towards the door and Margery left them.

'Well, have you come to your senses?'

'To agree to your demands is to be bereft of them, I'm thinking,' she snapped. 'However, it would appear that I have no choice.'

'None whatever,' he replied cheerfully, 'unless. . .'

'Then I must do as you say.' She hesitated, then turned away from him, her eyes filling with tears. 'Can I rely on you to keep your word and delay. . .?'

He came very close and turned her chin in his cupped hand then he bent and, looking intently into her eyes, kissed her on the lips. It was a slow lingering kiss, which sent her senses swimming, hard, demanding and yet, strangely without passion.

'Then we seal our bargain,' he declared as he released her. 'That's a good wench. You will not regret your decision. You can rely on me to keep my distance until the marriage is celebrated. It would not be proper to do otherwise,' he added mockingly and she turned and wiped her mouth deliberately so that he laughed aloud.

'Neither hard words nor insulting gestures will disturb me, Mistress Clare, but let me remind you that you remain in my keeping and I urge you to be respectful, before my men, at least. When we are alone together you may curse me as you please. I will summon the priest to perform the ceremony tonight. Before supper will be best, then we can celebrate.'

She looked back into his shining blue eyes, alight with triumph, and wearily turned away with a shrug of acquiescence.

When Margery came back into the room her attitude was subtly different. Obviously she had been informed of the coming betrothal ceremony.

She said, almost respectfully, 'Will you allow me to examine your gowns and see if they need any attention—for tonight?' She glanced meaningfully at Clare's mourning gown. 'I suppose you have nothing but black gowns in your baggage chest.'

'I have not,' Clare returned shortly. 'Must I remind you that, with my brother but lately dead, I could wear nothing else?'

Margery nodded regretfully. 'But if there is a Court gown. . .'

'There is one black velvet one. Open the chest and shake it out, if you must. I suppose I must, perforce, make a good show before Sir Reyner Astley.'

Margery busied herself and Clare, watching in some amusement, concluded that this betrothal had Margery's approval, if no one else's. Of course, Margery would understand well enough Master Devane's need to mend his fortunes.

As evening approached Clare allowed herself to be helped into her best Court gown of cut velvet and agreed, reluctantly, to wear a modesty vest of white and silver brocade within the the deep V of the neckline to temper its sombre richness. She sat while Margery brushed and combed her hair and confined it within the neat black velvet hennin. Firmly she insisted on wearing a black veil over the headdress.

Margery stood back to admire her handiwork.

'There,' she said proudly, 'you'll make a fair enough maid to stand beside my master.'

Clare wondered wryly if the woman was short of sight, but allowed the remark to pass unchallenged. Margery had brushed and attended to her own simple woollen skirt and bodice so that she looked tolerably well to attend her new mistress. Clare had noted with approval that the woman was clean in her habits. Throughout the difficulties of the journey she had managed to provide herself and Clare with water for washing. Only this morning, at the first opportunity, she had laundered both Clare's and her own underclothes and her blouse.

She said suddenly, a trifle huskily, 'I imagine you expected Master Devane to be betrothed with far more ceremony. You have affection for him?'

A sudden smile irradiated the woman's raw-boned features.

'Aye, I love him like my own. His mother died when he was scarce three years old, attempting to bear Sir Humphrey another babe. It was stillborn, a girl. He'd 'ave liked a sister, Master Rob. 'E was ever gentle with women. You're fortunate.'

'Oh, you think so. I am ambushed, abducted, forced into this mockery of betrothal and you consider I should be happy at the prospect?'

The woman leaned forward eagerly. 'You could fare much worse, I'm telling you.'

'In a loveless marriage?'

'He'll never treat you ill unless. . .'

'I deserve it,' finished Clare scornfully. 'He has told me this.'

'And 'e means it. I've never known 'im deal ill with maid or hound nor any poor creature at his door. There's no streak of cruelty in 'im.'

'And my dead sergeant was just unfortunate?'

'Aye, mistress, 'e was, in these times—like my man.'

Clare sighed. 'Well, since there's no help for it, you'd best go below and inform the priest and the gentlemen that the maid is ready for the ceremony like the lamb for slaughter.'

There was no private chapel at the Reyner manor, but a portion of the hall had been curtained off for the ceremony and the village priest had had a makeshift altar set up with chalice, paten and candles. Sir Reyner Astley and Robert Devane were waiting for Clare when she entered with Margery in close attendance.

For the first time she saw Robert out of military attire. Reyner Astley was clad in a doublet and hose of scarlet, but Robert was dressed as soberly as she was in mourning black velvet doublet and grey hose. He looked magnificent in it. The mourning black suited his fair complexion and flaming red hair and she sighed inwardly that her own dark clothes only served to diminish what claim to comeliness she had.

However, this was no occasion for wishing to look attractive and she came forward proudly to stand beside her intended betrothed. He turned instantly and took her hand in his. He wore a simple gold chain to relieve the starkness of his attire and she saw, with some annoyance, that it bore two white enamelled roses, the symbol of his service to the House of York and, depending from it, Warwick's badge of the bear and ragged staff.

The priest was addressing her gravely, questioning her as to her intentions. She answered that she freely gave consent for the ceremony and Robert nodded brusquely for the man to proceed. It was very simple and Clare felt strangely detached from it. She gave her responses when asked and, even when Robert Devane's heavy gold ring was placed upon her finger, she could not fully accept that these few moments had altered the whole pattern of her life.

Without protest she allowed Robert to give her a betrothal kiss and dutifully offered her cheek for Reyner Astley to congratulate them both, then she found herself whisked off to the upper part of the hall where supper had been set on a raised dais, the trestle table replete with pristine napery and gleaming dishes. The Astley servants stood, waiting to serve them.

She could not have said afterwards what was talked about at that meal. She ate obediently when Robert piled delicacies upon her embossed pewter plate. Clearly this friend of Robert's was a man of substance, for the house was finely furnished and the appointments of the best, as was the fare served.

Clare had little interest in any of it. She ate and drank, her thoughts abstracted, one fear occupying her mind to the presence of all else. Would Robert Devane keep his sworn word and allow her, at the close of this mockery of a celebration, to retire quietly to the tower chamber with Margery?

It seemed that her fears were groundless, for he turned suddenly and exclaimed, 'My dear, you look very tired. The hardships you suffered on our journey have caught up with you, I fear. Would you like me to escort you now to your chamber?'

She nodded gratefully, casting a nervous smile at the little village priest who had been invited to share this betrothal feast with them.

Clare placed her hand on Robert's arm and he led her from the hall, Margery following. He was so gracious and attentive that Clare almost laughed aloud. The situation would have been humorous under any other circumstances. Any onlooker would have thought, watching the two of them together, that they had been childhood sweethearts, looking forward eagerly to this moment, instead of the bitter antagonists they were in truth.

At her chamber door he took his leave of her, bending his handsome head to courteously kiss her fingers.

'Sleep well, my dear.' His blue eyes were shining again, whether with triumph for this coup or with genuine amusement, she could not tell. Then the smile faded and he appeared almost grave as he added, 'I swear you will not regret this, Mistress Clare. My lord will be victorious in this coming struggle for power and you will have the protection of the new King.'

She withdrew her fingers sharply and tilted her chin. 'Goodnight, Master Devane,' she said coldly as Margery held open the door for her to pass inside.

The next days passed in tolerable comfort at the manor house and Clare hardly saw her betrothed except briefly when she was invited to join the men in hall at supper. Margery had become decidedly more respectful towards Clare, whom she now regarded as her mistress. She was still inclined to be morose and said little, but she waited on Clare attentively and saw to it that all the pages and servants within the house treated Clare deferentially.

Seated with Margery within the oriel embrasure of the hall one afternoon, Clare saw the two men talking together and obviously making plans for departure. So they would be riding south soon.

The Astley steward entered and, bowing low, bent to speak softly in his master's ear. Sir Reyner glanced sharply up at the man and gestured for him to leave them.

His voice, a little raised in excitement, reached Clare where she sat some feet from them.

'Bad news, I fear, Robert. My lord Earl's men have

clashed with the Lancastrian forces again at St Albans. It seems that things have gone badly wrong. Lord Montagu, my lord's brother, was hopelessly outnumbered and it took some time for my lord Earl to bring up his forces. The messenger says some of the Kentish men deserted and the Queen's forces were victorious.'

Clare lifted her head to listen more intently. Had her uncle, Sir Gilbert, fought in this encounter and could this disaster for the Yorkists mean she might soon be free?

Robert had sprung to his feet angrily. 'Sweet Virgin, Reyner, how could this have happened and we here all unaware of it? Why no summons to you and proper commission of array to my lord Earl's supporters?'

Astley shook his head, as bewildered as his friend. 'I have heard no word, only an intimation that my lord Earl was marching on London. He appears to have delayed and relied entirely upon his Kentish contingent. I think we had better have the messenger in and question him further.'

The steward, who was still hovering in the doorway, left immediately to bring the man to the hall. Robert was still pacing furiously. Clare saw his eyes flashing blue sparks from the firelight's reflected glow.

The messenger entered and hastened to bow the knee before the two men. He was muddied almost to the waist, clad in leather jack and salet, and obviously wearied to the bone.

Robert snapped a hurried question before the man had risen to face them. 'What of my lord Earl, man? Did he get clear of the field?'

'Yes, sir. Though things went against us, he managed to make a good retreat with many of his men. There was no undisciplined rout. I'd say he still has more than four thousand men at his disposal. He has drawn off and is likely now to join the Earl of March in the west.'

'I don't understand how this could have happened, man,' Astley said in irritation. 'My steward says there was some defection of my lord Earl's forces.'

'Aye, sir, and some say that's what caused demoralisation in Lord Montagu's force. Lovelace, one of the Earl's squires, went over to the Queen's force with many of the Kentish men.' The messenger was breathing hard. 'It was snowing in our faces, sir, another reason why the battle turned against us.'

'And the King? Is he still in our hands?' Robert demanded.

'No, sir. It's said he was found sitting under a tree. He'd been put in the care of Lord Bonville and Sir Thomas Kyriell. Both of them were executed after the battle and they were all taken to Lord Clifford's tent.'

'So London lies in Margaret's hands,' Robert said heavily.

'Not yet, sir. It's said the Londoners are anxious to close their gates to the Queen, fearing savage attacks from her forces like those on her journey south. I was sent to give you word. My lord Earl urges you, if you can, to do what you can for the Duchess Cecily and the two younger York boys, but, to tell truth, sirs, I fear the conditions round St Albans might well prevent you getting into the city in safety. It all bodes ill for the Duchess.'

Astley had also risen and was leaning against the mantel. He was frowning in deep thought. 'Go, fellow, and get some rest. My steward will see to your needs. You intend to ride after the Earl?'

'Those are my orders, sir.'

'Good. You've delivered your message. We'll see to it

that everything will be done to help the Duchess. Deliver that message to the Earl.'

'So we ride south?' Robert said as the messenger limped out of the hall.

'At first light. I'll give the orders to prepare for departure. You ride with me?'

'Of course.'

'Then you'll not follow the Earl?'

'If the Duchess and her children require our assistance, I must go with you.' Robert turned and saw his betrothed sitting very silent within the window embrasure.

'You will have heard all that, Mistress Clare.'

'Yes. Will you leave me here?'

He hesitated but only for a moment. 'Indeed, no. Where I go, mistress, you go with me. Margery, pack your own and your mistress's baggage. We ride out with Sir Reyner early in the morning. Find Piers for me. I'll need him to deliver my instructions to the company.'

He held out his hand to Clare to escort her to her chamber and signalled to a young page to follow them and remain in attendance outside her door.

For the rest of the day Clare could see from her window the frantic preparations for departure. Piers Martine stood in the courtyard issuing curt directions to the Fletcher brothers, while Silas Whitcome saw to it that the horses were led out and was examining them for any signs of injuries or strains. She noted that her own palfrey was also being afforded a like scrutiny. So Robert Devane was determined, then; she was to accompany the party. She turned as Margery entered the chamber and set about packing their baggage chests.

'So,' she said waspishly, 'we are to be carted willy-nilly into danger again. Your master thinks little of the welfare of his womenfolk.'

Margery did not rise to the bait. She continued with her work in silence.

After supper Robert Devane accompanied Clare right into her chamber and looked round to see that everything had been done in readiness for the morning.

'Margery, see that your mistress has a cup of mulled ale so that she sleeps well tonight. Tomorrow will be hard going. Go down now and see to it.'

Left alone with him, Clare seated herself in the one chair the chamber boasted and regarded Robert with some satisfaction.

'So, it would seem that your youthful Earl of March is unlikely to be crowned after all.'

He looked back at her grimly. 'All is not lost yet.'

'But, since your Earl is on the run, you will find it less easy to keep me caged as you thought.'

'You are still my betrothed wife.'

'That could soon be altered, as you know well.'

'It might not be so simple as you think, if I were to make you completely mine. We are betrothed. The custom is not unknown.'

It was a brutal reminder of his power over her and she flinched where she sat as he came close, bent over her and leaned down, placing both hands on the arms of her chair so that she was forced to draw right back from him.

'Listen to me, mistress,' he said icily. 'You will ride with us willingly tomorrow or I shall have you tied in your saddle and put Piers Martine in charge of your person. You will not find him either careful of your comfort or easy to evade.'

She felt a sudden dryness of the mouth and he smiled sardonically. 'You do not like or trust Piers Martine, I

see. You are right to be cautious. Piers is excellent in
many ways, but his treatment of women leaves much to
be desired. Do not fear. He knows I am master and he'll
not touch what is mine, but he'll keep you safe for me
and go to any lengths to do so. I'll not have you escape
and fall into Gilbert Hoyland's hands.'

He bent and kissed her hard on the lips. 'Keep this
remembrance of me and your plighting of troth to me,
Mistress Clare. You may well find it will be better for
your continued health in the long run.'

Clare slept uneasily and was woken early by sounds of
frenzied activity both in the house and the courtyard
below. Margery was already awake and hastened to
dress, assisted her mistress to do so and then hurried
below to see to it that food was brought up to the
chamber. Clare felt little like eating but she made
herself do so, aware that there might be little opportunity on the journey.

Robert Devane came up to the chamber, dressed once
more in a plain leather jack and Clare noted that he was
well armed. Clearly he was expecting there might be
trouble on the journey. Margery rose, curtsied and
hurried out with the tray.

He spoke curtly to Clare. 'Are you ready?'

'Quite ready.' She was still seething with suppressed
fury from his last night's treatment of her. Her tone
must have conveyed her anger, for he raised one
eyebrow as he regarded her thoughtfully. Then he
moved to the chest where Margery had draped in
readiness her warm cloak and brought it to her, placing
it round her shoulders. She resisted the urge to flinch
from his touch and stood docilely, but, as he moved
aside to allow her to pass him through the door, she
stalked by him and descended the stairs to the hall.

Men were hurrying about with boxes and saddle bags and Reyner Astley stood with his steward directing operations. Lounging near the hearth, with one elbow on the mantel, stood Piers Martine. Rob signalled to him and the Frenchman came and bowed to Clare, then took up his post beside her while Rob went out to see their horses were ready. Clare studiously turned away from her jailor and did not deign to address one word to him.

Eventually Margery came to her side, cloaked and ready for the journey, and Rob returned to conduct them to the courtyard where Clare's palfrey stood waiting, Silas Whitcome holding the lead rein. She allowed her betrothed to lift her into the saddle while Margery, as she had done on the previous journey, mounted pillion behind Sym Fletcher.

Reyner Astley's men-at-arms numbered twenty, and all wore no distinguishing devices on their jacks. As on the journey from Brinklow, the company took to the forest tracks, avoiding the main Fosse Road south into the capital. Several times Sir Reyner halted the company while little troops of men-at-arms rode by and the Astley retainers remained hidden behind a screen of trees. They were not challenged. When they were within sight of London, Robert suggested they separate into three groups.

'I'll take Mistress Clare and Margery with Silas and Piers, Reyner, while I think it might be best before you pass through the gate, you divide your company. I'll leave the Fletchers with you. We'll meet at Baynards Castle. Agreed?'

Astley nodded thoughtfully. 'We may well be challenged at the gates. I'll enter by Bishopsgate while you ride in by Aldgate. If I'm prevented from reaching the Duchess, I leave you to do what you can.'

The two leaned from the saddles to clasp hands and Robert waited, his hand on Clare's leading rein, while the Astley company rode off. Margery had dismounted from Sym's horse and Silas Whitcome lifted down a hand to haul her up behind him. Clare noted they had left the sumpter mule and that only necessities had been packed into saddle bags and were being carried by the men of the party. She sighed as she thought of the loss of the greater part of her baggage. That couldn't be helped.

If the news from London was as bad as the messenger had indicated, there would be a state of confusion within the streets and she considered it might be possible for her to evade Robert Devane's watchfulness there and ride off in search of someone who could inform her uncle or one of his companion knights of her predicament. Determinedly she thrust aside her doubts about Sir Gilbert, deliberately planted there by Robert Devane for his own purposes.

They rode on and it soon became evident as they passed through Aldgate that the messenger had certainly not exaggerated the alarm of the Londoners. The small party was not challenged at the gate as had been feared. In fact, it was clear more citizens were anxious to leave than those wishing to enter.

The little party moved on, Robert instructing his men to keep as close to him as they could, for they were being jostled and crowded by carts and baggage wagons piled high with goods as the worthy citizens fled into the streets, determined to flee before the threat of the Queen's entry.

Piers Martine and Rob rode on either side of Clare and she was thankful for it. Any desire to melt into this terrified crowd had left her. Undoubtedly she now needed the presence of the stalwart men who guarded her.

She had never been in so large a town before and, in other circumstances, she would have glanced eagerly round her for the places of interest she had heard her father and Peter talk of. But now, in this milling flock of frightened and desperate people, she could only lower her head and make a hasty prayer to the Virgin that they would all be kept from harm.

Over all came the clangour of church bells. Ahead of her a man was beating away the frantic hands of two soldiers who were attempting to steal his horse. The animal neighed and whinnied in terror and it was only his excellent horsemanship which kept him from being unhorsed. Clare shuddered as she thought that, had he been so, he would undoubtedly have been trampled to death.

She could hear Silas cursing behind them and wondered if Margery was praying silently as she was doing while managing to keep her seat, for their horses were fast becoming unmanageable, frightened by the unaccustomed disturbances. The streets were slippery with mud, refuse and ordure, both animal and human, and the stink from the open kennels assailed her nostrils.

Once her palfrey slipped and shied and Rob cursed it and firmly reined it in. A passing apprentice, laden with a heavy sack, shouted abuse as the side-stepping horse almost knocked him from his feet.

A dank, sour smell told her they were approaching the Thames and Rob shouted to her above the noise of people bawling and the constant bells and the clang of iron cart wheels. 'We are approaching Baynards Castle, the home of the late Duke of York. Keep very close to me, now.'

They were all so tightly jammed together that she

could do nothing else, but Clare gritted her teeth on a useless rejoinder and thankfully pulled up her mount as two guards at the gatehouse ahead barred their passage into the courtyard of the gloomy fortress now looming before them.

Grooms sprang to care for their horses and Robert leaped down to run immediately to Clare. He lifted her down and snapped orders to his followers.

'Silas, stay in the courtyard until I send further instructions. Take care of Margery. Piers, you'd best accompany me.'

Clare turned desperately to look for Margery, but her wrist was seized and she was dragged along across the court towards a door guarded by two men-at-arms with crossed bills. Robert shouted his name and that of the Earl of Warwick and the bills were lowered and the little party admitted.

Clare now found herself in a dark low-raftered corridor, lit, even in daylight, by flickering sconces on the walls, and was hastened along so fast she was almost stumbling. Whatever haste Robert Devane thought necessary, he had no intention of abandoning his claim on her. Piers Martine kept careful guard on her other side.

Soon they were in an enormous hall crowded with servants and officials. Obviously Robert knew his way here and waited for no direction but pushed through the people towards the far end where, on a raised dais, a long table stood over which was a cloth of estate. There seemed to be few courtiers or male noblemen within the hall but a preponderance of clerks and sombrely garbed lawyers or officials.

A flustered steward approached Robert with his wand of office and, again, Robert brushed aside all attempts to stay him and demanded, 'I am Robert Devane, squire

to my lord Earl of Warwick. I wish to see the Duchess of
York instantly. I come on the Earl's business.'

The man hesitated only a moment, then bowed hastily
and hastened off through a doorway behind the dais.
Clare took the opportunity to catch her breath and look
around her. So this was the palace of the late Duke of
York, the King's cousin, and by the recent Act of
Accord, the heir to the throne of England. The hall was
a vast, high-roofed place, built centuries ago and, to
Clare's eyes, gloomy and too awe-inspiring for comfort.

Here, as at Astley Manor this morning, everything
was in a chaotic state. Men were conferring hurriedly
and almost secretly, chests were being conveyed outside
by harassed servants and all men gave the impression of
fearing impending disaster.

So the Dowager Duchess was preparing to flee before
the vengeful Queen's advance. Surely it would be most
unlikely that she would consent to receive Robert
Devane in audience? Clare was to be proved wrong in
such an assumption. The steward returned in agitated
haste and commanded Robert and his party to accompany him immediately.

Still Robert kept a tight hold on Clare's wrist as he
hurried in the wake of the elderly official, whose white
wand made a tap-tapping sound on the stone floor.

The man stood back before a doorway, again guarded
by men-at-arms wearing the falcon and fetterlock device
of York. The steward swept aside an arras and
announced the company.

'Your Grace, Master Devane is here with messages
from my lord Earl of Warwick.'

'Come in, come in, Robert. I have been hoping my
nephew would send someone I knew.'

Robert entered what was obviously a solar, advanced
a few steps and dropped to one knee. Bemused, Clare,

behind him with Piers Martine still on guard, bent her knee in a deep curtsy. The room was luxuriously furnished with upholstered chairs, fine, tall court cupboards displaying a wealth of silver jugs and goblets. Tapestries depicting Biblical scenes kept out the worst of the draughts and there were carpets from the East upon the floor instead of the more usual and humbler rushes.

When she rose and lifted her head, she saw Robert advancing towards a padded armchair near the giant hearth where sat a tall, imposing woman, dressed in deepest black, who stretched out her hand for him to kiss. He bent and did so and then stood up as the cool mellifluous voice commanded him.

'You are welcome, Rob. I know you to be a true friend to my nephew the Earl. Is Sir Reyner Astley with you?'

'No, your grace. We left Astley Manor this morning early after hearing the ill tidings from St Albans last night. Outside the city all was in confusion and we had no idea if we would be admitted through the gates. We decided to split up the party so that at least one of us would have a better chance of reaching you.

'My lord earl sent a messenger to bid us put ourselves at your disposal while he hastened to reach your son, my lord Earl of March, or should I say, the new Duke of York.' He glanced round quickly. 'It seems you are making preparations for departure. I have only a small party of men but I expect Reyner to join me soon. Anything at all you wish us to do we are prepared to do instantly. In what ways may we serve you?'

The Duchess's blue eyes were regarding Clare and the Frenchman with interest.

'I know Piers Martine, I think. He was with you and the Earl in Calais.'

Piers bowed low, a gesture Clare had never seen him make before and marvelled at the Duchess's authority, for Clare thought Piers Martine gave his allegiance only to those he himself chose.

'But who is this, Robert?' There was a steely note of command in the Duchess's question and Clare almost opened her mouth to protest at her enforced presence here and to request the help of the Duchess, but Robert smoothly forestalled her.

'This is my nearest neighbour, Mistress Clare Hoyland, your grace. She has been recently bereaved but is my betrothed and in my care. I thought it unsafe to leave her at my manor in so unsettled a time.'

The Duchess inclined her head graciously in greeting and Clare could only curtsy again in answer. Cecily Neville had been well named the Rose of Raby. Even in her drab mourning garments, more suitable to a nun than a great lady such as the Dowager Duchess of York, wife to a Plantagenet and with Plantagenet blood herself through her Beaufort inheritance, she was still a great beauty.

Clare could catch only a glimpse of her famed fair hair beneath the black velvet frontal of her hennin but the cast of her features, though now taut with the pain of grief and stress of alarm for the future of her family, was flawless. She held her head with haughty dignity as if she were, in truth a Queen in her own right, and, had her husband survived Wakefield, she might well have been.

She sat rigidly upright in the carved chair and there was no sign of panic in either her demeanour or her manner. Her servants and officials might well be in a state of uncontrolled alarm but not Cecily Neville.

She said quietly, 'You are welcome, Mistress Hoyland. It is well you should be protected by your betrothed at this time, though I fear life will not be comfortable for you. I imagine you are used to such disturbances, as I am.'

'Madame, how can I serve you?' Robert's question was urgent.

She made no delay while she thought. 'I intend to send my two younger sons to Burgundy to plead for the protection of Duke Philip. Once before I stood at the market cross at Ludlow with these two children beside me while Margaret's men plundered the town. I have no desire for them to see this havoc repeated.

'John Skelton, one of the late Duke's squires, has agreed to accompany them. He is a good man and has my deepest confidence. He will prove an excellent envoy to Philip but he is no experienced soldier as you are, Robert. I charge you to go with him and guard my boys for me.'

Robert inclined his head eagerly. 'Of course, your grace, but what of your own person? Will you not go with us until your son, the Lord Edward, can determine matters within the realm and send word that it is safe for you to return?'

'No, Robert. I have determined to remain here. Edward may need me and I am convinced my daughter Margaret and I are in no immediate danger. The Queen would not dare to harm us but my Lords George and Richard are Edward's heirs and could be in peril if they remain here.' She crossed herself piously. 'I pray to the Virgin that both Edward and Richard, my nephew, will be preserved but if not, and God knows anything can happen in these bloodthirsty times, Edward's brothers must be kept safe.'

'The town is in uproar, madame. We should leave as soon as the boys can be made ready.'

'They are ready, Robert. John Skelton is with them even now, making the final arrangements. A carrack stands ready on the quay near the Coldharbour steps and the boys should be on board within hours.'

The door behind them was opened and the steward announced, 'Master Skelton, your grace, and the Lords George and Richard.'

Clare turned quickly as the three entered. Somehow she had not expected the two Yorkist lords to be so young, although she realised that had she worked out their ages she would have known that. It was still quite a shock to see the two boys advance towards their mother's chair.

Both bowed before her while the squire, after a low bow to the Duchess, turned and acknowledged Robert Devane with a nod of greeting. He was a tall, well-built young man of about thirty summers with a dignified yet studious air which made Clare understand why the Duchess trusted him so with her embassy to the Duke of Burgundy and yet required someone like Robert, who possessed more martial skills, to accompany him.

The Duchess did not actually embrace the boys. Her grave expression broke into a smile as the elder boy knelt gracefully before her to kiss her hand.

He resembled his mother, Clare thought. Like everyone else in the household the princes were in mourning for their father. George was tall for his age, slim, and he carried himself with an unconscious arrogance. His features were regular and he would be floridly handsome when full grown, Clare decided. His fair curls fell girlishly to his shoulders. He was talking excitedly to his mother.

'My lady mother, John says I cannot take my best doublet and the new one that. . .'

She interrupted him quickly. 'I have told you, George, you must be guided by John in all things. It is impossible for you to take more than necessities.'

He turned and Clare saw that his mouth turned down sulkily and he cast John Skelton a look of extreme resentment, then turned to survey Robert and Piers Martine, observing the travel-stained appearance of the company with some distaste.

The younger boy resembled neither his mother nor his brother. He was small and slight and dark. As he had moved towards his mother's chair he had cast Clare a curious glance and then smiled. That smile completely illuminated the rather narrow, clever features.

Clare found herself reacting to that smile with a deep curtsy, and again his serious expression relaxed into an amused grin, which lifted the corners of the tightly held youthful mouth. He must be about seven or eight, Clare judged, and his brother possibly eleven or twelve. His eyes were grey-green, very like Clare's own. He would never be handsome, Clare decided, but that special smile would win him more truly loyal friends than his more charming brother.

He looked up at Robert, but there was no contempt in his eyes for the simple soldierly clothes Robert wore. His gaze passed down the length of the serviceable leather jack to the sword and dagger worn at the plain leather belt. The black clothing Lord Richard wore did nothing to enhance his appearance but made the thin, clever face look sallow.

Clare commiserated. Like her, he did not look his best in black and she sighed as she thought the way things were going he would need to wear it often in the future. He made them all a courteous little stiff half-bow. Unlike his brother he uttered no words of protest but simply went to his mother, dropped to his knees and kissed her fingers. Clare's heart stirred as she saw there was more an anguished little plea than Court courtesy in the gesture. For what, she could not tell.

The Duchess sat forward in her chair, one arm round each of her two boys as they knelt beside her. She made an appealing picture in her black gown and Clare was irritated by the fact that she was convinced Cecily Neville knew it and that it bound the men to her in the extremity of her grief and need.

She addressed John Skelton. 'I have decided it would be sensible for you to be accompanied by Robert Devane. He has just arrived in good time to be of assistance to us. We all know how well he served my lord Earl both at Middleham and in Calais. His services will be invaluable in helping to protect my sons both in Burgundy itself, but also to help you get free of the city.'

John Skelton showed no resentment but appeared relieved.

'I am honoured, Your Grace, by this charge you put upon me and will be grateful for the help of Master Devane, whose abilities I know well.'

The Duchess bent and gently urged her two sons to rise.

'My sons, you must be very brave. I know I can rely on you to behave with the dignity that the Plantagenet blood you bear behoves you to do. Obey John and Master Robert Devane here as you would do me or your brother the Lord Edward. At Duke Philip's Court you will behave with courtesy and in no manner disgrace your House. I do not know how long your exile will be, but I shall summon you home as soon as possible. Now, go with God.'

She *did* embrace them both now, but with restraint. George wriggled free quite quickly and smoothed down his velvet doublet, but Richard clung to his mother with some depth of desperation and she put him from her firmly. He withdrew at last and stood, stony-faced, while she gave final instructions to the men.

'Will you ride to the wharf?'

'I think it best if we go on foot, your grace. The crowds are very dense and in some disorder. I think it would be better so. We shall not attract undue notice in such a press,' Robert advised. 'It is but a short step to Coldharbour Wharf and, if necessary, the boys can be carried.'

She nodded and her gaze went to Clare. 'Do you intend to leave your betrothed with me, here, Master Devane? I fear I cannot guarantee her safety if the Queen besieges the castle, but she would be welcome to remain amongst my ladies if such is her wish.'

Clare hesitated only a fraction of a moment. If she were to remain here with the Duchess within this stolidly Yorkist household, she would lose every opportunity to escape from Robert Devane's dominance. She would be too well guarded, ostensibly for her own safety. Outside, in this panic-stricken city, she might manage to evade his vigilance. He would have his hands full with the two boys and would have little time for her.

She said hastily, 'I thank your grace, but I would not wish to be parted from my betrothed at this dangerous time. I promise I will prove no hindrance to him and—' she sought wildly for some valid reason to back up her answer '—perhaps I can be of help to him on the journey.'

Robert Devane started visibly and looked quite stunned, not to say suspicious, but he quickly regained his composure and joined his plea to hers.

'My betrothed is right, your grace. She should be with me, and the boys will need constant attendance by women since you cannot be with them. My old nurse-maid waits outside with another of my men. The lords will be well served, I promise.'

The Lord George looked affronted that he should be

deemed to need women's care at the ripe age of eleven years, but the Duchess flashed Clare a glance of profound gratitude. 'That would be more fitting,' she said with a smile, 'but I trust the journey will not prove either dangerous or too uncomfortable.'

John Skelton was looking back towards the door anxiously as raised voices could be heard from the corridor, signifying some new problem which had beset the castle's inhabitants. He said respectfully, 'We should go now, at once, your grace, if we are to catch the tide. We can split up the saddle bags and small travelling chests between us.'

'You have safe my letter to Duke Philip?'

He touched the breast of his doublet. 'I have, your grace. It will be handed to no other.'

'Then go now before I find it too hard to part with my sons.' The Duchess smiled tremulously and one of her two ladies who had remained unnoticed in discreet attendance within the oriel embrasure came forward to comfort her as she saw tears start to her mistress's eyes.

Again the men bowed and Clare curtsied, then John Skelton placed a guiding hand upon young George's shoulder to lead him to the door. Robert bowed respectfully to the younger boy who quietly moved to his side. George was chattering volubly as they left the room, but Clare caught a glint of tears in young Richard's eyes.

Outside, in the corridor, they met Reyner Astley's party entering the castle. He stopped dead at the sight of Robert and the two princes.

'Dear God, Robert, the city is in a tumult. I thought I would never be able to reach the Duchess. She is safe?'

'Quite safe, my friend, and determined to remain here. She has charged us with the care of her sons. We go with John Skelton to Burgundy.'

Astley stopped instantly, his brow furrowed. 'You will

need the Devil's own luck to get to the wharves. Do you wish me to come...?'

'I think it would be well for you to stay and help guard the Duchess. The larger the party, the more difficult our progress will be.'

Astley saw the sense of that and nodded. He bowed to the two noble boys and George smiled at him winningly.

'It will be a great adventure,' he said with boyish confidence.

Astley laughed. 'I applaud your courage, little lordling. Take heart and know your lady mother will be well guarded while you are away.'

The Lord Richard said quietly, 'For that I thank you, sir, for I shall worry about my lady mother. If the Queen comes...'

'Phoo, Richard, Queen Margaret will never dare to harm our mother,' George put in arrogantly. 'She knows Ned will be King in England soon enough and we shall return to avenge any insult.'

A nervous page waited by the outer door with cloaks for the boys. He looked as if he might burst into tears at any moment and Clare was unsure if he was distressed by this parting or fearful of what was to come within the next few days. She saw to it that both boys were well wrapped up to face the inclement weather and the prospect of wet, cold hours on board the ship which was to sail with them all to Damme harbour.

Outside in the courtyard Silas Whitcome was waiting with the horses and Margery. Robert explained tersely that they were now to proceed on foot. Clare quietly explained the situation to Margery who glanced hurriedly at their charges.

Her dour expression changed at the sight of them to one of tender concern, especially at the younger boy who was standing a little apart now, his desolation apparent on his youthful countenance. Clare remembered that Margery had been a nursemaid to Robert. It seemed she had deep affection for children and she had lost a child of her own.

Clare was sad to part with her palfrey, which nuzzled her shoulder as she bent to pat the satiny nose. She wondered if it might be possible to regain her mount if she managed to escape before they reached the ship but thought that unlikely. She watched, regretfully, as a groom led their horses to the stable.

Robert said a little gruffly as he came to her elbow, 'They will be safe enough with Reyner Astley.'

She nodded and moved to Margery's side. Already the former nurse was pulling up the Lord Richard's hood. 'You'll feel the cold when we reach the river wharf,' she scolded gently and he gave her a grave little smile of gratitude.

The noise outside the gates seemed to be growing in volume. John Skelton looked anxiously towards Robert who pursed his lips and then shrugged.

'Is there a picket gate, less noticeable for our departure?'

Skelton nodded. 'By the river steps.'

'Then let us take it without delay, my friend, and hope we shall be taken for a family of servants leaving the castle in hope of finding sanctuary elsewhere than with the Duchess's household.'

CHAPTER FIVE

SKELTON'S party passed through the river picket gate with several other groups of people determined to escape from the castle and the city also if possible. John Skelton held fast to the arm of young George, who was protesting voluably that he was unused to be crushed so close to common riff-raff who stank. Margery hastened to the assistance of the harassed squire, who looked bewildered and unsure how to deal with his difficult charge.

Piers Martine forged ahead ruthlessly clearing a way for the party. Men swore and cursed but, seeing the unholy glitter in the Frenchman's eyes and his hand meaningfully upon his sword hilt, gave ground. Rob signalled to Silas to bring up the rear and Clare was hustled near to him, the younger boy, Richard, between them.

The crowds here, jostling and pushing to get to the various ferry steps and wharves, were just as panic-stricken as the ones she had seen as they rode through the city. Clare soon saw the sense of Rob's plan to go on foot, for it would have been impossible to ride in such a throng. Young Richard turned to her once with anxious eyes and she smiled to reassure him, placing one hand upon his arm. Unlike his elder brother, he gave no trouble but remained as close to Clare as he could.

Rob looked down at them both and said through his teeth, 'For God's sake, Clare, keep Piers Martine and Skelton well in sight. If we once get parted, who knows when we could find each other again?'

Clare's lips tightened. He had spoken the truth. If she could manage to lose him in this throng, she could be free and, rage though he might, he would not dare relinquish his duty to the Duchess to go in search of his prisoner. This would be her one opportunity. Firmly she thrust aside the fear of being left unprotected in this terrifyingly unstable city. Men were too intent on escape to threaten her—yet she quailed inwardly at thought of remembered tales she had heard of Queen Margaret's soldiery on their way south from Wakefield.

Her heart was hammering wildly, but she struggled on, waiting for a chance to slip away from the watchful gaze of Silas Whitcome. For the moment Rob was too intent on the progress of John Skelton ahead of him to notice her. She had no money. How was she to survive until she could find someone who would contact her uncle? If the city fell to the Queen, surely he would soon be in London and able to come to her help?

Clare glanced down at her betrothal ring, a signet of heavy gold with the Devane crest set with a small cabouchon sapphire. She would sell it and she was wearing the one pendant she had brought from Hoyland, a mourning jewel set with jet and seed pearls. The value of the two would have to suffice. She doubted whether she would get much for the two pieces when no one was anxious to buy, but she would manage, she told herself grimly.

Skelton turned and shouted some comment back to Rob, who hastened forward to help him. It seemed that the Lord George had clumsily slipped his foot from his shoe and it could not now be found. Piers Martine, with scant respect, picked the boy up and stowed him beneath one arm, to his chagrin. He bellowed his rage at such unceremonious treatment. While Robert Devane's attention was off her and Silas's on the boy, Richard,

Clare seized her chance and slipped back from the party. Almost instantly the crowd closed round her and she struggled to win free and move against the tide back towards the castle.

It was hard work and she was breathless with effort but, though she could see Rob's tall form ahead of her crowned with his distinctive red hair, she knew she could wriggle free now and lose herself.

As she turned determinedly back the way they had come, she heard a boy's despairing cry behind her and turned immediately. The young Lord Richard had tried to follow her. Somehow he had been separated from his bodyguards and was pushing against the people, who jostled him angrily from their path. His hood had fallen back and she saw his strained white face appealing for her help. His lips formed the words, 'Mistress Clare, Mistress Clare—please—'

A burly man, clad in the canvas breeches and striped jerkin of a seaman, thrust the boy aside with an imperious brawny hand and Richard wavered for a moment unsteadily and went down on his knees.

Clare went white to the lips. In this throng the boy would have no chance at all. He would simply be trampled to death under the feet of unwary passers-by. She screamed a warning to Robert Devane and began to push her way back to Richard. Another sailor, seeing her desperation, bellowed a command and the crowd drew back apace so that she was able to reach the boy and put down a hand to help him to his feet.

'Is this your lad?' the sailor asked good-humouredly. 'Best keep a tight hand on his arm, mistress. It's every one for himself in this commotion.'

Richard hauled himself upright and stared at her open-mouthed. He was obviously very frightened. 'Oh,

Mistress Clare, I thought we would lose you, that you'd be hurt. . .'

'And no one but herself to blame if she were,' a harsh voice snapped as Robert Devane caught her arm in a savage grip. 'What, in the Virgin's name, did you think you were doing? Do you want to get us all killed? My lord.' He bent and lifted Richard into his arms. 'Are you hurt? If I have to put you down, do not leave my side again, for any reason whatever. Remember your lady mother's words, to trust and obey me. As for you, madam, it would be best if you heeded them too.'

He caught her arm with his free hand and tugged her back to the shelter of a wall where the rest of the party waited. John Skelton's anxious brown eyes brightened with relief at sight of his younger charge, safe and apparently unhurt. Piers Martine, still holding the Lord George somewhat disrespectfully bundled beneath his arm, was clearly amused, while Margery looked round-eyed with fear.

'Let us get on,' Rob snapped, irritably. 'At this rate we could lose the tide.'

Clare knew now she had lost her one chance but, catching sight of the pleading expression on the face of the youthful Lord Richard, she knew she could do no other but sail with him to the port of Damme and see the two boys safe. It might be possible there to appeal to someone in authority to help her get free from this hated imprisonment and return to England.

As they approached the wharves at Coldharbour Steps, Clare saw that people were struggling to board the smaller ferry boats that would carry them to the South bank, from where they could flee to safety in the countryside round Blackheath and await events.

Beside the smaller craft moored near the wharf, obviously merchant cogs plying across the North Sea to trade with the Hanseatic merchants, was a huge vessel with high castles fore and aft towering above its clinker-built sides. Hastily Robert Devane steered his party towards this ship.

'That is the Earl's carrack, *The Bear*,' he informed John Skelton. 'I have sailed on her many times. She is fast and seaworthy. Captain Smith is a man to be relied on, both in peaceful trading pursuits and, if necessary, in times of war. We have had our near-fatal moments raiding Lancastrian shipping out from Calais harbour. We must hurry up and board her. The captain will be anxious to make ready now before the next tide.'

He urged them onward and, to Clare's relief, a group of armed retainers wearing the livery and device of the bear and ragged staff of the Earl of Warwick now hurried towards them, their sergeant crisply ordering his men to clear the way. The people crowding the wharf had no choice but to stand aside and Robert Devane hastened to get his small party aboard.

Clare stared fearfully up at the towering masts and forecastle, which loomed over the upper deck, as one of the Earl's retainers took her arm to assist her up the gangplank. For the first time she faced the realisation that she had never sailed the seas nor even glimpsed the sea.

She had travelled once on a small river boat on the Soar with her father and enjoyed the experience, but the prospect of sallying forth onto the open sea filled her with mounting alarm. Once on the deck Robert left his small company under the guard of Silas Whitcome and Piers Martine, while he and John Skelton went forward to confer with the captain who issued forth from the forecastle to greet them.

Piers Martine had, at last, put down his struggling

burden and George dashed forward to follow John Skelton but was firmly held back by the Frenchman.

'Not this time, *mon petit seigneur*. Your guardian is too busy to concern himself with you, *n'est ce pas*?'

George sulkily wriggled free of Martine's grasp on his arm and went to lean down over the rail, peering down at the mass of humanity swarming below them on the wharf.

'Where are they all going?' he demanded of Clare.

'I do not know, my lord, but I think they feel they will be safer on the South bank, away from the possibility of the Queen's army entering the city from the north.'

Richard said thoughtfully, 'This is a very big ship, Mistress Clare. I have never been to sea before.'

'Nor I, my lord, but Master Devane has sailed on her and with this captain, so I do not think there is anything to fear.'

'Edward has sailed often to and from Calais to be with cousin Richard of Warwick,' George said confidently. 'Of course we shall be safe.'

Richard was peering down also at the milling crowds. 'I'm glad we are free of them now, but I feel sorry for them all.' He looked up, smiling, into Clare's face. 'I hope I shall not be seasick. That would be embarrassing.'

'It would, my lord,' Clare admitted ruefully. She had not considered the possibility and hoped that this would not assail her. It would be the last straw in what had been a frightening and infuriating ordeal endured over these last days.

'I have sailed on the Nene from Croyland to Fotheringhay,' Richard informed her, 'with Edward and once with my brother Edmund and sister Margaret. I wasn't sick then, but I expect it is different on the sea.' His face grew grave as he remembered the death of his

brother, Edmund of Rutland, following the battle of
Wakefield.

Clare nodded in sympathetic agreement as sailors
approached and began to swarm up the rigging and
attend to the gangplank. It seemed that the Warwick
retainers had been sent to ensure their safe boarding of
the vessel and were not to accompany them. It was likely
they would be dispatched now to join the defenders of
Baynards Castle or the Earl's luxurious town house.

If the Queen's forces swarmed into the city there
would undoubtedly be looting and the Earl's property
must be protected, besides the safety of the Duchess to
be assured.

Margery was urging the boys from the open deck rail
to the more protected shelter of the projecting roof of
the forecastle. Certainly it was becoming even colder
and a light drizzle had begun. Clare helped her shepherd
the boys and was glad they were all wearing warm
hooded cloaks for this journey. The light was beginning
to go and she could only dimly discern the wharf
buildings as the heavy rattling of chain told her the
anchor was being raised and their journey had begun.

Robert had apparently finished explaining their plans
to the captain, for he came to where Clare was standing
with the boys.

'Leave Margery to take care of them. I wish to talk to
you.' He gestured towards the stern rail.

Clare glanced hesitatingly back at Margery, but the
two young lords seemed, for the moment, contented
enough in the nursemaid's company. Reluctantly, Clare
went obediently with her betrothed.

'Captain Smith tells me the weather prospects for this
journey are not good. We may enounter some high seas.
I hope you can help with the children if they begin to
suffer from *mal de mer*.'

'Naturally I can,' she said evenly, 'though I cannot be
sure I won't be sick myself. I have never sailed before.
Be assured though, I shall do everything for the boys'
comfort I can. If it were not for Lord Richard. . .' Her
voice trailed off miserably.

'You would have lost yourself in that crowd near the
wharf,' he finished, eyeing her speculatively.

'If you know that. . .' Clare drew a hard breath. 'You
must be aware that I am prepared to do anything to be
free of you.'

'Yet you wouldn't desert the boy when he seemed to
be in trouble.'

'He tried to follow me. I feared he would be trampled
to death in that crowd. Anyway,' she said a trifle
breathlessly, 'he needs someone to offer him some show
of love—well, affection, anyway. That brother of his
does not appear likely to be a helpful companion.'

'I think young George could prove quite a handful,'
Robert murmured under his breath, 'and God knows,
he needs protection. Should any Lancastrian get within
yards of either of them they could become dead meat.'

She gave a horrified gasp and he nodded grimly. 'They
are heirs to York and Edward could get himself killed in
any new engagement—or captured.'

'Yet you seemed so sure of his victory only days ago.'
Clare could not dispel the note of triumph in her voice
and he looked down at her again keenly.

'Whatever you may think of me, I ask you now to
consider the welfare of the children.'

'Of course I shall,' she snapped. 'I am not used to
children but I have healing skills, as you very well know,
and I shall not desert them until. . .'

'Until they are safe within their own household again.'

She swallowed at the enormity of that sacred promise.
By it she was committing herself to servitude in Robert

Devane's party for what might be months ahead, and well she understood those months might doom any chance she might have to obtain her dispensation later. Her uncle would assume she had willingly gone with this man or, at least, accepted the situation, when escape had proved difficult or threatening.

He gave her a little half-respectful bow. 'I am grateful, mistress. I had not thought that this adventure would have put us all in this dilemma. I know how much you crave to be free of me, but the need of the boys is great. My men are capable of protecting them but, as you said, they need the care of women. Margery is an excellent nursemaid but, I suspect, she will have a devil of a job convincing Lord George in particular of the need to obey her. He will recognise your innate authority.'

Clare was by no means sure of that, but she inclined her head thoughtfully.

'Where will you take them?' she asked.

'You heard the Duchess express a wish that we should convey them to the court of Duke Philip but...' he paused and gazed across the darkening sea and the creamy wake the stern of the carrack made across the water '...I am not sure the Duke will be prepared to receive them, at least until he is sure matters will go well with their brother and the House of York. Should the Queen be succesful in routing the Earl of March's army...' He shrugged and turned back to her, a deter-mined gleam in his blue eyes which glimmered in the light from the vessel's stern lantern. 'In that event our stay in Burgundy could prove protracted and the gold provided by the Duchess insufficient for our needs. We can manage but we might have to exist in straitened circumstances.'

Clare's eyes widened and she nodded again.

'If the seas become rough, cold though it might be, I

propose to keep the boys above deck. There will be less chance of us all sickening in the open air.'

She nodded again and he leaned towards her as if he would say something else, then appeared to think better of it, nodded respectfully and stalked off to join Martine and Whitcome near the rail in the well of the deck.

Clare remained where she was for some moments. In this brief conversation she knew she had glimpsed another side of this man. Before, she had considered him feckless and venal for gain, willing to serve any master who would offer him preferment, but she had seen him look towards the two Yorkist lords and she understood his loyalty to them and their House.

Whatever happened, even if the Earl of March were defeated or killed and the hopes of the Yorkist princes doomed, Robert Devane would keep his pledge to their mother and remain with them, whatever sacrifice it might cost him. She considered her own reaction to that. She had never doubted his courage, only his probity.

He had forced a betrothal for gain, he had made no bones about that, but, in some respect, there was justice in his claim. Her family had brought about the downfall of his House. She gave a little tremulous sigh, biting her lips in doubt. If only such a man as he had wanted her for the right reasons. . .

She straightened her shoulders determinedly. It was useless to think along those lines. Her traitorous body was guilty of weakness whenever he was near and to admit that, even to herself, was to allow only disaster to her hopes of final freedom.

While in the Thames estuary the seas remained calm enough. Though it was now full dark and lanterns glimmered about the ship, the boys were rapt in the delight of discovery and ran happily about the deck, peering over the rail, trying to distinguish the shadowy landmarks along the banks. Margery watched indulgently while the squire, John Skelton, engaged Piers Martine and Robert Devane in conference, apparently concerning their immediate plans on landing.

Clare seated herself on a bale of wool, caught her fur-lined cloak around her, for it was becoming now very cold, and allowed herself to close her eyes and rest her tired body. It had been an eventful day and the happenings had followed so hard upon her betrothal that that momentous occasion seemed to have disappeared in the misty distance of time.

Up until now, her thoughts had been entirely upon means of escape, but now she knew she was duty bound to remain with the children and she must allow the future to shape itself any way it would. She discovered that the thought brought some measure of comfort.

She watched Robert Devane as he talked enthusiastically with the two men. Now and then his infectious laugh rang out and she understood what measure of confidence the Duchess had placed in him. Even Piers Martine appeared willing to be guided by him. She was somewhat surprised. In their first meeting in the barn at Hoyland she had judged Robert to be reckless and almost without compassion, making light of his grief and injuries and regardless of his danger.

Now she recognised the true leader he was. He might give the impression of easy camaraderie, but his men held him in the upmost respect. Certainly Clare had seen the light of admiration in young Richard's eyes at his soldierly bearing and the sure way he had escorted them through the panic-stricken city.

Soon they cleared the estuary and sailed into open seas and the sailors came quickly and efficiently to hoist more sails, their bare feet resounding on the planking of the deck. The wind freshened and Robert's prognostication of heavy seas bore weight. The carrack shuddered throughout its timbers and the decks heaved below them.

Even sitting, Clare was forced to take a firm hold of the clinkered bulwark above her. Margery pulled up her hood and began to mutter hasty prayers to the Virgin. She called to her charges, who came stumbling across the deck towards the two women. Richard almost fell but hastily recovered himself and came, breathlessly, to sit upon the deck near Clare.

'We are in open waters now,' he said excitedly. 'The waves are very high, Mistress Clare. I thought one would come right over the ship's side.'

'I think it best if you keep close to me now, my lord. It will be hard to keep your footing and we are protected here from the worst of the wind and spray.'

George demanded querulously, 'I want to go to the cabin in the forecastle. Please take me, at once. It's getting too cold to stay here.'

Clare said reassuringly, 'Master Devane thinks it best to stay on deck, my lord. Below it will be close and fetid and you may sicken more quickly.'

He stamped his foot, his face pale and set and a trifle greenish of hue, in the pallid light from the lantern above them on its projecting hook on the forecastle housing. 'I feel sick already. I insist on going below. I won't be sick here on deck in full view of everyone.'

Margery stood up and placed an arm round the boy's shoulders. 'I'll go below with him, Mistress Hoyland, if you prefer to remain here with the Lord Richard.'

Clare agreed, raising her voice above the noise of the wind and slapping sail against the masts. 'Very well, Margery, but be careful when you go down the companion steps. It will be hard to stand upright and slippery with spray.'

She pulled Richard's body close to her to shelter him from the lashing spray. He made some small sound and she peered down into his face only to see he was laughing delightedly as he watched the unsteady gait of Margery and his brother as they made for the steps. John Skelton rose from his seat on another bale of wool and tried to hasten after them, but his progress was slow, and Clare heard him curse loudly and pull his way hand over hand along the side.

'You are not afraid, Lord Richard?'

'I do not like it very much,' he confessed as his teeth chattered and she felt his thin young body shivering against her, 'but, as George said, it is an adventure, isn't it, and I shall have to learn to stand hardship when I go on campaign with my brother, Ned, when he fights his enemies.'

'You are somewhat young to think of war, my lord,' Clare said gently. 'Your mother is more concerned with keeping you safe than testing your courage.'

He smiled at her gamely. His pale young face was wet with spray and the wind took his breath as he strove to answer.

'I'm so much smaller than my brothers. Everyone says I was scrawny and weak when I was a baby, even compared with my sisters. But I intend to be a great warrior, Mistress Clare, you shall see. Once Ned routs the Queen's forces I shall be sent to start my training with sword and battle axe and I mean to practise hard so I shall grow strong and my size will not matter.'

Privately Clare thought he was much too slight to handle such heavy weapons, but prudently she kept her own counsel and hugged him closer to her. At least he did not appear to think such an affectionate gesture either impertinent on her part or too belittling to his age and martial ambitions, for he snuggled closer and laughed against her shoulder.

'My nurse called me Dickon and all those I love do that,' he told her. 'Please call me Dickon, Mistress Clare. You saved my life out there on the wharf and—' boyishly '—I like you.'

She felt ridiculously warmed by his tribute and bent to wipe the wet from his cheeks with a linen kerchief. 'I shall be honoured by your trust, my Lord—Dickon.'

He chuckled and lifted his head to peer across the deck.

'Do you think George will be sick?' he enquired artlessly. 'He looked very green but perhaps that was this peculiar lantern-light. Master Skelton did not look very happy or comfortable either. Do you feel sick, Mistress Clare?'

She shook her head with an answering smile. 'No, my Lord Dickon, but I do not think we should be too quick to assume we shall not if this weather continues.'

She wrapped her fur-lined cloak around him and he snuggled close and, despite the noise of the wind in the rigging and frightening slapping of the huge waves towering over the ship's side, he fell asleep. Margery did not emerge from the forecastle and Clare assumed either the Lord George had been sick, which she feared likely, or he had flatly refused to come up on deck. At least Margery will be warmer down there, Clare thought ruefully.

She heard a step near her and looked up, startled, to find Robert Devane looking quizzically down at her.

'The older boy is very sick, I'm afraid, but Margery can manage,' he whispered, as Clare warned him to quietness by a finger upon her lip. 'Is he all right?' indicating the sleeping Richard.

'Yes,' she whispered back. 'He seems to be very game for his age.'

He nodded, smiling, then he reached down and placed a homespun blanket about her shoulders and topped it with a piece of sail canvas. 'That should help to keep you protected from the wet and a little warmer. I still think it best for us to remain up here. The atmosphere below is anything but pleasant.'

She thanked him quietly and watched as he strode off across the deck to find some shelter with Silas Whitcome near the aft castle housing. She was comforted by his thought for her. She had feared that, later, when their immediate problems were in abeyance, he might be furiously angry with her for her abortive attempt to escape him but he appeared to have accepted the situation calmly.

She sighed. She trusted him to get them through this, though why, she could not have told herself, but she dreaded the days ahead when open conflict would break out between them once again, as surely it must.

The seas calmed towards dawn and, by morning, life on board was much more comfortable for all of them. Margery came up on deck with Lord George, who was still looking very green about the gills, but somewhat recovered and an hour later ready to break his fast.

It was still very cold and, after the sailors had cleared up below in the larger cabin within the forecastle, the small party went below to take a breakfast of ale, cold bacon and rye bread. Clare had expected George to protest that he was not used to such poor fare but he ate cheerfully and appeared to be in a much better humour. She hoped the night's experience had chastened him and that he would not prove a handful during their stay in Burgundy.

It snowed the following day and they were forced to keep within the cabin but, as it was not so rough, the night was not so uncomfortable as the previous one. The boys fretted under the enforced inactivity and Clare and Margery were kept busy trying to keep them amused. They were all glad when *The Bear* sailed finally into Damme harbour and they could all disembark for the famous trading port of Bruges.

The boys scrambled on deck eagerly, but Clare saw that once they were in sight of land Robert had mounted a very close watch upon his charges. Either Silas Whitcome or Piers Martine kept very near at all times, especially when Robert and John Skelton were engaged in planning their next moves.

Richard, in particular, was delighted that they could proceed into the town by barge and was fascinated by all the sights along the banks. Clare, too, watched with interest this strangely flat landscape, busy with shipping from all ports in Europe, and with its own quiet charm as they neared the centre of the city.

Here the canals were lined with the gracious stone-built houses of the wealthy merchants and nobles, step-gabled and fringed with trees, mostly willow and alder, leaning down to touch the water. They passed under many stone bridges and Clare was delighted by the sight of housewives, baskets on their arms on their way to market. The ferries and barges moved in stately progress, heavily laden with goods of all types, bales and chests and curious canvas-wrapped shapes at whose contents Clare could only guess.

Robert scrambled to seat himself close to her and point out the cargoes.

'Here we send our finest wool and, see there, wine casks from France and Germany. Within the city itself, mistress, you will see shops displaying the most beautiful cloth, silks from the East and damask and brocades in every quality and colour, and amber and furs from the Baltic ports brought in by the merchants of the Hanseatic League.'

Clare doubted that the sight of such luxurious wares would charm her, since she had no funds with which to buy, but she nodded and watched as the boys' eager eyes were everywhere—at the huge derricks and equipment for the unloading of the larger cogs and carracks and the smaller craft which brought their wares into Bruges itself.

'Are we to remain in Bruges or pass on to Utrecht?' she queried.

'We shall take lodgings here in Bruges for now while John goes on to Hesdin to seek out the Duke's approval for hospitality for the young lords.' He paused and added, 'I shall take lodgings in the less frequented district. I think, for now, it were best if the identity of the boys remains unknown to the city's notable inhabitants. The place is as intrigue-ridden as Westminster and the stews of the Southwark and we shall keep ourselves to ourselves for a while—just in case.'

She was relieved when they found themselves established on the upper floor of a house in Steen Straat which Robert had taken after a great deal of haggling with the owner.

'This place will serve,' he said as he showed the two women into a large parlour and threw open a door off it which led into a bedchamber. 'I will arrange for truckle beds to be brought in here for you, Mistress Clare, and Margery and the boys can sleep in the inner chamber. We men can settle below on the ground floor. There is a sizeable kitchen there and I'll engage a servant, a French-speaking one if possible, to cook for us and keep this place in order.

'There is a stable some small distance away and I'll hire horses for the length of our stay here. Most people here walk or take boats along the canals, but John will need to ride in and out of the city to the Duke's palace at Hesdin and to Utrecht. I shall need to ride out also from time to time. I don't want any of you to leave the house.'

'You mean we are to be prisoners?' Clare demanded truculently.

He shrugged. 'Certainly, for a while, for your own safety and, most of all, for that of the boys. Do not ever leave or allow them to do so without either my permission or that of John or Piers Martine. Perhaps,' he said grudgingly, 'it may be possible to escort you around the town.'

'We shall need to hear mass.'

'There are churches in plenty nearby, but you must go escorted.'

With this she had to be content.

Margery settled into their quarters cheerfully enough and chivvied her charges into washing and changing their attire, which had grown crumpled and dirtied during their stay on board. George was considerably chagrined when Robert arrived back at their lodgings after an absence of an hour with a bundle of clothing for all of them comprising good woollen skirts and blouses of linsey wolsey for the women with the plain linen caps and coifs habitually favoured by the good housewives of Bruges and plain woollen hose and tunics for the boys.

'Must we wear these?' he demanded sulkily. 'The cloth is rough and scratches and besides, it is not mourning and...'

'Please do as I say, my lord,' Robert replied briskly. 'As your lady mother enjoined you to do. John Skelton agrees with me that it is best for us all to merge into the background as much as possible and,' he added significantly, 'if you wish to venture into the streets and be shown the sights of the city, it is absolutely imperative that you should not be recognised.'

Clare, too, had felt somewhat dubious at leaving off her mourning dress but saw the need. She added her voice to that of Robert's and saw Richard, somewhat reluctantly, don the tunic of dark green cloth obediently.

Over the next few days she saw little of Robert and found that she missed the sight of him more than she could possibly have thought she would. The lodgings were scrupulously clean, though sparse of furniture, and the food was simple but palatable, served by a buxom woman of middle age named Jeanne, who talked continually and fast in French whenever Clare ventured into the kitchen but whose accent was so thick that Clare found it almost impossible to understand her.

Margery gave up at the first attempt. The maid was far more talkative herself now and seemed to have found her particular niche in the company in caring for the domestic well-being of the Yorkist lords.

Neither complained after the first day about their enforced imprisonment and Richard busied himself practising his writing skills, sitting at the bare pine table the parlour boasted. Clare saw that his hand, though still round and childish, was good and commented warmly.

'When we stayed within the Bishop of London's house in London after the rout at Ludlow,' he told her, 'the Bishop's chaplain insisted on teaching us.' He gave her that rare but winning smile. 'We were really prisoners then and it passed the time. I liked to read and write and I learned more Latin and some French.'

He looked back at George who was staring miserably out of their window at passers-by in the street. 'George did not enjoy it so much. He likes to ride and be with his hawks. I expect he misses them sorely.'

Clare was aware that the elder boy was indeed restless though, surprisingly, he was more tractable than she had believed likely and responded to Margery's spoiling with good grace. He was a handsome child with a ready charm when he liked to exhibit it and Margery warmed to his golden, winning personality. Richard, more restrained and less quick to give his affection and trust, clung to Clare rather than to the older woman.

On the following Sunday, Robert Devane knocked at the door of the parlour early and suggested that he escort them to mass at a church in the centre of the city. Until now Piers Martine had accompanied the two women and the boys to a small church only yards away, almost adjoining their lodging, and Clare had seen nothing of Bruges but the canal scenes on their arrival.

Robert announced, 'I thought you might like me to take you to the famous Chapel of the Holy Blood. It contains the most sacred relic in Burgundy and you should see the shrine while you are here in Bruges.'

Clare was ridiculously delighted by his offer and Lord Richard's grey eyes lit up with pleasure.

'Our chaplain at Fotheringhay once told me of it. The reliquary contains some pieces of linen in which Our Lord was buried. Isn't that so, Master Devane?'

'Yes, my lord. The casket which contains these relics was brought to Bruges by Count Thierry of Flanders soon after the Crusades and is said to have been given to him by the Patriarch of Jerusalem. Once a year, I am told, the casket is processed round the town and people come from miles around to see the ceremony.'

Clare asked, 'Is Master Skelton to accompany us, Master Devane?'

'John left yesterday for Hesdin, carrying the letter from the Duchess Cecily. If all goes well, our stay here in Bruges should not be too protracted and,' Robert glanced mischievously at Lord George who, as usual, was peering from the window, 'our charges will be established at the Duke's Court and in the state to which they are accustomed instead of living like humble citizens as we are doing now.'

And, thought Clare wildly, my task of caring for the Yorkist lords will be done and I can be free of my promise to remain with Robert Devane. She could not quite understand why the thought brought with it little pleasure.

Margery hastened to prepare the boys for their outing for it was still bitterly cold but George, surprisingly, demurred.

'If you think I would go out into this town dressed like a peasant to be seen by any noble who might be known to Duke Philip, you are foolish indeed and presumptuous,' he informed Robert haughtily. 'It is bad enough that we must be seen in that church near here. At least only humble craftsmen and a merchant or two worship there and we are unlikely to be recognised by anyone who would see us later at the Ducal palace.'

Robert smilingly shrugged and made no attempt to argue. He turned to Lord Richard but the boy was already waiting, cloaked and hooded by the door, eager for the promised treat.

Clare said coaxingly, 'But my Lord George, you have been fretting for days at being cooped up as a prisoner. Surely. . .'

But he turned from her sulkily, not even deigning to answer. Clare turned worriedly to Robert.

'If Margery is to go with us, who will guard Lord George?' she murmured in a whisper.

'Piers Martine is below. I will ask him to come up and keep the boy company. Silas rode off with John Skelton. Even riding incognito, I thought it best for John to have at least one stout bodyguard. George will be safe enough with Piers. Indeed,' he added, grimly, 'it appears he has no wish to leave the lodging.'

Clare, for one, was as eager as young Lord Richard to visit the famous chapel. The air outside was like wine and frost still sparkled upon window casements and door frames. They set off with Richard between them and Margery coming close behind. It was a short step, too short for Richard's eager appraisal of everything, to the great market square with the canal running along the west side.

'I'm informed this is the square where tournaments are held and ceremonial processions,' Robert told Clare, 'and you can see the keep is being extended and a high belfry built. I doubt if it is completed yet, yet, even so, it towers above anything I have seen in London.'

Richard peered up curiously, clearly overawed, as he was to be also by the great stone fortress known to the citizens as the Bourg and the fine cathedral of St Donatien but this beautiful church was not to be their destination today, for all were eager to view the shrine of the Holy Blood within the Basilica which stood in a corner of the square. Robert hurried them through the gathering townsfolk, giving them little opportunity to view the impressive city hall with its beautiful ribbed windows and the many recesses filled with finely carved statues.

They marvelled at the ornate shrine within the Basilica containing a gold and crystal cylinder that enclosed the holy relics. Kneeling within the nave, Clare reverently prayed for her brother's final repose and that of Robert's father and brother. Mass over, they prepared to return to their lodging, though Clare would have delighted to see more of this wonderful city and Richard looked longingly about the square as, emerging from the Basilica, Robert put a firm hand upon his shoulder to point him in the direction of Steen Straat once more.

He looked up at Clare with that rare little smile, which sometimes transfixed his rather stern young features.

'It is as if we were a family. Do you not wish to have a son with Master Robert some day just like me, Mistress Clare?'

Clare blushed to the roots of her hair as Robert flashed her a keen glance. She was thankful her hood was well up, shadowing her features.

She said, her voice a little choked, 'Certainly I shall pray that my son will be as good mannered and obedient as you are, Lord Richard—sometimes,' she added and he gave a little gleeful chuckle. She thought, coming as he did from so noble a house, that these moments, when he could think of himself as an ordinary child without the cares of nobility, must be rare indeed.

She recalled the sight of him with his mother. Cecily had shown concern for her sons certainly, but with more alarm for their preservation as prospective heirs to the throne rather than the affectionate normal anxiety of a mother for her children. Clare had heard her father talk of Proud Cis, as he had called her, and the way she had loyally followed her husband, Duke Richard, from place to place so that her children were born in so many places and castle.

George had been born in Ireland, Edward in Rouen and young Richard in the Yorkist stronghold of Fotheringhay. How much had he seen of his father, Clare wondered, and had either parent spared time to show him demonstrative love? She had been fortunate that both her parents had clearly shown their love for her. Peter had declared scathingly on more than one occasion that her father had spoiled her.

She cast a hasty glance at Robert and, for the first time, wondered what it might be like to bear a child of his, as Lord Richard had so ingenuously suggested she would. Previously she had thought he might make a negligent husband and father; now she was not so sure. His care of them all during their journey and stay here in Bruges had rather changed her opinion of him.

He was looking away from her and she saw a tic in his jaw work and was not sure if he was attempting to conceal laughter. She knew, passionately, that she *did* want to have children, a son like young Lord Richard, who would be eager to learn about books and curious about the world, and brave under adversity. Robert Devane's son would be like that, she thought, and some woman would be fortunate to bear him such an heir.

Their pleasant little family idyll was broken almost before they had entered the door of their lodging. On the stair they encountered Piers Martine, bounding down towards the outside door, his face a mask of black fury.

'God's blood,' he shouted at sight of Robert. 'Thank all the saints you have returned. That imp of Satan has gone—managed to escape me.'

As he reached the stair foot Robert seized him by the sleeve of his jack and jerked him to a standstill.

'Hold, man, hold. You are speaking of Lord George? Gone, you say? How is that possible?'

Martine was swearing horribly in his native tongue then, seeing the women wide-eyed in shocked horror and Lord Richard standing uncomfortably between them, he stopped and eyed Robert miserably beneath dark lashes.

'I think we should go into the upstair parlour, *mon ami.*' He looked covertly towards the kitchen where Jeanne was banging about with her pans, busily preparing their dinner.

Robert took Lord Richard by the shoulder and led him firmly upstairs, gesturing for the women to follow, for once impervious to the rules of courtesy. Once within the parlour, away from prying eyes and ears, Martine slammed to the door and faced his leader with a shame-faced air Clare would have thought totally alien to his nature.

'I think you should explain,' Robert said coldly, 'how you allowed yourself to be parted from your charge.'

The Frenchman shrugged helplessly. 'The *petit*—' he hesitated, clearly implying an obscene epithet which could not be uttered, certainly not before Lord George's brother '—he demanded mulled ale, said that he was very cold, Messire Robert.'

'But you did not leave him alone with the door unlocked?'

'*Non, non, mon ami.* I went to the top of the stair and called to Jeanne. I could hear her in the kitchen. She brought the ale and—and—' he ground out the words between his teeth in impotent fury 'as—as I gave the cup to the—boy—he hurled it at me. I was drenched and taken by total surprise. He said it was an accident, murmured apologies, but—but now, *mon ami*, I believe it was meant and. . .'

'You left him to change your clothes?' The accusation was harsh and Martine avoided his eye.

'*Oui,*' he admitted finally, looking shamefacedly away from them all.

'Without locking the door and taking charge of the key?'

'I was so wet, *mon ami*, and—how do you say, half-blinded with the hot ale and—and, *non*, I did not think. . .'

'How long ago?'

'Minutes—perhaps half an hour.' Again his expression was shamefaced. 'After I had changed my clothing I—I stopped to talk with the *charmante* Jeanne within the kitchen and—and then I came up—only just this moment as you came in, and found—found the young *seigneur*—missing.'

'Surely he would not have gone far,' Clare put in, anxious to ward off Robert's fury from the hapless head of his henchman. 'I imagine it was just a boyish prank. He will be back within minutes—an hour perhaps. He said he would not venture into the street in his work-men's clothes.'

'He had changed into his velvet doublet,' Piers said grimly. 'I thought it strange, but he argued that it was the Sabbath and he felt so unsuitably attired, that is how he put it and I thought it could do no harm.'

'Are you suggesting he deliberately planned to leave the house?' Robert demanded.

The Frenchman shrugged again helplessly. 'I can see no reason for him to do so but now—I do not know. I think the ruse of wetting me was possibly—deliberate.'

'But where would he go?' Clare said bewildered. 'He has been told how dangerous it is for him to wander about unguarded. He knows no one here. . .'

'Several times he spoke to some man in the street when you and Margery were out of the room, Mistress Clare,' Lord Richard said quietly.

'Man, what man?' Robert's greenish-blue eyes were flashing turquoise sparks.

The boy shrugged helplessly as Piers had done. 'I only saw him for a moment. A young man, garishly dressed with a high-crowned red felt hat with a tall feather.

Later, George said the man had told him he had been sent with a message from the Court of the Duke. I said that was nonsense, as Master Skelton would bring us any such message, but he said you, Master Devane, were keeping us prisoners for your own purposes. I did not believe that, for our lady mother trusted you and said we were to obey you and Master John.'

'This fellow, he spoke English?'

'I think he must have done,' Richard agreed. 'George's French is not good and we know no Flemish.'

'And what else did George tell you?' Robert's expression was thunderous and his tone peremptory, so that the boy's eyes widened.

'Some nonsense about meeting this man at some tavern, that it was to be kept secret from you, that officers from Duke Philip had sent for us. . .'

Robert seized the Lord Richard's thin shoulder and began to shake him, to Clare's utter astonishment and shocked horror. Even the watchful Margery, who obeyed Robert's instructions as if they were from the Holy Scriptures, moved forward warningly, anxious to intervene, for the young Yorkist lord could not be handled so roughly.

'Why, in God's name, did you not tell of this before we left this morning, you foolish child?' Robert roared.

Richard put out one slender hand and firmly, using his boy's full strength, thrust Robert off, standing back, straight and slim and Plantagenet to the core.

'Master Devane,' he said icily, in a voice Clare could not have believed to have issued from the mouth of an eight-year-old. 'I think you forget to whom you are speaking.'

He was so young and vulnerable, and yet, in this moment, so utterly regal, that the pronouncement startled them all.

Robert instantly recollected himself and consciously took in hand his fast rising temper. He gave a quick half-bow of apology for so mishandling the young lord and so thoughtlessly injuring his dignity.

'My lord, you must forgive me. My fears are for your brother. . .'

Immediately the haughty stance and expression were gone and Lord Richard was a boy again and anxious to help.

'Master Devane, I am sorry, but I did not think this at all important. George does things like this all the time. I thought he was just boasting when he said he would go out alone to meet this man.' He paused and looked back at them as fearful and bewildered as they all were. 'I did not believe he would do anything so silly.'

Years later, when Clare was an old woman, she would look back and remember those childish words of young Richard Plantagenet concerning George of York. 'George does things like this all the time. I did not believe he would do anything so silly.'

Piers Martine put in impatiently, '*Naturellement, mon ami*, time is vital, but how are we to find him?'

Clare repeated, 'You do not believe it could still be a boyish prank, a simple wish to make us anxious and that he will return of his own accord?'

Robert shook his head decisively, 'No, I do not. It sounds very much as if contacting the boy was a deliberate plan.'

'But who could know they are here? We have taken such careful precautions?'

Robert moved restlessly to the window. 'You say Lord George has been constantly peering from the window. Lancastrian spies are everywhere, as are our own. If the boy were to be abducted and held for ransom. . .' His voice trailed off as he caught Clare's steady grey gaze then looked away from her and to Lord Richard as if he did not wish to say more in case it further alarmed the boy. 'In all events he must be found and quickly. Piers and I must go out and search.' He sighed as if he realised that in this foreign, hectically busy town, even on Sunday, the task might prove impossible.

Lord Richard said suddenly, 'The tavern, the man called it by its name in Flemish but when George said something like it to Jeanne later she said the word meant "Cockerel", but I cannot remember if it was a red or black one.'

Robert nodded in satisfaction. 'Thank you, my lord. That is at least a start. Unfortunately there may be several inns and taverns nearby with such a name.' He was already on his way to the door to arm himself and prepare to leave with Martine.

Lord Richard recalled him. 'I should go with you, Master Robert.'

Robert swung round instantly, his expression both surprised and alarmed. 'Certainly not, my lord. I have lost one of my charges, how could I explain to your mother if I had lost you both?'

He recrossed the room to stand before Lord Richard who was now looking equally concerned. 'Not that I think this search will prove dangerous,' he amended hastily, 'but, as I have explained before, it is wiser to conceal your identity. If it proves that Lancastrian factions are already aware of your presence here with your brother, you will naturally remain safer here with Mistress Clare and Margery.'

'But I am the only one who has seen the man,' the boy argued logically. 'I admit I did not observe him too closely because I thought him just a passer-by at first, but I did see him and could point him out to you and

Monsieur Martine if once we find the right inn. I have been out with you this morning, Master Robert, in these clothes and you did not object then. Now it is more important. Why should I not go with you again?' He stared imperatively into Robert's intense blue eyes. 'I shall not be afraid, not with you.'

'I'm sure you will not, but. . .'

Clare cut in, 'I think the Lord Richard is right, Master Devane. If I also accompany you. . .'

'God in Heaven, no,' he exploded.

'If it is a question of Lord George desiring to play a trick upon you, he may well refuse to accompany you home. You could hardly bundle him up as you did in London and bring him by force, not without attracting unwelcome attention, but I think he would consent to return with me and his brother.' She regarded him steadily. 'If—if there is need, I have healing skills—as you well know. You might have particular need of me. Lord Richard and I will cause you no delay nor disobey you in any way.'

He caught her by the arm and pulled her towards the door.

'Do you realise that this may well prove to be a very grave business indeed?'

'Of course,' she replied simply. 'I understand that you do not wish to frighten Lord Richard, but he is no baby, despite his youth. He understands the gravity of the situation. He has faced dangers such as this before. I am sure he will remain with me well out of your way should it come to—fighting. . .' Her voice trailed off. 'Lord Richard is your one hope of finding this possible abductor and I can guard him in case of need.'

He drew a hard breath. 'God knows I wouldn't risk either of you unless. . .'

'Are you afraid you might lose in me a future source

of enrichment?' she taunted and he cursed softly under his breath as he pulled her close and she felt his breath fan her cheek.

'If there had not been need, I would have packed you off to Calais long ago,' he said softly.

'I know that, and there *is* need and, in particular, for haste.'

He released her and signalled for Piers to fetch his weapons. He finally came back to the boy.

'Very well, my lord, under the circumstances I will allow you to accompany Piers Martine and me with Mistress Hoyland.' Margery moved forward anxiously at this point, for the first time wishing to add her assistance.

'No, not you, Margery. Someone must remain here in case Lord George returns and, if he does, you must keep him here. I don't mind if you restrain him physically, bind and gag him if you must,' he said through his teeth, 'but see he does not leave this room again. If Master Skelton returns in the meantime, tell him what has happened but impress on him the need to stay here and await our return.'

'Yes, Master Rob.' She was clearly disappointed but ready, as ever, to obey him to the letter.

Robert turned again to the taut figure of the waiting boy. 'I do not need to impress upon you the need to stay very close to Mistress Hoyland. If I give you a command, you will give me your word to obey instantly, even if you wish to do otherwise?'

The boy nodded gravely and a relieved little smile lit up his grim young countenance.

'Right, then we must waste no more time.' Again Robert exhaled sharply as Piers Martine mounted the steps at a run and paused in the doorway, cloaked and hooded for the journey, and proffering Robert's sword belt with his serviceable blade and dagger. He took only a moment to belt it on and Clare put up her hood. Gently she guided Lord Richard before her as Robert stood aside for the two of them to precede him down the stairs.

CHAPTER SIX

ONCE outside their lodging Piers Martine glanced hastily at Clare and was about to argue, but Robert testily waved his hand.

'I know only too well the dangers, but it seems necessary,' he snapped, 'that is if we are to find the boy soon. I am assured that both Mistress Clare and Lord Richard will stay well clear of any action.'

Martine shrugged in his habitual enigmatic way. He said, 'I have spoken with Jeanne. She says there are two inns near here with the sign of *un coq*, Le Coq D'Or, in Zilver Straat, which runs parallel with this street and Le Coq Noir, in Woolestraat, near the Bourg. It would seem more likely, *mon ami*, that the man would have suggested to Lord George the nearer inn and told him how to get there.'

Robert nodded, his brow furrowed. It was now almost noon and most of the Flemish citizens had returned to their houses for dinner. There were one or two roisterers on their way to or from the various inns and taverns and more sober folk returning from the many churches with which Bruges abounded. Obviously, Robert had got to know his way about the town for he turned hurriedly down an alley off their own *straat*, one hand keeping a tight hold on the Lord Richard's wrist.

'I do not suppose, my lord, that you can now remember whether the tavern suggested was the Golden Cockerel?'

The boy shook his head worriedly. 'I did not take

147

undue notice, Master Devane, only that it was a cock that I heard Jeanne speak of.'

'Well, let us hope that a golden one meets our requirements.'

'Master Devane.' The slightly haughty note had returned to Lord Richard's voice, although he was somewhat breathless, having been abruptly dragged along, as they halted for a moment while Robert looked for his bearings. 'Do you think this man might harm George?'

Robert eyed him uneasily. 'I hope not, my lord,' he said grimly, 'but, as Mistress Clare enjoined me to be frank with you, we cannot entirely discount the possibility.'

'No real messenger from the Duke's court would have acted in that way, would he?'

'No, my lord.'

'And the man probably thought I would go as well?'

'It would seem likely.'

'Then. . .' there was a little uncertain pause '. . .George really is in great danger. An enemy—from Queen Margaret's force would—would wish to kill him as—as Ned's nearest heir?'

Robert looked back into the anxious grey eyes directly.

'That is why it is imperative that you obey me implicitly. Only because I know how necessary it is to find your brother quickly have I allowed you to come with us. You must be very careful, my young lord. If, even now, you would rather return with Mistress Hoyland to our lodging. . .?'

'No, no, Master Devane.' The boy shook his head decisively. 'I said I was not afraid, at least—' he swallowed hard '—not very much afraid. I—I just wanted to understand what—what is at stake. You need me to find that man. I wish. . .' his voice trailed off miserably '. . .I wish I had argued more with George or—or told you or Mistress Clare, but—but, as I said, I didn't think it was important. I was intent on copying my letters. . .'

'My lord, none of this was your fault.'

The boy swallowed hard again as he looked up uncertainly at Robert. 'No, Master Devane, but—but if anything happens to George I shall always blame myself.'

'Not as much as I shall,' Robert returned grimly.

Clare touched him lightly upon the arm. 'I am as much to blame as anybody,' she reminded him. 'I should have known just what the young lord was up to.'

Piers Martine was looking round for directions and pointed them to the right. 'That leads to Zilver Straat, I am sure, *mon ami*. I have been down here before.'

The alley opened out into one of the broad-paved streets Clare had so much admired since coming to Bruges. The fine shops were shuttered for the Sabbath and there were few passers-by about, but they could hear voices lifted in what she thought was amused badinage and song ahead of them. They hastened towards the sound and stopped finally before a building which clearly proclaimed itself an eating house and bore the finely executed sign of a golden cockerel.

Robert glanced round briefly to reconnoitre the area directly round the inn. He saw there was an alley entrance running down the side, apparently going to the rear of the premises. An elderly couple passed by on the other side of the street but, apart from the laughter and general babble emanating from the inside of the inn, there were no other unlookers.

'If they are keeping the boy here, it does not look as if there is a guard outside,' he commented thoughtfully to Piers. Martine had also been regarding the terrain and stood, thumb thrust into his sword belt, near the entrance to the alley.

'They, *naturellement*, see no need,' he agreed softly, 'if it is as the Seigneur Richard said, the boy came of his own accord. Once inside, who knows what has occurred?'

'Well, obviously they must have taken lodgings. The boy is unlikely to be now in the public eating-room.'

Piers nodded soberly.

'I shall proceed inside with Mistress Clare and the boy.' Robert smiled grimly. 'We make a convincing family group and we can observe the company. If there is no sign of the man Lord Richard saw, I shall have to make some excuse to leave the two of them and try to prowl about the building.'

'*Oui, mon ami*, while I search from outside. I see there is an outside wooden stair leading to the rooms above.'

'Be careful, Piers. If I am right about this business, our opponents could be very dangerous indeed. Reconnoitre and come and find me before you embark on any rescue attempt.'

Piers Martine revealed very white teeth in a broad grin. 'Robert, *mon ami*, you know me well enough now to realise I nevaire risk my skin without dire need.'

Robert gave an answering grin but Clare thought it was somewhat forced. She released her pent-up breath as she felt Richard's body tremble under her hand upon his shoulder.

Robert gave them a significant nod and the three entered the eating room. The place was crowded, as they had expected, and Robert had difficulty finding a place on a long bench near the window. The place outwardly, at any rate, looked respectable enough and reasonably clean, even to Clare's discriminating taste.

She felt Richard's tense young body relax a little closer to hers as Robert rose to summon one of the fair Flemish girls to come to take their order.

The young lord's eyes were everywhere and Clare saw his lips tighten. She wondered if the novelty of eating food in a common inn was exciting his attention and taking it from the business in hand but she soon saw that his grey eyes were narrowed in careful scrutiny of everyone in the room and she lifted her chin slightly in a small gesture of approval.

The serving-woman, a rather buxom, blowsy creature who looked and smelt fairly clean for all that, came with tankards of beer and steaming bowls of pottage. Richard made no demur at the simplicity of the fare and began eating at once, plying his wooden spoon with a will and pulling free pieces of the rye bread with an appetite. For all that, Clare was conscious that he was still keeping a careful watch for sight of his quarry.

Robert had engaged the serving-wench briefly in talk in a mixture of French and broken Flemish. Clare understood he was letting her know they were English and hoping she would comment on any other English visitors she had served recently. She wondered how he had explained their presence in Bruges—on merchant business, she guessed, dealing in wool most probably.

The girl replied rapidly in Flemish and did not appear to be unduly curious. The room was crowded and the proprietor emerged from the kitchen beyond to yell at her to hasten to serve others. She bustled away, seemingly relieved to be free from the difficulty of trying to converse with a foreigner.

'She said nothing of another English boy?' Clare questioned in a whisper.

'Nothing.'

'No mention of any other Englishmen here?'

'No, she merely listened and made the usual polite responses that the day was cold and hot food a necessity.' Robert appeared to be eying his food resolutely without peering around the chamber. He, too, ate with a will but Clare knew, that like the boy, his eyes were observing all the customers carefully and his ears were strained for any snippets of talk which might prove revealing.

He said with a rueful grin, 'I'm sure she's right. It certainly *is* cold. Piers would much rather be here with us inside, partaking of food, than keeping watch outside. Let us hope he will not be there too long.'

'What if this is not the right inn?'

'Ah.' Robert's eyebrows rose significantly. He looked sardonically at his charge. 'Do not eat too enthusiastically, Richard, you might have to eat another dinner very shortly.'

The boy gave him an amused grin and continued to give the semblance of being totally absorbed with his food. Suddenly he stiffened, his spoon suspended between plate and lip, then hastily he resumed eating. Out of the side of his mouth he whispered, 'Master Robert, there is the man, the one who has just come in. He is no longer wearing that absurd hat, but I am sure it is him.'

The boy moved in his seat as if to rise but Robert placed a hand upon his wrist and gently but firmly held him down.

'Softly, softly, my young lord,' he growled in a half-whisper. 'Stay very still and leave this to me.'

Clare murmured, a little note of panic in her voice, 'If Lord Richard was seen at the window, he could be recognised.'

'It makes little difference,' Robert returned softly,

'for I know the man and, if he turns this way he will, no doubt, recognise me.'

He heard her give a little intake of breath and her eyes widened but he noted approvingly that she stayed calm, though she was watching her young charge anxiously.

The man who had just entered the dining-room was engaging the proprietor in conversation. They spoke in French but were too far away for their words to be heard. Since he was making no move to seat himself at table and order food, it appeared he had, as Robert had surmised, taken lodging in the place. He did not look in their direction. Robert was studiously avoiding looking his way and he commanded Lord Richard, with a warning expression, to give his attention once more to his food.

The fellow eventually finished his talk for both men gave brays of laughter and the newcomer swaggered towards the door at the rear of the room, from which the serving wench had emerged with the food earlier. Still he did not glance their way and was soon lost to view in the darkened shadows of the corridor behind.

Lord Richard let out a little breath of relief. Robert grinned at him a trifle mirthlessly.

'Do not be alarmed. We will get you clear of this place in moments. I want you to go with Mistress Hoyland back to our lodgings. I shall need to keep Piers with me. You think you can find the way?'

The boy nodded vigorously and again Robert smiled. 'Your work is done, my lord. I rely on you now to escort Mistress Hoyland safely.'

Clare made to interrupt but he silenced her with a look.

She said in a whisper, 'You know this man to be dangerous, don't you? How do you know him?'

He ignored the first part of her question. 'Staninforth was one of Warwick's captains, was found to be dishonestly handling stores in the Calais fortress, selling them to townsfolk, for his own profit, a common enough failing in men-at-arms. He could have been hanged, but the Earl dealt leniently with him. He was soundly flogged and dismissed from service. It seems he has turned his varied skills to mercenary business. It would seem very likely that he saw a chance of gain by holding the Yorkist lord and selling him to the highest bidder.'

Again his lips twisted in that travesty of a smile. 'Margaret would pay well to hold Lord George of York, more still if he had been accompanied by his brother, especially now, when Edward is marshalling his forces to meet her in open conflict.'

'Then Lord George could already have been taken elsewhere, since the man has clearly been absent...'

'I doubt it.' Robert's eyes were still roving the room weighing up the possibilities of exits and opportunities for a quick getaway, should he need to make a move to rescue the older Yorkist lord. 'There has been little time and I do not think Staninforth would relinquish such a bargaining treasure to any charge but his own. No, I'm fairly certain the boy is somewhere behind in an upper room.' He signalled to the serving-wench who was busy drawing wine from a cask near the kitchen entrance. 'I intend to pay the bill and take you both out of here and join Piers. By now he will have discovered a back entrance.'

The woman came eagerly enough and he paid her. With a cheery remark in Flemish, he rose to leave. She gave a broad smile at young Richard, who smiled back winningly, and went obediently with his seeming parents to the outer door.

Outside in the cold air of the deserted street Clare

found her heart was pounding uncomfortably. She placed a protective arm round the boy. Uncertainly she said, 'You have no idea how many men there could be up there. You could be badly outnumbered.'

He gave her that half-mocking bow she knew so well. 'Well, well, Mistress Hoyland, are you so concerned for my welfare?'

'I'm more concerned for Lord George,' she shot back at him. 'He could be badly injured in the fray, even killed.'

His smile faded as the soft padding of Piers's feet behind him alerted them to his nearness. Clare thought the man always walked like a cat.

'He will have to take his chance,' he replied shortly. 'To delay now would only endanger his safety. Staninforth will take no chance of the boy alerting strangers to his predicament. He'll move him fast and we have to act quickly. In all events, to whom would I turn for help? The Watch? To do that could further endanger Lord Richard's safety by revealing his identity and—' he shrugged again '—like as not they would not believe me.'

Piers informed him, 'The wooden outer stair leads to the bedchambers. There is another to the kitchens. I managed to get a glance inside, but the place is crowded with cooking wenches and pot boys and mine host is yelling instructions. Monseigneur George is not kept there. It must be the upper chamber if, *mon ami*, we 'ave the right inn.'

'We have,' Robert replied crisply. 'I have just seen Staninforth come in and go through to the back.'

Martine gave a little expressive hiss. '*Maintenant*, then Lord Richard was right.'

Robert drew the Frenchman slightly aside and though

Clare strained her ears she could not catch his next words.

'We must move with haste. Agreed?'

The Frenchman was gazing swiftly around the now quiet street. 'Agreed, *mon ami*, for the man is *un cochon*. If the *petit seigneur* gives him any trouble, he will rid himself of his burden.'

'Exactly,' Robert agreed suavely, 'for even a token from the boy as confirmation of his death might still win the fellow a goodly sum from a grateful Margaret.'

He turned swiftly back to the waiting woman and boy. 'We shall go in at once, cannot delay. You will take the boy to safety?'

She nodded, then tentatively reached out and touched the sleeve of his rough worsted jack. 'You will take care.'

His ready laugh bubbled out. 'I have told you before, I have a sensible regard for my hide.'

She hesitated. 'It is—it is not only for the safety of the boy that—that I. . .'

'Do not fear, one of us will return to you—' his eyes were gleaming with amusement '—with luck, both of us. We are good at our trade, killers both if need be.'

He had turned away already. She sighed and began to lead Lord Richard from the inn's vicinity. Like her, he was reluctant to go and moved only slowly, with several backward glances at his two guardians, now intent only on their campaign.

Robert said tersely, 'The obvious move would be for us to reverse positions. The company inside the inn have seen me, not you. If I go back inside, I could only arouse suspicions, particularly from the proprietor, who would try to prevent me from going behind and into the upper rooms. I'll go up the outer stair and leave you to make the onslaught from within.'

The Frenchman nodded soberly.

Robert continued. 'There is a handsome enough serving-wench. Try your charms on her and you could probably approach the entrance to the kitchens and back quarters reasonably simply.'

Martine bared his white teeth in a mirthless grin. 'That will be easy enough, but how do we consolidate action? We have no idea how many men Staninforth has with him, *n'est ce pas*?'

'Agreed.' Robert glanced thoughtfully upwards at the wooden stair. 'I shall give you some time then move into position. Is the door heavy, difficult to break through?'

Martine shrugged. 'Not now, *mon ami*. I pressed my dagger point around the lock. I think it should yield to considerable pressure.'

'Good. We wish to avoid too much interference from below—until later, at least. When I think you might have moved into the corridor behind the dining-room, or, at least, have the possibility to do so, I'll give my seaman's whistle.'

Again the Frenchman grinned. He understood perfectly. Often on board one of the Earl's ships the two had used such a signal to give warning of an attack and to consolidate action. Both were capable of making the piercing note without the need of an instrument, had perfected it.

'*Bien*,' he murmured confidently and, without further ado, approached the inn door.

Robert watched his entry through narrowed eyes then, seeing an old man coming towards him and staring at him belligerently, as if requiring passage on the narrow footpath, sauntered away, seemingly heading for an alley on the opposite side of the *straat*. Once there, he took refuge in a shadowed spot beneath the lintel of a house where he could just see the door of the inn, and waited.

After some minutes the door was thrust open and several of the customers emerged, laughing and chattering. They stood beneath the inn sign for a moment, continuing their talk, then, as the day was growing increasingly cold, gave cheery waves and made off in differing directions. By now the street was deserted again and Robert, becoming more and more chilled, moved his feet and as silently as possible slapped his crossed arms against his chest to improve circulation.

He had to time his arrival at the head of the stair to allow Piers to move into the inn's rear quarters. He had little doubt that his companion would accomplish this manoeuvre without too much difficulty. He had seen Piers work upon serving-wenches before. He would move near to the ale cask, flattering the lass, keep her interest until he was able to make his move without interference and, should there be open resistence, he was sufficiently skilled with sword and dagger to hold off his attackers until Robert was able to join him. Robert remembered, with a soundless chuckle, the way Piers had managed his escape from Hoyland Manor.

After considering a suitable interval of time had passed, he emerged from cover and once more, outwardly casually, sauntered across the *straat* to the inn front. A quick glance around convinced him he was unobserved and he mounted the outer stair with quiet light steps, and placed an ear to the clumsy keyhole of the somewhat warped door. He could hear nothing from within for the door was sturdy enough, though old. The wood had been neglected over the years, but he saw that breaking into the chamber from without would pose no real problem after Piers had dealt with the lock.

He had not seen a window, so if the inner chamber

boasted one it must be at the side of the property. He straightened, lifted his head, put two fingers to his mouth and made the thin, piercing sound he and Piers had used on countless occasions to announce the presence of one to the other. At the same moment he put his shoulder to the door jamb and thrust it wide.

There was a startled bellow of rage and surprise from within as Robert entered the chamber at a run. He was conscious that, at almost the same moment, the opposite door was burst open and Piers called a joyful warcry to announce his arrival on the scene of battle.

There were four persons in the chamber, as Robert quickly identified, three men and the boy who was tightly bound to the truckle bed near the wall. Robert took in instantly that the boy was gagged with a pad of linen secured in place by a torn rag and that his blue eyes widened in shock as the two men burst into the chamber, and then, bewilderingly recognising Robert, appealed silently for succour.

The men had undoubtedly been taken by surprise but acted instinctively as all trained men-at-arms did. Staninforth swore as he struggled up from a stool where he had been seated, overturning it in his haste and sending it spinning as a second man stumbled over it and fell full length right across Piers Martine's feet.

The Frenchman made no more ado but simply bent and thrust his dagger between the other man's shoulder blades so expertly that his victim gave hardly more than a sigh in passing out of existence. The third man had been nearer the bed and now faced Robert, his hastily drawn dagger at the boy's throat. George's blue eyes fairly bulged in terror as he met those of Robert but he could make no outcry.

Staninforth glanced down dispassionately at his fallen

companion, then faced Robert squarely. His own sword was now already in his hand.

'So, one of Warwick's bear cubs,' he drawled menacingly, 'I might have known you were sent with that milk sop, Skelton. That,' he pointed contemptuously towards his youthful prisoner, 'could hardly remember your name. The young coxscomb is too scornful to care who has charge of him provided they dispense his needs and keep him comfortable. So the other young lordling saw me and told you where to come.'

'He did,' Robert returned shortly. 'So you are up to your mercenary tricks, Staninforth, this time dealing in flesh and youthful flesh at that. What amount of blood money do you hope to get, cur, by your betrayal of your former master's cause?'

Piers's voice, soft with menace, reached Staninforth from behind him. 'To abduct *les enfants* is about your weight, *n'est ce pas*? To tackle men and steal from them would be too much of a challenge.'

A growl of fury came from the man guarding Lord George but his half-move was immediately prevented by a lashed-out command from his leader. 'Stay where you are. Keep your dagger trained on the boy.' He turned mockingly towards Robert. 'Come, Devane, what is your next move? True, we are one against one and I do not doubt your ability to dispose of me or that of your henchman to do his deadly work, but there is the boy. One move towards either of us and he dies instantly.'

Robert smiled back at him as mockingly. 'So, we have deadlock and where do you expect matters to go from here, Staninforth? You have the whip hand over the boy, but, as you said, you are not out of danger.'

The other man's brows rose in amusement. 'I take it you want the boy. Are you prepared to pay for him?'

'Not in gold.' Robert shook his head regretfully. 'Alas, I have no amount sufficient for your requirements.'

'He has to be ransomed. You'd hardly expect me to part with him without some remuneration.'

Robert's voice was steel edged. 'I'm prepared to give you your lives and your freedom.'

Staninforth threw back his head and laughed. He was a rakish fellow, tall and well made, a favourite with serving-maids and popular with his fellow men-at-arms for his easy manner and addiction to gambling.

'I think,' he said coolly, 'I would prefer to take my chance.'

'Would you now?' Robert's reply was silky. For one fraction of a second Staninforth had been off guard. His amusement at the terms offered had caused him to be less cautious and his second in command had been listening to the terms avidly, equally, less intent upon his prisoner.

Piers Martine had needed only one opportunity. With the ruthlessness which had made itself apparent in the dispatch of his first victim, he moved forward with lightning speed and struck down the man's hand with the hilt of his sword. The dagger he had held at Lord George's throat fell with a clatter to the floor and, lightly and with the same swiftness which had lost him his bargaining counter, the Frenchman had moved and the man felt the coldness of Martine's sword blade at his throat.

Robert had not for a second taken his eyes from his own opponent. He continued to stand with his sword ready. Hearing the noise the dagger made, Staninforth turned very slowly to assess the situation and swore softly. He gave another harsh laugh. 'Though I would not concern myself unduly with the death of such an arrant fool, I have to admit that once this executioner of yours had dispatched him, I would follow very quickly,' he said softly. 'It seems I must accept your terms after all.'

'But why should I adhere to them—now?' Robert countered.

Staninforth chuckled. 'Because you would still have to kill me and I think you would rather the noise of our combat did not alert mine host and his friends downstairs. If I lay down my arms and allow you to free the boy, will you give me your word you will allow both of us to go unharmed from that door?' He indicated the door to the outside stair.

Robert looked questioningly towards Piers Martine who inclined his chin very slightly.

'Very well, I give you leave to make your escape but should I encounter you again in the streets of Bruges I shall not be disconcerted by any watchers. You and I will decide the issue at sword point, once and for all.'

Staninforth sighed gustily. 'I take gambles, Devane, I never take odds stacked deliberately against me. The boy is hardly worth it.'

Deliberately he laid down his sword and dagger at the other's feet and looked challengingly towards Piers Martine.

Robert took charge of the discarded weapons then moved lightly towards the bed and with two strokes freed the boy's wrists which were stretched with rope to the two posts of the bed-head. He could feel George stirring behind him as he sat up and struggled with the linen pad and strips that effectively gagged him, for his wrists and hands were still numb and he gave a little moan as the blood coursed freely at last causing him, momentarily, great pain.

'Let the fellow go, Piers,' Robert said softly. His foot

stirred the body of the fallen conspirator. 'The two of you had best take this carrion with you. Mine host might feel somewhat alarmed to find him here and it would rouse a hue and cry which would be helpful to none of us.'

Sullenly the man held at Piers's sword point knelt and heaved the body to his shoulder at the terse command of Staninforth.

Instinctively knowing that Lord George would make some outcry if not prevented, Robert said quietly, 'It is best for all of us for you to remain silent for the moment, my lord. You want to return to our lodgings without hindrance, I take it?'

The boy gave a voiceless gulp. Robert was still keeping his prisoners in view and could not turn but he felt the boy's quivering form beside him. For once George obeyed him unquestioningly.

Staninforth paused near the door and mockingly saluted them with a flourished bow after his fellow had staggered through onto the landing with his burden. His feet could be heard clumsily descending as he awkwardly managed the crude wooden steps. Warily Robert kept guard by his charge but, as Staninforth stepped onto the outer landing, Piers slipped to stand by the doorway, sword in hand to watch his retreat.

Then, and only then, did Robert turn to regard the young lord. George met his gaze and his eyes slid away. He was clearly very frightened and ashamed. He could not find his voice even to thank his rescuers. Now the gag was removed, Robert noted signs of bruising round the well-formed young mouth where one or both of his abductors had struck him. There was another darkening bruise on his right cheek and tears ran slowly down the dirtied countenance.

Robert said briskly, 'All is well, my young lord. We

must get you back to the lodging and the care of Mistress Hoyland and Margery. Your brother is very concerned for your safety and you must thank him for your timely rescue. He was able to tell us where you were to meet Master Staninforth and identify your abductor.'

Lord George murmured hoarsely, 'He refused to believe the man's lying tale. I was too trusting. . .'

'But, apparently, you did not trust *us*,' Robert chided, and the boy hung his head.

'Well,' Robert continued briskly, 'we must get on. Who knows when mine host may decide to mount the stair and I do not want any more unpleasantness. Will you trust yourself to us now?'

A slow blush mounted from Lord George's throat to his cheeks and he inclined his head almost humbly.

'Then come.' Robert held out his hand and the boy stood up. Once clear of the bed it was clear that his limbs were trembling and Robert came closer. 'I'll carry you, my lord.'

'No, no, please, give me a moment longer and I shall be able to walk. I—I would not give you further trouble. . .'

Robert nodded and after a moment Lord George was able to move to the top of the stair and follow Robert down, Piers bringing up the rear.

'It is a pity, *mon ami*,' Piers growled as they began the walk back to the lodging in Steen Straat, 'that we were not able to dispose of those two permanently. Who knows when they might give further trouble in future?'

'A pity, but necessary,' Robert agreed, 'but our only concern is the welfare of our two charges. Personal animosities must be dealt with later. The times being as they are, I am sure the opportunities will come.'

Piers grunted again. They had reached the corner of the alley now and were about to turn towards their destination when Robert suddenly let out a hiss of fury. Ahead of them, near the corner of Steen Straat, Clare lingered with young Richard beside her. 'Why can not that woman obey me?' he snarled moodily.

His irritation failed to keep him as instinctively alert to danger as he was, customarily. George, seeing his brother, ran forward eagerly to greet him. At the same moment a flickering of steel in the winter sunlight and the strange hum of a weapon flying through the air revealed Staninforth half-concealed by the overhanging gable of one of the houses in the alley.

Clare moved as instinctively as Robert had failed to do and, grasping George by his shoulders, pulled him clear of the dagger missile and caught him back, held protectively close against her body as it hurtled by him to clang onto the cobbles below them. Robert and Piers halted abruptly, their swords already in their hands. Robert had no time to see where young Richard now was, but he could see clearly enough the danger to the woman and her charge for, stealthily, the second man had crept up behind her and Staninforth let out a braying laugh.

'I told you I only bet on certainties, Devane. What a pity you do not. You should have engaged and dispatched us both when you had the chance. As it was, I decided to wait in ambush. The boy is too valuable for me to surrender him so easily. You see, I knew in which direction you would move towards the lodging.'

The alley, like the street behind them, was deserted but for the combatants and Robert's eyes narrowed in alarmed fury for his own foolhardiness.

Staninforth's voice went on triumphantly, 'Well, now, what is it to be? Is the woman valuable? Will you let my comrade there kill her or will you consent to stand off and surrender the boys to us? Did you not think to search both of us thoroughly? Hadn't it occurred to you we were both accustomed to conceal other weapons about our persons? I always carry one of mine in my boot.'

A pulse pounded in Robert's temple. It seemed that the moment, while he stood irresolute, stretched out into infinity. Clare stood perfectly still. Her hood had fallen back and her brown hair streamed free to her shoulders, her white linen cap tangled at her neck. Her two hands held the boy beneath his two arms and her eyes, luminous in the cold, white sunlight, looked fearlessly back at Robert.

'Let him kill me. Take the boy,' she said. 'While he is engaged with me either you or Piers can keep George safe while the other fights off this man who launched the dagger. Once,' her voice quavered only a little, 'once he has finished with me, you can—can take him on. . .'

So many times they had argued. Robert swallowed hard and Piers saw his Adam's apple work in anguish. She seemed so calm. Robert knew she was desperately afraid but her back was as rigid as when he had first beheld her and made her his prisoner. Thoughts, memories, swept at immense speed through his mind, pictures of her facing him out fearlessly, caring for the boys on the ship, sacrificing her chance of escape on the wharf at Coldharbour Steps.

He knew he had known no other woman like her. He could not let her die like this—and yet—if he moved now, only a fraction, Staninforth would give the order for her death and, if he were to sacrifice the Lord George, his honour would be tarnished irretrievably. He took a harsh, painful breath and leaned slightly forward on the balls of his feet, knowing Piers was as tensed and as frustrated beside him.

It was then that Lord Richard launched himself into

the fray. He gave a sudden shout and threw himself bodily at the man behind Clare. Woman, attacker and the two boys were thrown together into a tangled heap upon the hard stones of the alley. Robert leaped into the attack towards Clare and knew without waiting to be sure that Piers had instantly tackled Staninforth.

For moments it was impossible for him to get to grips with Clare's attacker, for the boys' frantic strugglings hampered his movements. The man had turned like a terrier at bay and stabbed downwards at the hapless Richard who was still grimly gripping his ankles. The boy gave a sharp yelp of pain. The sounds of snarling and swearing were truly animal-like. Robert frantically pushed Clare aside and, jumping astride the fallen man, stabbed down with his sword at the man's unprotected neck. Even after blood stained his jack sleeve and the dreadful gasping screaming sounds were telling him his opponent was dying, he continued to stab downwards in a berserk need to be sure the man could no longer threaten Clare.

He sat back at last and stood up slowly, the man's body sprawled below him, his head lolling as if the executioner's axe had decapitated him. Robert's own legs were trembling. He had no thought for anyone now but for Clare. She had scrambled to her feet and was leaning down a hand to help up George, who was moaning faintly.

He appeared to have been injured in the fall and seemed incapable of rising. Richard, on the other hand, had scrambled up quite quickly and was holding his right arm where blood was bubbling and staining the cloth of his sleeve. Piers came up at a rush and tore a strip from the sleeve of his shirt.

'Stand very still, *mon petit seigneur*, while I bind that.' He turned reassuringly to Robert, who had placed a steadying arm round Clare. 'I do not think it is too bad, a scratch only, *mon brave*. Do not fear, Staninforth will not trouble us again.'

Clare gave a little relieved moan and clutched at Robert for support. 'Dear God, I thought—thought—he would slit my throat from behind. . .'

'And had not Lord Richard the presence of mind to attack him, he might well have done so and killed George afterwards,' Robert said tersely. 'We must thank the Virgin and all the Saints we have come through this so well. I should not have allowed myself to be distracted by the sudden glimpse of you two standing there.'

He turned to Lord George. 'You have not broken any bones, my lord? Can you put weight on that leg?'

'No.' George's voice was unsteady and he was deadly pale. 'I do not think so, Master Devane. I—I twisted my ankle again when we fell. It has been weak since I hurt it in London.' His haunted eyes went from one fallen man to another and a shudder passed through him. 'I thought—thought—this time—' he swallowed '—this time we would all—die. . .'

'As we nearly all did, but for the prompt thinking of your brother, my lord.'

Richard said hastily, 'Master Devane, what—what are we to do with these men?' He, too, was pale and seemed in pain and still clutched at his arm awkwardly, though, already, he appeared to have recovered his nerve. 'Will the Watch. . .?'

Robert shrugged. 'We can leave them here, Lord Richard. Unfortunately, brawls are not uncommon when men leave taverns, even on the Lord's day. Best if we do not bring attention to our presence in the city by involving ourselves in this business. We must get you back to our lodgings where we can attend to your injury.'

Clare shook her head at his questioning look. Despite her determination to stand stolidly calm and not reveal weakness, she was very close to tears. 'No, I did not hurt myself in the fall. I'm a little bruised, I think, that is all.'

Piers put a supporting arm round George, who was limping badly. Richard averted his eyes from the two bodies and refused gently any help from Robert, so he continued to put an arm around Clare. A casement window of one of the houses bordering the alley was flung open and a man's voice in Flemish shouted a question, possibly demanding who was about and causing a disturbance on the Lord's day. On receiving no answer, the man had a muttered discussion with someone else inside the room, then the window was abruptly drawn to again.

Robert, grim-faced, signalled that it was time to make a hasty withdrawal. Now was not the time to be discovered with two bodies and be forced to answer the determined questions from a curious Watch. He drew Clare firmly away, knowing that Piers would bring the two boys safely after them.

Margery met them at the door to the solar and immediately threw her arms around Lord George.

'Oh,' she sobbed, 'thank the Virgin you are returned to us safely. I have been near frantic with worry.' Her gaze swiftly took in the state of dishevellment all were in and that Lord George was limping. 'My lord, what have they done to you?'

George, responding to her petting, launched into an eager account of his misadventure until, for once, she hushed him in mid-torrent, to pounce upon Lord Richard. 'He is wounded, bleeding, the little lordling,' she shrieked. 'Master Rob, whatever have you involved him in?'

The 'little lordling' drew hastily out of her embrace, though smiling at her gamely. 'It was not Master Devane's fault, Margery—I disobeyed him. It is naught but a scratch.'

Clare said briskly, 'Please attend to Lord George, Margery, I think his ankle is badly twisted. But, first, would you bring warmed water and bandaging into the boys' chamber? I'll get my bag with the salves and ointments and deal with Lord Richard's wound.'

She turned and looked directly at Robert. 'Are *you* hurt, or Piers? If so, you must come in and let me look at you.'

Robert shook his head. 'Like my Lord Richard, I have taken some scratches, but nothing I cannot deal with myself.' He glanced at Piers Martine, who shook his head.

'No, mademoiselle Clare. Nothing to concern you. I will go out now and reconnoitre the streets. It may be possible that there are others of Monsieur Staninforth's company prowling about.' He instructed Margery, 'Keep the outer door bolted. Admit no one but me. I will call to you when I return.'

She nodded, clearly frightened.

Clare drew Lord Richard gently into the chamber he shared with his brother and began to undo his cloak. The sleeve of his tunic was soaked in blood despite Piers's improvised bandaging. She threw off her own cloak and discarded the ruined linen cap, shaking back her dishevelled hair impatiently.

'Wait for a moment, my lord,' she warned him gently. 'When Margery arrives with the water, we will soak off this bandage very carefully, lest it hurt you further.' She knelt down and drew him to her. 'You have been very brave indeed,' she said consolingly, for she perceived now that reaction was setting in and he was near to tears. His thin young body was very rigid in her grasp. 'You saved my life, Lord Dickon. I shall never forget that.'

He smiled at the endearment. 'I think Master Devane is very angry with me,' he said doubtfully, 'but George is safe and. . .'

'You let *me* deal with Master Devane,' she said firmly.

Margery came in with the warmed water, a flask of wine and towels, looking more anxious than ever as she saw the bright blood dyeing the boy's tunic. 'You'll best cut that sleeve off,' she said doubtfully. 'Should we not summon a surgeon?'

'No, no,' Clare assured her, 'I'm sure it looks worse than it is. I think I can manage, but if not, I'll call you.'

She saw that Lord Richard seemed reluctant to undo his tunic until Margery had left them and nodded imperatively to the woman. 'I think Lord George needs you. His ankle is giving pain and he has had a bad shock.'

Margery hastily hurried back to her charge and Clare took her bag of simple medicaments from the travelling chest.

She approached the boy, who was now struggling one-handedly with the fastening of his tunic.

'Let me do that. First, we will cut the sleeves of your shirt and tunic clear at the shoulder; then we'll soak the rest away. Come and sit down on the stool.'

He allowed her to help him, grimacing as she soaked off the sleeves of his tunic and stained shirt, revealing a long but fortunately shallow gash from forearm to wrist on his right arm.

'It has not cut too deep,' she reassured him, 'but it will hurt for some days, I'm afraid. It will not need stitches. I can draw the edges of the wound together very carefully.'

She turned to look for the wine flask Margery had also brought through so that she might cleanse the wound. When she turned back to him, she found him shrinking from her.

'It will only hurt a little while,' she promised, 'just while we ensure the wound is really clean. The tansy salve will be soothing.'

He was white lipped and his grey eyes were appealing for her understanding. Then she understood. It was not the fear of pain from her ministrations which was troubling him but, for the first time, she had seen clearly that this right shoulder was imperceptibly higher than the left. Now she knew why he had always insisted that he was no baby and could dress and undress himself. She averted her eyes from the slight deformity and deliberately dipped her cloth into the warm water.

He set his teeth after she had thoroughly bathed the wound and applied the wine, which stung considerably, then he relaxed as she applied the soothing salve and set herself to bandage the gash again.

At last he said in a tight little voice, 'I didn't want you to see. George—' he drew a hard breath 'George sometimes teases me. He says I am like my ancestor, Edmund Crouchback.'

'You are no crookback, my lord,' she said, and her own voice was tight with suppressed fury against those who would so hurt his vulnerable youthful feelings. 'There is so little to see. A skilful tailor will ensure no one notices the difference.'

'I fell from my pony,' he explained, 'when I was five. They say I broke the collar bone and it was not put quite right. I will not let it make any difference,' he said fiercely. 'I told you, Mistress Clare, I intend to become as doughty a warrior as my brother, Ned.'

'I'm sure you will, my lord,' Robert Devane's quiet voice alerted them to his presence. He had come in so silently and they had been so intent that neither Clare nor the boy had noticed his entrance. 'Forgive me for this intrusion,' he said courteously. 'I came to borrow some of your famed salve. It did its work so well in the barn at Hoyland, I thought it would be just as efficacious now.'

His eyes dwelt briefly on the slight thickening of the boy's shoulder and he smiled. 'Why, my lord, I've seen men finish training with the muscle of one arm develop far more than the other after long bouts of practising. I'm sure my own shoulders would not bear a too-careful scrutiny. Once you begin training to arms, I think you will find no one will comment on the difference between yours. That will appear perfectly natural.'

Warm colour flooded back into the pale cheeks and Clare saw the boy's confidence blossom once more. She blessed the common-sense attitude shown by Robert Devane and applauded his skill at knowing what was exactly the correct words to say at this juncture.

He grinned back at her. 'Margery says, if you have finished here, will you take her the witch hazel? Lord George's ankle is badly bruised.'

Clare looked from him to the boy and Robert said, 'I'll help him into a clean shirt, never fear. Besides,' he added, grimly, 'I want to have a little talk with my Lord Richard, alone.'

The boy went white to the lips again and half rose from the stool, but Robert pushed him very gently down again. Clare hesitated as she read the pleading glance Richard gave her, but then she caught Robert's eye and went obediently. Surely, after what she had just heard, she could trust Robert not to be too harsh with the boy for his disobedience.

Richard sat fearfully silent, while Robert drew up another stool and sat facing the stricken boy.

Lord Richard gulped. 'Master Devane, I know that I promised. . .'

'You did, my lord,' Robert said grimly and then, as the boy's grey-green eyes were raised anxiously to his, he burst into a merry laugh. 'Thank all the saints you knew just when to be obedient and when to ignore those strictures. God knows what would have happened to all of us had you not had the presence of mind to do what you did.'

The boy's lips trembled. 'But—I know I should have taken Mistress Clare straight to the lodgings, as you instructed me, but—but neither of us wanted to go without knowing. . . She was worried about you and I feared for George and. . .'

'So she was concerned about me, was she?' Robert mused.

'Yes, Master Devane.' Lord Richard looked puzzled. 'Of course she was. She is your betrothed.'

'She is indeed,' Robert breathed. He rose and sought for a clean shirt and tunic in the chest near the bed. 'Come, my lord, allow me to assist you into this. You will need help with dressing for the next few days. I'll see to it.' He could not miss the expression of relief on the youthful countenance. Dressing was a somewhat painful business and Lord Richard sank back on the stool with a little relieved sigh after it was done.

Robert resumed his seat opposite and Lord Richard looked up at him expectantly. 'We shall be safe now, won't we, Master Devane?'

'I shall see to that too, my lord,' Robert assured him. 'I owe you a great deal. You saved Mistress Clare. For those few terrible seconds I was powerless to decide what I had to do, you understand?'

The boy nodded and dark colour flooded his cheeks.

'If you will graciously accept it, I would like to give you a small gift.'

The boy watched eagerly as Robert withdrew from a small sheath up his sleeve a plain-hilted dagger, workmanlike, but finely crafted and lovingly cared for. The bright blade glimmered in the pale sunlight which filtered in through the horn window.

'My father gave it to me when I was somewhat older than you and about to leave my manor for service with your cousin, my lord Earl of Warwick. I was very proud of it and it has served me well. I hope it may prove of use to you during your years of training in arms.'

The boy took the weapon from him wonderingly. His fingers caressed the hilt and cautiously tested the edge of the blade. 'Master Robert,' he said, with a little catch to his voice, 'I—I shall treasure it always.'

'You will have fancier weapons later, my lord, when you are grown, I do not doubt, but none more serviceable, I assure you.' The words were gruffly spoken, but the boy understood, suddenly, the magnitude of the service he had rendered the man and their eyes met in understanding.

Robert rose and made a little half-bow. He handed over the sheath. 'You should get some rest now. Piers Martine is out patrolling the district. I do not think your brother will be so rash again—at least, not in a hurry,' he amended. 'He has had a hard lesson. Thank you again, my lord.'

Richard's answer was very dignified and gracious. 'Thank you for your gift and for your great care of us. I shall not forget—ever. My brother, Ned, shall hear of it.'

Hastily Robert said, with a slight quirk of one eyebrow, 'I do not think, under the circumstances, that that would be entirely wise, my lord.'

'Nevertheless, my brother shall be made aware of your services to our House.'

Again Robert was aware of the unusual maturity of the speaker. He could not laugh at the boy's regal dignity and felt as commanded by it as he had earlier when he had treated Lord Richard roughly, as he would have done some recalcitrant page under his control. It had brought him up sharp then, as it did now. He could only bow in acknowledgement and quietly ask permission to withdraw.

In the main solar he stood with his back to the door of the bedchamber. Clare was completing the tight bandaging of Lord George's foot, Margery leaning over them both anxiously.

'My lord,' Robert said softly but with an edge of steel to his voice. 'I think you should lie down for a while in your chamber. I will help you there.'

The boy stood up awkwardly, his expression, for once, thoroughly abashed.

'Master Devane, I must ask you to forgive me for all the stupidity. . .'

'Fortunately, sir, your brother is not too badly injured. Now that you recognise the dangers, I am sure we can count on you to be more circumspect.' Robert's tone was suave.

The boy turned to thank the two women very gravely and charmingly and Robert helped him into the chamber and to lie on the bed.

'My lord, I think perhaps you are hungry. Lord Richard and I and Mistress Hoyland have already eaten. I will arrange for Margery to prepare something for you in the kitchen.'

Lord Richard had already stretched himself on the

bed and Robert recognised the fact that though he would not confess to it, the boy was totally worn out by his exertions, loss of blood and emotional shock. He left the two to rest and returned briskly to the solar.

'Margery, I wish to talk to Mistress Hoyland. Please go to the kitchens and prepare a meal for Lord George and also for Monsieur Martine when he returns. Will you see that we are not disturbed until I call you?'

Margery looked more than a trifle flustered. She wiped her hands on her apron and looked helplessly towards Clare.

'Now, Master Rob,' she said severely. 'I hope you are not going to apportion blame, for it will do no good and. . .'

'Be off with you, Margery, and do what I say,' he returned curtly and she curtsied and hurried out with the bowl of bloodied water and used towels. They could hear her muttering to herself crossly as she descended the stair.

Clare was wearily aware that she was not looking her best and was in no state or mood to be reproved for her disobedience to her betrothed.

'Margery is right,' she said bitterly. 'We are all tired and this is no time for recriminations.'

He strode over and seized her wrist as she moved to turn away from him. 'Is it not?' he demanded harshly. 'What, in the name of God, did you think you were doing placing yourself in peril like that? I told you to return to the lodgings. I had no wish for you to endanger yourself In the first place. I only agreed to your accompanying us so that you could keep an eye on young Richard and because you pestered me to allow it.

'Do you know what I was feeling, facing that traitorous dog, and he with his dagger at your throat?' He caught her to him and shook her hard. 'Do you realise how close to death you were?'

'Afraid of losing your title to my lands and wealth?' she taunted, angered now by his treatment of her.

'We'll have no more of that talk,' he snapped. 'You are my betrothed and I am responsible for your safety.'

'Well, I am safe.'

'Only thanks to a child's thoughtless gallantry. You could all be dead.' He gave a terrible shudder. 'Never, never, do that to me again.'

'I'm sorry,' she said stiffly. 'It was foolish. Lord Richard and I have both admitted as much. We were worried. . .'

'About the boy—or about me?'

'Of course I was alarmed for Lord George, but. . .'

'But?'

'Naturally I was concerned for you too—and for Monsieur Martine.'

'Yet, were I to have perished, you would have been free. Have you thought of that?'

'No—yes—' she stuttered, then flashed out, 'How can you believe that I was thinking of such a thing, at that time when you might have been. . .'

He pulled her close to him and she half stumbled backwards, as he bent and pressed his lips hard down on hers. It was a long, lingering, almost desperate kiss; for moments she fought for breath then gave up all pretence of resistance and surrendered to his ardent embrace. The reaction from the horror of fear had left them both desperate for reassurance. Eagerly her arms stole around his neck and she returned his kiss as fiercely.

He was here within her arms, strong and demanding, frighteningly masculine and alive. She had never felt like this about any man before and her need was great.

Anger and fear and longing blended together within her and became a totally terrifying sense of desire. She had so nearly lost him and also known a debilitating fear for her own existence. She was tempted to allow him to possess her utterly. When he withdrew from the kiss momentarily for need to draw breath she attempted weakly to remonstrate as he began to draw her inexorably towards her bed.

'No, no, we mustn't. You promised. . .'

'We are betrothed before God,' he murmured hoarsely. 'There is no sin, sweetheart. Sweet Virgin,' he muttered again, 'I thought I would lose you. In that one dreadful moment—and—and—I saw how it would be if. . .'

She was lying flat on the bed now, the cloud of her soft brown hair flowing around her face and silkily heavy under his hand. She had washed it in some herbal water and the scent of it inflamed his senses. She was strong and brave and so very desirable—and she was his for the taking. . .

Recollecting herself, she thrust him back from her, her grey eyes wide with horror for her own weakness.

'You gave your word,' she reminded him. 'I took you for a gentleman, even though. . .'

'I am still a rascally pirate,' he mocked her and he sat up suddenly, wearily, all blinding desire drained from him.

She lay back against the pillows, regarding him steadily. 'I take that back, sir,' she said quietly. 'Pirate you may have been, in the Earl of Warwick's cause, but no rascal. I know now the strength of your loyalty to the House of York. I admire that, even if I cannot accept the same allegiance.'

'Not even for Lord George and Lord Richard?' he enquired, one eyebrow raised. 'I cannot fail to notice your affection for the younger boy. As my wife, I shall expect total loyalty to the House of York.'

'I am not your wife yet, sir.'

'But soon—when things are well in England again.'

She shook her head and tried to turn from him, for tears were welling in her lovely eyes and she had no wish for him to see.

'Perhaps, sir. Who knows? I shall pray that the boys remain safe whoever comes to power in these desperate struggles—and I shall pray for you too.'

'Have you *any* feeling for me at all, Clare Hoyland, other than hatred?' he asked softly.

Again her eyes widened in astonishment. 'I cannot hate you, sir. Like all of us caught up in these struggles, you are helpless in the hands of destiny. Everything has happened to me too quickly. I have lost—' she drew a hard breath '—everything, and I have been helpless in your hands. I need to rely on your protection, not your exploitation—in honour.'

'Aye.' He rose heavily and wiped a hand across his sweating brow. 'You remind me of honour. I think, perhaps, just now, in my relief at having you safe, alive, I was in danger of forgetting that.' His breathing was fast, shallow. 'I was so very afraid for you,' he murmured. 'Forgive me. You must be completely exhausted. I'll go down to Margery and leave you to put to rights your appearance—and then—then we must all rest and strive to come to our senses by morning.'

She watched him go and the tears streamed down her cheeks. She had wanted him to stay—to make her completely his. She knew that and the thought filled her with a strange mixture of dread and bewilderment. Did she love this man, her abductor?

It could not be, yet—her fear for him when he had gone back into that inn had been numbingly unnerving.

She could not have borne it if. . . Again she told herself
fiercely that all she wanted now was to hand over her
charges to the Duke of Burgundy, to know them safe
with John Skelton, so that she could once more turn her
thoughts toward escaping her fate as a helpless pawn in
this man's hands.

Shudderingly, she covered her eyes and wept. All her
life, even if she were freed and became the wife of some
other man, she would see Robert Devane's tall, strong
form, that head carried so proudly, crowned by that
distinctive red gold hair, and hear constantly his laugh
ring out. He would haunt her for ever. She would fight
against this overpowering longing for him—but could
she deny that her contempt and fear of him had suffered
some indefinable sea change and become—love?

CHAPTER SEVEN

OVER the following days Clare found that Robert appeared to be avoiding her or, at least, he made every effort not to be alone with her. Watching him carefully when he was abstracted, she thought she detected a trace of shame in his expression.

Margery had made no comment on returning to the solar, but Clare felt sure she had her suspicions about what had occurred. Clare was thoroughly miserable. Since the incident on the ship when Robert had shown the responsible, caring side of his nature, she had felt more at ease in his company.

Now she was painfully aware that that comradeship could not return. Robert Devane was her betrothed, for his own pecuniary reasons. He had no real feelings for her. His only interest lay in her manor and fortunes, but she now knew that she needed, desperately, for him to want her for herself.

Could she agree to marry him, knowing full well that he would never love her? Would she not be wiser to return to her own plan: to try to escape from his dominance and marry at her uncle's pleasure? She would most probably never love her chosen husband, but she would not suffer the indignity of seeing Robert constantly and knowing his love to be out of her reach.

The boys soon recovered. George's sprain was not serious and Richard's wound healed well, as she had promised. George was considerably subdued, especially after it was discovered that he had taken a considerable amount of the gold his mother had provided to his meeting with Staninforth and the little company's means were now somewhat limited.

'I thought—I thought we should soon be with the Duke,' he confessed shamefacedly to Robert, 'and I—I did not wish to leave the bulk of our funds. . .' His voice had trailed off miserably and Robert's grim expression revealed clearly that he understood only too well what had been implied, that the boy had not wished he and Piers to gain personally from the possession of that gold.

He had not been trusted. It could not be helped. Until John Skelton returned with some news from the Duke's Court, they would have to exist in still further straitened circumstances. Richard accepted the news cheerfully enough, but George was considerably chastened and gave up his practice of gazing out of the window. Clearly he had been very frightened indeed. It made dealing with him easier, but Clare could not like the fact that the boy's life was shadowed by fear and guilt.

Piers Martine had, apparently, searched the bodies of the two mercenaries and found only a few coins, so the purloined gold must have been hidden elsewhere. Clare asked no questions but concluded that the Frenchman had disposed of the bodies, for no enquiries were instituted by the men of the Watch and the English party had not fallen under suspicion.

On the sixth of March John Skelton returned to them and it was tacitly agreed that nothing should be said to him about the unfortunate incident in and near the Golden Cockerel. He had not brought good news. He had presented the Duchess Cecily's letter and been received briefly by Duke Philip.

'My welcome was only lukewarm,' he reported. 'The Duke was affable enough and sympathised with the Duchess's lot. He made vague promises to eventually receive the Lords George and Richard, but gave me no firm date. It seems clear to me that he is waiting to see what happens in England. If Edward loses in this coming struggle, Duke Philip will not commit himself to the boys' cause.

'If, on the other hand, things go well,' he shrugged helplessly, 'then our fortunes will improve. In the meantime, we shall have to make shift for ourselves. I think it might be sensible to move nearer to the Burgundian Court at Utrecht.'

It fell to Robert to inform him of the depletion of their funds. Catching George's alarmed eyes, he explained that the gold had been unfortunately stolen on an expedition into the town. John Skelton cast the two men a somewhat suspicious glance and Clare felt impelled to come to their defence. Obviously Skelton believed that either Robert or Piers had appropriated the gold or lost it recklessly in some game of chance. Richard's eyes appealed to her to remain silent and she swallowed her anger and let the matter drop.

Fortunately, or unfortunately for Clare, as matters turned out, Skelton's concern over the loss of funds was overtaken by news from Calais. Silas Whitcome had been sent there with a message from Skelton to the garrison and came hastening back post-haste with the news that Edward of March had been victorious over the Queen's forces at a place in the Welsh Marches called Mortimer's Cross.

He was so excited he almost gabbled his account, stopping mid-while to gulp down ale.

'They are all talking of it in Warwick's force. The Lancastrians were under the command of the Earls of Pembroke and Wiltshire. No one seems to have details but it's said the beaten army was pursued as far as Hereford.'

He grinned delightedly at his listeners. 'Not bad, eh, for a lad of scarce nineteen? The Earl—' he shook his head irritatedly '—I should call him the new Duke of York, of course, was then pushing on towards London. Of course, it was too late for him to come to my Lord of Warwick's aid at St Albans and we haven't heard about it till now, 'aving been busy getting the young lordlings out of England.'

George gave a great whoop of joy and Richard sat, chin on a raised bent knee, carefully considering this momentous news.

'But, Master Whitcome,' he said earnestly, 'will not my brother have to deal with the Queen's forces in London and will my cousin of Warwick have joined his force by now?'

'Couldn't we go home?' Lord George demanded eagerly.

Whitcome shook his head. 'I heard nothing of the Queen's entry into London, my young lord. The talk in Calais is that the Londoners were determined to keep her out. Certainly my Lord of Warwick should have joined the young Duke by now, and it's likely the Queen might decide to retreat north without making an assault on London.'

Robert said thoughtfully, 'This battle will hardly have been decisive. It will be necessary for Lord Edward to take on the full might of Margaret's army before matters are ended. He'll need all the trained men he can get.'

John Skelton cast him a hasty glance then quickly answered Lord George's question. 'No, my lord, certainly we cannot return home yet. We must remain here, as bidden, until we are summoned by either your lady mother or the Lord Edward.'

Margery called from the kitchen that she had just taken some gingerbread from the oven. Though Lord Richard would have preferred to hear further news of his eldest brother, he was pulled off by George who had a great love for sweetmeats, gingerbread in particular.

Whitcome added a rider to his tale. 'They took some ten important prisoners at Mortimer's Cross and they were executed in the market place in Hereford. One of them,' he said, his lips thrust out aggressively, 'was Owen Tudor. What happened to Pembroke I don't know, Master Rob. There was some tale about the Tudor's head being surrounded by candles burning throughout the night, an old wives' tale, doubtless.'

Robert gave a soundless whistle. 'Executing Tudor might not have been a wise move,' he remarked to Skelton. 'The man is King Henry's stepfather, after all.'

Skelton nodded in agreement, his eyes wary. 'And Tudor an old man and relatively harmless, but,' he sighed, 'in all these skirmishes, there are old scores paid out and more created. In some ways I am grateful to be out of the fray, in charge of my Lords George and Richard.'

Silas Whitcome was aware of a steely glitter in Robert Devane's blue eyes and he gave his attention to the dregs of his ale.

That afternoon Robert came to Clare in the solar. 'I would like you to come out with me to take the air,' he requested bluntly. As she glanced towards Margery questioningly, he added, a trifle harshly, 'You will not need a chaperon. I am your betrothed and Margery is needed to care for the boys.'

Clare acceded and went to the chest to fetch her warm hooded cloak. In truth, she would welcome this little time alone with Robert and hoped it might clear the air between them.

He took her to the town square and she revelled in the dry, cold air. There was a slight wind but not sufficiently rough to give discomfort while walking. She thought longingly, Spring is on the way. How will it be on the manor at Hoyland with no one in authority to give the necessary orders?

She noticed a preponderance of nuns walking freely about amongst the bustling townsfolk and thought it was not a sight usual in England. She had seen the prioress of their nearby nunnery ambling quietly about the countryside on her quiet palfrey with an elderly nun and steward in attendance, but rarely did she see the younger nuns about their duties in the town or villages as she saw them here.

She gave a little sigh and remembered that not so long ago she had feared she might be immured in a nunnery. Was that fate still likely if she continued to consider her betrothal to Robert Devane not binding? She stole a glance at him as he walked close. He was silent, abstracted, his features unduly serious. With Martine and Whitcome and even the grave-mannered John Skelton he was more often cheerful, even merry, despite the discomforts of their present circumstances due to George's unfortunate loss of their funds.

They entered the Chapel of the Holy Blood and, at the door, he offered her holy water. She felt that strange unnerving tingle as her fingers met his, then she turned from him hastily and went to kneel before the reliquary, praying for her own peace of mind and the continued safety of all of them.

Afterwards he drew her to a rough wooden bench near one wall, reserved for those too frail to stand throughout the service of mass. It was quiet here, the chapel almost deserted, a convenient place out of the extreme cold to speak to her privately. They lived all too close together within their lodgings.

'First,' he said hesitantly, frowning slightly, as if unsure of himself, 'I must apologise for my behaviour the other day. I was in danger of forgetting my solemn promise. Put that down to my fears for all of us only hours before.'

She did not answer, but lifted her face to his calmly so that he understood she had forgiven him.

'I am going back to England,' he announced and her fingers trembled with the brutal shock of his words, so much so that she was forced to clasp them to keep them still in her lap.

He turned the penetrating gaze of his remarkable eyes full on her. 'I must return to fight for Edward's cause,' he explained. 'As I said to Silas, this is likely to be decisive and I must serve him in arms.'

'But you are serving him now,' she reminded him softly, 'by caring for his brothers. The Duchess gave them into your charge. Must you—must you hazard yourself on the battlefield to prove your loyalty?'

'I must serve my King,' he said simply.

She blinked unhappily. 'But Edward of March is not the King.'

'He is the declared heir by the Act of Accord.'

'The Duke of York was named heir but he is dead.'

'Edward is now Duke of York and, I believe, soon will be declared King.'

She was looking bewildered and distressed, so he explained, 'England is tired of these wars. Henry is too weak-minded to rule properly and Margaret is both hated and feared. London will declare for Edward and the rest of England will follow. If he defeats Margaret in this coming engagement he *will* be our King.'

She gave a little sigh. Men were so determined to fight and die for causes—her own father had done so—but Peter...Peter had died for nothing worth hazarding himself for, let alone losing his life for. Perversely she wanted to keep Robert Devane here, safe from harm. Even though she had no wish to be forced into marriage with him, she did not wish him dead to free her that way.

'The Earl of March is little more than a boy,' she said a trifle desperately. 'How can he hope to defeat Margaret's commanders, all seasoned experienced men?' She did not know how old Robert was, she thought suddenly, too young, like his young lord, to die on some bleak battlefield.

As if he read her thoughts he said, 'Edward is nineteen, two years younger than I am, but I have met him in Warwick's company, seen him train to arms. He is not only fearless in combat but astute and, if the truth be known, more skilful in strategy than his cousin, Warwick, who is often rash, too eager, proud and overly ambitious to be circumspect.'

She could not help murmuring bitterly, 'Are you, too, not ambitious? Is this the reason why you must go now and fight for your King?'

He turned abruptly and she saw his strange eyes glitter in the uncertain light from the guttering candles. 'Yes,' he admitted. 'Younger sons must be ambitious if they are to survive and prosper, but I stand or fall by Edward's cause. If he prospers, then it is possible he might reward me. I have no shame in wanting and hoping for that, at least to win my spurs on the field. If he falls,' he shrugged, 'then so will my hopes.'

She turned from him, her eyes sparking with tears. 'And what of me?' she whispered at last. 'Do you trust your prize to others? I had not thought that of you.'

'You will be safe here in Burgundy. John Skelton is

an honourable man and you will be adequately chaperoned by Margery. The boys need you. You swore you would remain with them until they were assured protection from the Duke.'

'I shall not leave them,' she replied tonelessly, 'but can you be sure John Skelton is an adequate protector?'

'I shall leave Piers Martine to guard them and you.' He smiled a trifle grimly. 'He will not allow Lord George to fool him again and—' his smile broadened '—I trust him utterly—with you. Oh, I know, I gave you the impression that he was dangerous, back there on the Lutterworth road. I needed to have you sufficiently afraid of me then, but though Piers is indeed a lady's man, I trust him with you completely and he will give his life for you and the boys if necessary.'

'But you will need him with you,' she protested.

'I shall take Silas and I'll join Reyner Astley in London or at his manor and the Fletcher brothers will most likely be with him.'

He had thought it all out. There was little she could say to detain him, but she felt a sudden numbing ache around her heart.

'I shall pray for you,' she whispered through stiffened lips.

'But not for the success of our cause?'

'That I shall leave to God to decide.'

'And you will be here, waiting for me, my dutiful betrothed wife?'

For the first time she put her deadly fear into words.

'And if you do not—come back?'

His eyes slid from contact with her clear searching grey ones.

'I shall come back—to claim my own.' He was so confident, she wanted to cry out to him that only children trusted so blindly in their own immortality.

Had not Peter, her brother, believed himself invincible the day he rode out of Hoyland with her uncle?

She rose and deliberately stiffened her spine so he would not see how alarmed she was. 'I can only wish you Godspeed,' she said mechanically. 'When do you leave?'

'I shall sail from Damme on the morning tide so will leave at first light. I shall squander some of our gold on two horses for Silas and me in London, just in case ours are no longer at Baynards. I want no delay in joining the King's force.' He gave a brief bark of a laugh. 'John approved it. I think he is hopeful now that Duke Philip will soon receive the children and you'll have less need for funds here, then.'

She inclined her chin and tried to smile bravely back at him. Throughout the short walk back to their lodgings she was struggling against revealing her distress and said very little. He, too, remained broodingly silent, his mind already filled with plans for departure.

To his relief Robert found Edward still in London when he arrived at Baynards on the ninth of March. He was equally delighted to find his friend, Reyner Astley, also in attendance. The castle was filled with Edward's suppporters and Robert was amazed to see the royal standard now flying over the ramparts.

Astley grinned as he saw his friend look wonderingly upwards.

'So you haven't heard of Edward's triumphant entry into the city or of his proclamation as King on the fourth of March?'

Robert shook his head, bewildered by the speed of events.

'On Wednesday he heard "Te Deum" sung at St Paul's, then went on to Westminster and took the oath as King in the great hall of the palace. He even wore the kingly robes and cap of estate and formally set out his title to the throne, seated on the chair of state.'

'You were there? The assembly accepted his claim?'

'They did indeed. It was a mere formality. The day before a council met at Baynards to examine his claim and he was acclaimed then.'

Robert drew a hard breath. 'So Edward is King already? That must please the Duchess well.'

'Aye, it does,' Reyner's expression became grim, 'but he is not crowned yet and there'll be a deal of hard fighting to do before that is fact. The Queen's force is in the North and she has most of the nobility with her.'

'Where is my lord Earl?'

'In the midlands gathering yet more support while Norfolk is doing the same in East Anglia.'

'Good, so we are in time to take the field with the King.'

Astley nodded. 'The Duchess will be pleased to hear from you that all is well with her boys.'

'I'll ask for an audience and report to her.'

As the friends walked through the castle corridors Robert was able to inform Reyner of some of the problems in Bruges.

'And your betrothed?' Reyner's eyes bore a hint of mischief and he revelled in the sight of a blush which mounted to Robert's fine cheek bones.

'She is well,' he said shortly, 'and has been of inestimable worth caring for the boys. Lord Richard is deeply attached to her.'

'Such a paragon,' Astley mocked, as they approached the Duchess's chamber, 'young, attractive, practical and—wealthy. You are indeed fortunate, my friend. But has she become any more tractable?'

'She has given me her word that she will remain with the children,' Robert said gruffly.

'And you trusted her to Martine?' Astley's brows rose in surprise.

'Piers is truly loyal to me — and mine.' The answer was so short, almost harsh, and Astley did not pursue the matter.

The Duchess was gracious enough to receive Robert after only a short wait. Cecily Neville sat in regal state now that she was the mother of the acclaimed sovereign. Her smile was truly welcoming.

'I see you have returned to fight for my son,' she said as she extended her hand for him to kiss. 'I am sure you left my sons in good hands.'

'They are safe and in good spirits, your grace, in suitably obscure lodgings in Bruges.' Robert assured her, 'and being heartily spoiled both by my betrothed and by her maid, Margery Lightbody. When Master Skelton returned from the Ducal Court at Hesdin and I heard the news of the King's early triumph at Mortimer's Cross I thought it safe to sail so I might join his force.'

'Then Duke Philip has still not received my sons?'

Robert was about to reply when the door of the Duchess's chamber was thrust open without ceremony and Edward Plantagenet strode in. Robert slipped to his knees and was immediately bidden good-humouredly to stand.

'It's Devane, isn't it, my cousin Richard of Warwick's squire? I hear you have been guarding my young cubs of brothers in Burgundy. Did I hear you about to say what Philip has done — or not done?'

Edward of March, the late Duke of York's eldest son, now acknowledged King of England, was one of the handsomest young men Robert had ever seen. He was taller than Robert, well over six feet in height, broad shouldered, slim hipped and without an inch of surplus fat upon his well-muscled body. Robert saw his likeness to his younger brother George, both in the lineaments and in colouring, the golden hair crowning that proudly held head.

His face shone with the radiance of his recent triumphs and wore no trace of anxiety concerning the coming combat. In fact, Robert thought he saw signs that this final challenge would be relished, not dreaded or feared. The King was in a fine jovial humour; he kissed his mother's hand graciously and threw himself down into a chair near hers.

'Well?' he questioned shrewdly, still smiling. 'How has Philip dealt with my brothers?'

'As yet with caution, Your Grace,' Robert said gravely, 'but Master John Skelton has high hopes he will send for them in the very near future. In the meantime, the boys are comfortable and happy, though impatient to return home,' he added.

'And you now thought it safe to leave them in Skelton's care?'

'I did, your grace. Knowing you must soon oppose Queen Margaret in open combat, I wished to join my lord Earl of Warwick's company in this coming engagement.'

The king's smile broadened. 'And you are very welcome, as are all good men. I shall meet up with my cousin on the march so, as I shall be leaving London shortly, you can ride in our company.'

Robert bowed acknowledgement.

'By the way,' Edward lolled back comfortably in his chair. 'My mother tells me you had your betrothed bride with you when you last came to Baynards. I had no knowledge of your betrothal. Tell me, who is the fortunate lady?'

'I am the fortunate one, your grace. Mistress Clare Hoyland is my neighbour. Her father was killed at the first battle of St Albans and she has recently been further bereaved. Her brother and guardian, Peter Hoyland, was killed in an attack on my manor.' He hesitated but there was no frown on Edward's features, rather an avid curiosity and, as yet, no sign of hostility to Robert's plans concerning the Hoyland heiress.

'I think there is more in this than you are revealing. Peter Hoyland made an attack on your manor, an unprovoked attack?'

Robert flushed darkly. '*I* say it was unprovoked, your grace. There was a trumped-up motive, some brawl in the village between Hoyland retainers and those of my father.' He broke off for a moment, his face working. 'I think you will have been informed by now that both my father and brother Walter were killed in that engagement.'

A little crease showed itself now between the royal brows and he leaned forward slightly in his chair.

'No, I had not heard. I'm truly sorry to hear it, Robert. You mourn the loss of a father and brother, as I do after Wakefield. So you are now master of the Devane lands.'

'If your grace will be pleased to confirm my ownership.'

'Certainly I shall. Is there extensive damage?'

'Yes, sir.'

Edward's lips twisted into a cynical little smile. 'And Mistress Hoyland is now an heiress and capable of repairing some of your losses. You are a clever young dog, Robert.'

'The lady has an uncle, your grace, Gilbert Hoyland, but I was by no means sure of her safety in his hands.'

'Ah.' The King's eyes met those intent blue ones

meaningfully. 'You are unsure as to exactly how Sir Peter Hoyland met his death? Is that what you imply?'

'Aye, sir. Mistress Clare was sent to the Court in Coventry with few men to guard her and. . .'

'How fortunate she met up with yours.' There was a bubble of suppressed laughter from the King, then he threw back his handsome head and laughed uproariously. 'You are a knave, Rob, but fortunately for you, I admire knavery when it is useful to me.'

Robert flushed darkly again but the King extended his hand towards him. 'Come, man, you wish me to give my approval to the match?'

'Yes, your grace.'

'And the lady, does she consent?'

'She will, your grace, if you command it.'

'I must see this wealthy lady. Is she beautiful?'

'She is beautiful to me, sir.'

'And that is enough for any man.'

'She is brave and loyal and very practical—and honourable. Your brothers love her, your grace.'

'Then both she and you have rendered me valuable service and I will reward that—when I am in a position to do so.'

The King grinned towards Reyner Astley, who was waiting quietly by the door. 'See to it that Robert has a good horse and suitable armour and equipment—at our expense. We shall be glad to see you both in our company on the march.'

So, graciously, Robert felt himself dismissed. He bowed to both the King and the Duchess who inclined her head, smiling, and withdrew from the chamber.

Robert left London, riding in the King's troop with Reyner Astley on the thirteenth of March. William,

Lord Fauconberg, had already set out two days earlier with a considerable force.

Robert had obtained horses for his needs from the stables at Baynards—those he had obtained earlier from Clare's men-at-arms near Lutterworth—but the funds put at his disposal by the young King provided him with serviceable armour. He had taken his leave fondly of Clare's palfrey, stroking the gentle creature on the nose and feeding him titbits.

'Your mistress will soon be back to claim you,' he promised. 'She loves you well and has often spoken of you with pride. She misses you.'

The palfrey whinnied shrilly as if he understood and Robert stood for a moment longer, looking at the beast with real affection. He recalled how proudly Clare had sat in the saddle throughout the difficult journey to Astley's manor near St Albans. She must have been truly terrified as to her fate but she had never allowed him to see that, nor had she when she had faced Staninforth in the alley in Bruges.

His thoughts winged to her and he hoped she would pray for him as she had promised. If all went as the young King Edward hoped, and he, Robert, survived this coming battle, he would be able to hasten back to Burgundy to claim her as his bride and bring her proudly before his King. If not, he mentally shrugged off the alternative, he would die on the field and Clare would be free. His only prayer was that Edward would be victorious and able to offer her his protection, as he surely would after the service she had given him and the House of York in caring for his brothers.

Reyner did not pursue the subject of Robert's betrothal. His former levity had not been well received and he perceived there had been a change of heart in Robert. Where, formerly, he had wanted the marriage simply to restore his fortunes, it was clear that his friend now held more tender feelings towards Clare Hoyland. It would be safer, for the present, for him to hold his tongue.

The King's army was joined by the forerunners under Warwick and Fauconberg just north of the Trent. Edward had deliberately made slow progress to allow further supporters to join him and there were many. It was not difficult for the Yorkists to catch up with the Lancastrian army; they simply followed the trail of devastation left by the Queen's men.

Robert was shocked by the sights that met them as they rode north, and he was not squeamish by nature, trained to arms as he had been and witness to other skirmishes and depredations. But evidence of farm houses attacked, pillaged and left in smoking ruins, the unburied bodies of raped womenfolk and their murdered children, left in the fields to rot, the carcasses of animal stock slaughtered and only partially eaten, abandoned for the carrion crows to peck at, sickened him.

Edward rode on, grim-faced. It was no wonder that men flocked to him on the march. The common folk had suffered too much, had had enough personal experience of the Queen's callous treatment of her subjects to wish this wanton destruction to continue.

Robert felt a sense of relief that Clare was safe in Burgundy. Who could tell what might have happened if she had remained unprotected on her manor in Northamptonshire if the Lancastrian force had passed that way?

Just north of Nottingham, the Earl of Warwick joined his royal cousin and sovereign and, when camp had been made that evening, Robert reported to his lord.

Warwick was smaller and slighter than the King, brown-haired, a brisk-mannered man who greeted Robert as warmly as the King had done at Baynards.

'I am glad to have you with us,' he stated, though unsmiling. 'You will have noted the state of the country-side. The time is ripe for Margaret of Anjou to pay for these crimes against good English yeoman stock.'

Robert noted, wryly, that no mention was ever made of King Henry being responsible. Henry's weakness had resulted in his Queen's domination of policy in Council, but the hatred of the Yorkist nobles for the French queen was too deep-seated to be appeased by even the slightest suggestion that she and she alone was not to be blamed for the state of civil war now in existence. Wakefield and the Queen's bloodthirsty vengeance after the battle had hardened all their hearts. Warwick had lost a father, Salisbury, in that catastrophe; it could not be forgiven.

Warwick feasted both Reyner Astley and Robert in his own tent and listened intently to Robert's account of his escape from London with the Lords George and Richard.

'Young Richard is so slight for his age you'd never believe the strength of his courage and determination,' Warwick declared. 'I'd be as glad to have him in my household in training as I was pleased with you,' he asserted.

Robert, thinking silently of young Richard's partici-pation in the fight in the Bruges alley, agreed that the boy would acquit himself well.

The King pushed on to Pontefract, made camp, and here received information from his scurriers that Queen Margaret with King Henry and her son, Edward, Prince of Wales, who was scarcely as old as young Richard, was safely bestowed in York while her army, under the command of the twenty-four-year-old Duke of Somerset, had massed behind the River Aire.

The King decided to send a detachment foward to reconnoitre the ferrybridge and Lord Fitzwalter was put in command. Anxious to retrieve the King's good opinion after his defeat at St Albans, the Earl of Warwick requested permission to back up Fitzwalter's force and Robert rode with him. Reyner Astley remained in the King's camp.

Surprisingly Robert saw that the bridge was undefended but damaged and concluded that Somerset's main intention was to take advantage of the ridge between the villages of Towton and Saxton. It would be here that the King would be forced to give battle, but it was likely that the Lancastrians would keep the bridge in view and possibly give serious problems to the King's force when it attempted to cross the river.

Fitzwalter grunted in annoyance as he saw the extent of the damage and gave brisk orders for a company of the men to attend to the repairs. Afterwards it would be necessary to keep watch. He accordingly sent back a messenger to the King's camp to report on the situation.

Warwick stood, huddled in his cloak, watching the men busy about their tasks, restless and impatient now to prove himself in action. Robert's eyes scanned the far bank continually. It was bitterly cold; massed dark cloud and that strange unaccountable unnatural quiet suggested the possibility of snow very soon. He thought of Clare in that last walk they had taken together in Bruges. She had smelt the air and it had been warm then, as if spring were on the way. Now the bitter conditions here told otherwise. It would be a hard battle, if the weather worsened.

Camp was made and watch fires lit, and the small

advance company prepared to wait out the night until the King's main battle force would join them. It would be Palm Sunday the day after tomorrow, Robert thought reflectively, as he warmed his frozen hands at the blaze. Would John Skelton take Clare and the children to the Chapel of the Holy Blood or to one of the other famed churches in Bruges? He sniffed the air like a wary dog. Suddenly she seemed so far from him, totally beyond his reach.

Warwick insisted on the erection of tents, though Fitzwalter clearly did not approve, but the men were suffering in this intense cold and he agreed sourly after giving firm instructions for a careful watch on the bridge, now repaired and ready for Edward's advance.

'Don't be an old washerwoman, Fitzwalter,' Warwick clapped the commander familiarly on the back. 'Somerset is as likely to keep his men to their fires as we are tonight. If he had considered the bridge important, he'd have had a guard on it before this.'

Robert's raised brows echoed the uneasy glance Fitzwalter accorded the earl, but Warwick's bastard brother laughed at their fears and hastened into the lords' tent when it was quickly erected. Robert paced the river bank near the bridge for the early hours of the night and then reluctantly surrendered his duty to one of Fitzwalter's squires who was yawning mightily and found a place outside the tent but near enough to the fire to give him some warmth.

He lay for the first hour wrapped tightly in his cloak, and, for the first time in years, did not immediately sleep. As a soldier this ability had been learned and had never failed him until now. His mind dwelt on the coming encounter and his need to survive it and return to Clare. Wryly, he faced the prospect that he was a man in love.

Never before had he not relished the thought of battle as an opportunity to show his prowess as a means of advancing himself. He wanted all that, for he needed to return to Clare no longer a beggar but a man rewarded by a grateful sovereign and capable of enriching her holdings by valuable land of his own, but now—there was Clare.

He was responsible for her safety and he had an uneasy foreboding that placing himself in peril could threaten her security. He was not afraid, he would fight the more fiercely to ensure his own survival, but the old reckless delight in the adventure of such encounters was no longer there. He would fight for Edward loyally and with a will, but as a grim necessity to ensure that his young sovereign would mount the throne in peace and hold the kingdom for the welfare of the realm.

He had fallen into an uneasy doze in the early hours of the morning when he was just as suddenly woken again by a thudding noise and someone shaking him roughly by the shoulder.

'Master Rob, for the love of the Virgin, wake up.'

Groggily he forced himself awake and pushed himself into a sitting position, to find Silas Whitcome, his face a mask of terror, kneeling beside him.

'Master Rob, the Lancastrians are upon us. The watchman on the bridge was asleep and. . .'

Robert woke fully, instantly, as if he had been drenched in a bucket of icy water. The thudding noise came louder and he recognised it as the sound of approaching horsemen across the frozen ground. He cursed and rose to his feet, yelling out the alarm. The men sleeping by the fires woke less quickly. The morning grey light was strengthening now, though the fires had largely descended into ash.

Robert grabbed Whitcome and pulled him aside as

the advancing Lancastrian cavalry swept ruthlessly through the camp. There was complete chaos: horses' hooves trampling through the still half-live coals of some of the watch fires, men yelling startled warnings, screams of agony abruptly cut off as many were cut down by mounted knights.

Robert's sword was in his hand and, still swearing, he dragged Silas Whitcome with him towards the tent where the Earl of Warwick was sleeping still. Behind him he heard a roar of anger as Lord Fitzwalter came to his own tent flap then a choking cry as a Lancastrian horseman cut him down where he stood, still half-awake and confused.

Robert reached the Warwick tent with its standard of the bear and ragged staff, dashed aside the flap, and bent to enter. The frightened guards had rushed into the fray but Robert was now intent only on saving his master. He had slept in leathern jerkin and breastplate himself and was now armed and ready, but he guessed that the Earl and his bastard brother had trusted too easily in the night and their own sentries.

He stumbled over the still slumbering Neville, stubbed him awake with the toe of his boot and bent to wake his lord.

Warwick was already awake on his camp bed and pressing himself upright. Recognising Robert by the light of the horn lantern on his folding camp table, he said hoarsely, 'In the name of God, Robert, what is it?'

'Lancastrians, my lord, upon us very suddenly, and the sentries incompetent. I hazard a guess they were sleeping. This cold is deadly and can lull a man very easily into a half-dead state.'

Hurriedly he handed Warwick his sword belt. Like himself, the Earl had settled to sleep fully clothed, but he needed to pull on his boots and wore no armour.

'The camp is in total disorder, my lord, and I fear Lord Fitzwalter is killed. I heard him give a choking cry as a Lancastrian horseman swooped. We can do little now but try to save ourselves. The bridge is lost.'

Silas Whitcome was standing within the tent entrance and the Earl's brother pushed him aside and ran into the shouting, screaming chaos of the camp.

Warwick was pulling on his boots and stood to buckle on his sword belt. In the uncertain grey light now seeping in through the flap, his face looked white and ghostly.

A horseman came too close to the tent and Whitcome stolidly bent to one knee and pierced the under belly of his mount. The horse screamed shrilly in agony and man and horse fell in a terrible mass of heaving bodies. Robert flew to aid Silas Whitcome and cut down the fallen knight, who was still struggling to rid himself of his horse's reins caught round his boot. Robert stood up fully to peer hastily round the camp. Men were fighting doggedly, some fleeing. Fallen bodies lay all round him. The Earl joined him and stared dispassionately at the carnage.

'Sweet Christ,' he muttered. 'How in God's name. . .?' but his fearful question was cut off as another mounted knight spurred his horse towards them. He leaned down and his broadsword cut savagely and deeply into the Earl's right leg. He gave a hastily cut-off scream and fell to one knee, his own sword still wavering in his hand.

Robert took advantage of the mounted knight's momentary triumphant crow of victory to put up an arm and thrust him from the saddle. The horse reared and whinnied and trotted smartly away, leaving the two combatants facing each other across the Earl's injured body.

With a sudden jolt Robert recognised his opponent,

Gilbert Hoyland. The man's visor was up, for these men were so confident of the success of their surprise attack that they had not bothered to take elementary precautions for their own safety and there was no mistaking Robert's opponent. He had seen him too close in the attack on the Devane manor and after, at Hoyland, to be in any doubt.

'You murderous dog,' he yelled, as he launched himself against Hoyland. 'I'll send you without time to pray for your soul's salvation to your Maker, to join my father and brother.'

The other gave a breathless laugh. 'Not too soon, my friend, nor too easily. It may be that you will join your kinfolk long before I face mine in the hereafter.'

They fought doggedly on foot, circling warily. Robert was conscious that, somehow, the Earl had been assisted to his feet and pulled clear, probably by Silas Whitcome. He only knew it was man against man now and dared not shift his gaze for a moment from his enemy. Both were fresh to the fight—Gilbert Hoyland had come mounted and unfogged by sleep, Robert had not yet tired of bloodletting.

Around them the slaughter went on but neither man cared. Each had a personal score to settle and Robert was intent on saving his lord, for Warwick would die if this man gained the upper hand. Sword clanged against sword and breaths were drawn hard. Hoyland was heavier and older than Robert, who was lighter on his feet, but Hoyland was a wily, experienced fighter and they were well matched.

Robert's lips drew back into a grimace as he thought how this dastardly dog had left Clare deliberately unprotected on the Coventry road to fall to ambush. His snarl of defiance discomfited Hoyland who was finding now he was too quickly tiring and being forced to give ground.

'You scum of the earth, you meant her to die,' Robert ground out and, momentarily, Hoyland hesitated, his guard down, as if he could not comprehend the accusation, then he gave a bellow of rage and rushed into the attack again. Robert skipped lightly aside and, for one second, had the advantage and saw an opportunity to plunge his blade into the unprotected flesh between Hoyland's vambrace and breastplate but, in that one single moment, he wavered.

The man was Clare's uncle. Even yet, she might have feelings for him. That hesitation might have proved his undoing, but for the quick thinking of Silas Whitcome who came at Hoyland from behind for, undoubtedly, Hoyland's blade might well have cloven Robert from shoulder to groin. The man turned and countered the rear attack.

Robert reasserted control and entered the fray but, suddenly, a trumpet shrilled and a line of horsemen charged into the unequal combat. Behind the protection of their own cavalry the Yorkists were able to marshall their beleaguered company and press back into some semblance of organised retreat. Hoyland beat down Whitcome, who fell, but he did not go in for the kill. He thrust the man-at-arms aside with a muttered curse and disappeared in the flurry of activity, to help reorganise the Lancastrian charge once more.

Whitcome scrambled up, clutching his blood-drenched shoulder, but well able to walk. Robert turned his attention now to the Earl, who was leaning against the trunk of an elm.

'I'm all right, thanks to you, Devane,' he said crisply. 'The gash in my leg is deep, but no bones are broken. I'll mend.'

Three squires came running up with horses. Warwick shouted, 'Lord Fitzwalter?'

'Killed, my lord, and your brother too. Do we stay and try to fight off the rest or retire?'

Warwick exchanged glances with Robert, who shrugged. Ahead of them horsemen were still engaged in conflict.

'Sound the retreat,' Warwick said wearily. 'We must get to the King and warn him of this disaster.'

Trumpets shrilled again and the Yorkist line began to give ground. Robert mounted one of the horses and reached down to pull Silas up behind him. One of the other squires had helped the Earl to mount and the little troop re-formed and began to move back towards the King's camp.

They were all weary and dispirited and not a little bemused by the disastrous speed of events, but soon realised they were clear of danger though they could still hear the sounds of warfare behind them as some Yorkist knights guarded their orderly retreat.

Robert rode silently, his thoughts turning continually to his encounter with Gilbert Hoyland. He was still undecided whether to be glad or sorry that he had allowed the man to live when he had had opportunity to dispatch him.

The King received the news of the ignominious defeat philosophically. He was concerned for his cousin of Warwick's wound and a surgeon was sent for immediately. The man came hastily and removed the blood-soaked rag that one of the squires had tightly drawn round the gash before they had retreated from the ferrybridge.

Warwick said thankfully, when it had been dressed and stitched and the man dismissed, 'Well, the news is bad, I know, Ned, but things might be worse. We could have lost more men and I would not be here myself had not Robert Devane come to my rescue.'

The King said quietly, 'I hear Fitzwalter is dead and I am sorry for the loss of our other cousin.'

Both men crossed themselves devoutly. The King turned to Robert, whom Warwick had insisted should remain in attendance.

'Can you say who was in charge of the ambush party, Master Devane?'

'I certainly could not see for myself, your grace, in all that confusion and haste—it was still not entirely light—but I understand from one of my men that he saw Lord Clifford's device.'

The King's countenance darkened and Robert noted an almost wolfish expression cross those handsome young features. He barked out an immediate order for a company to pursue the Lancastrians. Robert understood, only too well. Lord Clifford had cut down the King's brother, Edmund of Rutland, on Wakefield Bridge and it had been Clifford who had stood beside Queen Margaret at the Micklegate Bar in York when the King's father's head had been so insultingly stuck there upon a spike. He had had similar vengeful feelings after the raid on Devane manor.

He heard the Earl assuring the King earnestly, 'Whatever you decide, Ned, I shall remain by your side and see this through to the end.'

The King smiled, though Robert thought that smile was not reflected in the eyes.

'I thank you for your goodwill, cousin. As to taking the field with me again, we must see to the condition of your wound first.'

He turned away slightly and Robert detected a cynical note in his voice. Most likely he had already been fully informed of the rashness both commanders had displayed at the bridge, by failing to keep careful watch and to see that the way ahead was clear for the King's advance.

Warwick had failed him at St Albans and now, again, here. Could this man whose will was good but whose strategy was weak be relied upon to take the right decisions in the coming battle? Robert decided he had not been wrong in his assessment of his young sovereign when he had spoken of this to Clare. Of the two men here in this room, the younger, Edward Plantagenet, was the more likely to bring victory out of this shambles at the ferrybridge, if victory were possible.

At Edward's command Lord Fauconberg was placed in command of the company to pursue Clifford and the King's main battle force then advanced, to come within reach of the enemy near Towton.

They reached Saxton village before it was full dark but the King decided to make camp here and engage the enemy in the morning. The Duke of Norfolk's company had still not joined his army and he wished to delay until he heard further news that those men would be at his disposal. Robert, with Reyner, would again spend a vastly uncomfortable night stretched upon the cold ground in freezing temperatures.

By late evening they had received information that Fauconberg had successfully crossed the Aire four miles upstream at Castleford, cut off Clifford's men's retreat and cut them down after a fierce fight near Dintingdale. Robert could not fail to see the King's joy on learning that Lord Clifford had been killed.

Once again there was evidence here of the over-confidence of this company, for he had removed his gorget and took an arrow in the throat. Clifford's party had sustained heavy casualties and it was thought few would manage to escape to rejoin Margaret's army. Another of the Neville family had fallen in Clifford's company, Lord Neville, who had been an avowed Lancastrian for some years.

Palm Sunday dawned, as Robert had feared, cold and with a pewter sky forecasting heavy snow to come. The wind was fierce, so going would be hard, and fighting harder. He waited with Reyner Astley for the King to emerge from his tent and give the signal for his main force to advance towards the ridge near Towton.

Today he had donned full armour and was grateful for the King's gift that had made it possible for him to purchase it. He had seen too many casualties recently to think himself safe in this coming encounter without it.

The King came out and his men cheered him lustily. He towered above his commanders, his armour and weapons glinting in what wintry sun there was, but he was as yet unhelmed. He lifted his hand to still the vociferous greeting and spoke some encouraging words, but the wind carried away his words and Robert heard only the gist of it.

He was totally amazed to hear his name called peremptorily. Glancing sharply at Reyner, he hurried to the King's side.

Edward stood unsmiling, and said simply, 'Kneel, Master Devane, here before me.'

Robert obeyed and felt the flat of the King's broadsword strike first his right, then his left, and again his right shoulder.

'Rise up, Sir Robert Devane. You have done us sterling service already and I would have you take the field with us today a knight of the realm.'

It was some moments before he could find the impulse

to stand up and look fully into the hard blue eyes of his young sovereign.

'Perhaps you would rather have received the accolade more fittingly when we have returned to London and were fully established in the seat of power, with more magnificent ceremony.'

Robert blinked away sudden emotional tears of joy. 'Your grace honours me beyond my humble imaginings,' he murmured hoarsely.

'Then God be with us all, Sir Robert, and may his protection enclose you within his heavenly wings, for the sake of your dear lady.'

Robert bowed and, thus dismissed, stepped backwards, smiling and awkwardly acknowledging the calls of congratulation and banter which met him from all sides as he returned to his horse. Reyner leaned down to grasp his elbow, his face shining with his own unrestrained delight for his friend's good fortune.

'We must find you a pair of gilded spurs when all this is over,' he said laughing. 'Aye, and celebrate, too.'

Robert mounted, still in a daze, but nodding and grinning towards Silas and the Fletcher brothers who had crowded near to shout their approval of the King's decision.

Afterwards he could remember few details of the battle, only the long slog throughout the day of brutal hand-to-hand combat. He fought on foot largely, and thanked God often that the heavy falling snow blew in the faces of the Lancastrian force established, as they had learned earlier, on the ridge between Towton and Saxton.

This gave a distinct advantage to Fauconberg's archers who discharged an opening volley at the Lancastrian host. Indeed, it was the archers constantly harrying the half-blinded Lancastrian foot soldiers who must have won the day for the Yorkists, finally, but it took *all* of that day.

By mid-afternoon Robert felt he could no longer lift his heavy sword and he could not have told how many men he had cut down, or who had stood to the right or left of him.

In the end it was the Duke of Norfolk who turned the Lancastrian force, marching up in heavy slushy snow from Sherburn-in-Elmet. He had brought up reinforcements to Edward's right and, at last, after hours of grim fighting, the Lancastrians began to give ground and retreat towards Tadcaster.

Robert *did* remember the pursuit, however. Till the day he died he would never forget that terrible slaughter as men fled in panic, many cut down by the Yorkist foot soldiers and cavalry—Robert had resumed his own mount by this time—and hundreds drowned trying to cross the Cock Beck and reach the open road south. Robert saw for himself the river running with bright blood.

Miraculously he survived relatively unharmed, wearied to the bone, and bruised and battered by the continual blows delivered on his mail. He and Reyner reined in their horses when the King at last called a halt to the pursuit and stared, horrified, at the mounds of bodies, dead and dying, that littered the slush-covered field and bloodied the grey whiteness of the snow.

At the King's camp in Pontefract they were to hear an account of noble casualties: Lords Dacre, Neville, de Maulay and Welles had been killed, and the Earl of Northumberland had been so badly wounded that it was feared he would soon die. The Earl of Devon was taken prisoner but no word was received of Somerset. It appeared he had finally fled the field.

King Henry, Margaret and the young Prince Edward

had not been on the field, and later Edward was to grind his teeth in helpless fury at the news that they had managed to flee north towards the Scottish border, but, gloriously, the victory was Edward's. He would be able to march south triumphantly when the casulties had been fully counted and the dead buried.

In the crowded room of their lodging in Pontefract that Robert and Reyner shared with six other men, the two reviewed, wonderingly, their own miraculous luck in coming safely from the field.

Robert shook his head, grinning foolishly as he viewed his own darkening bruises after removing his gambeson. 'God in Heaven, Reyner, I took worst hurts in the raid on my manor and in that attack in the alley in Bruges. Clare will never believe my good fortune.'

Reyner had taken a wound to the thigh but it was not deemed to be serious and, though he would limp for a day or two, he would soon mend. They both sank down on some scattered straw wearily.

'Did all my men come through?' Robert had asked tentatively when he had seen Silas Whitcome, who had come to help him out of his armour earlier, and was glad to hear the Fletcher brothers had been spied coming from the field, laden with booty.

'That's to be expected,' Robert had laughed.

'Well, Sir Robert, what are your immediate plans now?' Reyner said, stretching his wearied length out beside his friend.

'I shall ask audience of the King the moment he has time to receive me and beg to be excused further service. I want to be back in Burgundy at the first possible moment. I could sail possibly from Redcar to Damme harbour.'

Reyner leaned up on one elbow. 'The King intends to enter York in triumph and will want us all with him to swell his victorious army.' His expression grew sober, his mouth held in grimly. 'We took noble prisoners. It's likely there will be reprisals for the executions in York last December. Edward will want witnesses of this significant event.'

Robert swallowed sharp bile. He mused over his own hasty feeling of revengeful triumph as he had ridden from the field. One of Reyner's men had informed him that Sir Gilbert Hoyland's body had been found near the Cock Beck. He had survived Robert's blade at the Ferrybridge only to die ignominiously in that terrible retreat. He sighed and wondered how Clare would receive the news of her uncle's death. He grimaced wryly. Would she, he pondered, hear of his own new-made knighthood with pleasure — or disgust?

CHAPTER EIGHT

THE promise of spring Clare had experienced on that last walk through Bruges with Robert seemed to her in the week afterward merely a cruelly deceptive illusion, for the days following were grey and overcast and appeared to be unbearably long. She missed Robert dreadfully and could speak of it to no one except to Lord Richard who confessed, one morning a week later, that he, too, was fretting after his faithful bodyguard.

Richard had been extraordinarily prickly during that week and Master Skelton had had cause more than once to reprimand him. His behaviour had been somewhat overbearing and difficult and Margery had complained of his conduct. When Clare charged him with discourtesy to the nurse he had at first subjected her to a haughty stare, so unlike his usual well-mannered self, and then broken down and boyishly admitted that he was fearfully worried about his brother, Edward, and also about Master Devane.

Clare drew a hard breath and confessed to a similar feeling of concern.

'Though,' she added in an attempt to be more stern than she usually was, 'this concern of yours does not excuse your lack of manners, my lord.'

'No,' he agreed, granting her, at last, one of his sunniest rare smiles, 'and we cannot expect to hear any news yet, can we? But, oh, Mistress Clare, if Ned should be defeated or taken prisoner—what then?'

'According to Master Devane's assessment of your royal brother's abilities, that does not seem likely.'

'Then you think he will send the Queen's army packing?'

'I do not know, but I believe, even should the worst happen, Lord Edward will know how to make an organised retreat and wait to re-form his armies at a more propitious moment. As for Master Devane—' she hesitated, averting her face from the young lord's scrutiny, lest he see too clearly the blush which revealed her hopeless love '—I am not so sure. He may not prove so fortunate.'

'But, Mistress Clare, Master Robert knows how to handle himself. Remember how he dealt with those ruffians in the alley.'

Clare turned and eyed him steadily. 'That might have proved fatal for us all, Lord Richard,' she said quietly. 'We were foolish to disobey his orders.'

Again he favoured her with that smile that lit up his thin, clever young features. 'That is what I mean. Master Robert knows just how to protect himself and all those who rely on him. He will serve my brother well.'

'I don't doubt it,' was Clare's dry rejoinder.

'He is your betrothed,' Richard said airily. 'You are bound to worry about him, but he will come back to us. I am sure of that. If—if things should go badly—I'm sure Ned will send him to care for us.'

Clare could not prevent herself giving him a hasty hug and he did not withdraw from her grasp, but grinned at her gamely.

Still, it was an anxious wait for all of them. Lord George was broodingly quiet and gave no trouble. He had had a bad shock and was anxious that Master Skelton should not hear of his misadventure. John was over-busied with plans to move the small party to Utrecht the moment he received word from Duke Philip and gave them all scant attention, leaving the day-to-day care of the boys to Clare and Margery.

Piers Martine, surprisingly, kept his distance. He came twice a day to see that all was well with them and to report anything he thought which might threaten their safety to John Skelton, for Clare believed that he spent his days keeping a careful watch on all foreigners who came and went in the city.

Once, meeting his eyes, Clare thought she saw a suspicion of the same concern for his master and events in England which was engaging the thoughts of them all, but he did not force his attention on her as she feared he might do.

She was more than a little surprised when a messenger from Duke Philip appeared at their lodging one morning and was closeted with John Skelton for some time. Indeed, to make a private chamber available for them, Margery and Clare were forced to take the boys for a walk in the town, escorted by Piers Martine.

Clare ventured to talk with the Frenchman. She always found this somewhat embarrassing and could not have explained to herself why she felt so awkward in the man's presence.

'Do you think, Monsieur Martine, that the arrival of this man suggests news has filtered through to the Duke that matters are going well with the Lord Edward in England?'

He shrugged in that Gallic gesture now so familiar to her for Robert often employed it, too, when he was puzzled by something or unwilling to give her a satisfactory answer to some difficult question.

'It is difficult to say, *mademoiselle*, but it is a good sign, I think, *oui*. Did you know that the Duke sent a contingent of troops to support Monseigneur Edward's advance against Marguerite d' Anjou?'

'No, I did not.' She was startled. 'Then, obviously, he believes Lord Edward is likely to achieve a victory?'

Again Martine gave a shrug. 'These matters are governed by trade, *mademoiselle*. If the Duke thinks to support monseigneur Edward will be profitable. . .'

She nodded, eyes narrowed a trifle. 'But it augurs well for the young lords.'

'Ah, *oui*. I think they will be soon accepted at the Burgundian Court, *n'est ce pas*?'

It was to be as they had thought. John Skelton was in cheerful mood when they returned and informed Clare that the party was to move to Utrecht within a matter of days.

'To the ducal palace?' George demanded but Skelton shook his head.

'No, certainly not, my young lord. You must be patient for a while yet, but the man brought gold. We shall be far more comfortable in our new lodging.'

Certainly it proved so. Three days later they were installed in a fine house near the town walls in Utrecht. There were chambers for the boys, Master Skelton and Clare and Margery, a spacious solar, well-furnished in some luxury, and they were provided with several servants, much to Margery's relief, for she was growing tired of Lord George's complaint about the lack of servants. Fortunately, they all spoke French as well as Flemish so Clare and Skelton were able to manage, with the assistance of Piers Martine when there arose some problem in communication.

John Skelton diffidently suggested that Clare should purchase some more suitable clothes and the boys were able to resume wearing the garments they had brought from England. It seemed it was no longer necessary for them to continue to live in obscurity.

Leaving her charges with Skelton and Martine, Clare ventured into the town to do as he wished. She bought two good woollen gowns of excellent quality but serviceable. She felt shamed by the necessity of relying on ducal generosity and felt still unwilling to buy anything too bright, aware of her own state of mourning. One gown was in dark blue and the other in dark wine red, but they were well cut and, for the first time in weeks, she was conscious that her appearance was considerably enhanced by them.

On her return and glancing at her reflection in the iron mirror the solar boasted, she noted that her sallow cheeks bore a hint of a healthy blush and the blue of the gown became her. The headdress was simple, but also framed her face charmingly. She wondered, fleetingly, what Robert would have made of the transformation were he here to see her now.

She fretted for news of him constantly and spent many a sleepless night worrying about him. Lord Richard had been so confident that he would return to them safely, but she could not assure herself that he lived a charmed existence. Like her father, at St Albans, he could be one of the many bodies prey to scavengers after the battle.

She was continually torn with guilt for her self-confessed love for Robert Devane. Had he not been present when her brother had fallen in the raid on the Devane manor? Why, his might well have been the hand which dispatched Peter but she told herself that could not be so. Peter had been killed by a stray arrow, not fighting hand to hand with some worthy opponent.

Then her eyes clouded, as she remembered the suspicions Robert had placed in her mind concerning her uncle's aspirations to inherit Hoyland. That could not be. Her uncle could not have been so perfidious—why, he had always been kind to her in his roughly jovial way. Yet—doubts persisted. It had been rash in the extreme to leave her so poorly guarded on the road to Coventry.

Did her uncle now know she was held by Robert Devane? What would be his reactions if he were aware of her betrothal and her intention to wed his enemy? Of course he would be furiously angry, that would be natural enough, but would that anger be because Robert Devane would thwart his intentions by this marriage?

Clare shook her head in bewilderment. She only knew that now she needed to see Robert, safe and whole, returned to her. She was no judge of her own emotions. She loved him, and that was enough.

In the middle of April on a fine sunny morning that confirmed the coming of spring at last, a messenger from the ducal court visited their lodging with an invitation for John Skelton to formally present his two charges to Duke Philip at his fine palace of Hesdin. Clare was to accompany them but she would remain outside the presence chamber. The young lords were clearly over-excited by the news, but Richard demanded to know the reason for this recognition, at last, of their nobility.

'Tell me please, Master Skelton, did the messenger say if our brother has been victorious? I know there was a rumour over a week ago, but surely, now the Duke wishes to see us, is it because Ned is more important now than King Henry?'

'Yes, my lord Richard, I think we can all be sure now that everything is well in England and that your brother will soon be sending for you.'

George gave a great whoop of joy and Richard turned

to Clare. 'Didn't I tell you Ned would win and—and soon Master Devane will come back for us.'

Clare's heart was pounding madly but she felt a sudden little cold frisson of doubt. She nodded, smiling, but, of course, there could be no news yet of Robert. He was not sufficiently important for his name to be on any list of casualties. Why, oh why, had he not come himself with this so-welcome news of victory for the Yorkist cause? Was that because he could not? She brushed aside the fear and gave her attention to making the two lords presentable for this occasion.

A painted carriage had been sent for them and she sat within, the leathern curtains pushed aside, to breathe in the delightful spring air. This city, like Bruges, had great charm, with its tall windmills just outside the walls, its fine paved streets, and the rivers and canals fringed with willows in soft green now, bending right down to the water's edge.

Yes, she admired the fine stone houses and bridges and imposing churches, but she felt a sudden intense pang of homesickness for England, for the greenness of fields after the winter rains and snows, even the rutted mud streets of towns and villages and the churches with their Norman doors and towers. She missed Hoyland and longed for the day when she would step across the manor hall threshold once more.

The palace was a wonder. She had not imagined such splendour and the boys, too, caught their breaths in admiration of the luxurious surroundings in which Duke Philip lived. John was greeted by an imposing major-domo and conducted down seemingly endless corridors towards the chamber of presence where the two Yorkist lords would be presented to the most puissant Duke of Burgundy.

Even here, in the entrance hall, Clare marvelled at the imposing glazed windows of the palace, the fine polished furniture of rich woods, some unknown to her, obviously from lands far away in the East, the cushioned window seats, the carved panelling of the walls, painted and embellished by many tapestries and paintings, all glowing with bright colours.

She knew the famous Jan van Eyck received the patronage of the Duke and guessed that some she saw now were painted by this gifted artist. She perched uncomfortably upon a window seat to wait, conscious of the stares of many of the courtiers and servants, clerks and clerics who thronged the hall either waiting, as she was, for someone within or hurrying to and fro on the Duke's business.

She remembered her first sight of Baynards and how she had thought that place splendid, but it could not compare with the opulence of this palace. Margery had not been able to attend her, as there had been no room in the carriage, but Piers Martine had ridden behind, a silent and watchful guard. She thought he must have taken himself to the stable to wait until the carriage was once more summoned to convey them back to their lodging. Within the palace Lords Richard and George would be more than adequately guarded.

Clare glanced self-consciously down at her new wine-coloured gown. In the shop it had seemed fine enough; now she saw by the contemptuous glances of some of the elaborately gowned ladies of the Court who swept past her, their over-long trained overskirts held high, their steepled hennins raised to the painted roof, like their sharp, pinched, haughtily raised noses, that she was regarded as an interloper who should have been relegated to the kitchen quarters. She drew in a catch of breath and rose. A young page, magnificently attired in crushed scarlet velvet doublet and fine silken hose, hastened to her side. Apparently he had been instructed to escort her if she showed any intention of leaving the outer hall.

'Mademoiselle? How may I serve you?'

Clearly he spoke French and, relieved, she explained. 'I would like to walk in the garden and take a breath of air.'

'*Mais oui*, mademoiselle,' he assured her with a bow. 'We shall be told when *les deux monseigneurs* are ready to depart.'

He led her through a long, ornate and finely panelled corridor to the rear of the palace and out onto the terrace. Clare gave a great gasp of astonishment. If the building itself had impressed her, these magnificently laid out gardens were a revelation. There were terraces and lawns, pleached alleyways and beautifully laid out and tended rose beds, bare now of flowers but with promise of glories to come.

Most exotic of all were the ornamental lakes and fountains, and beyond tall, gilded cages, which the page informed her contained the Duke's menagerie: bears and lions and other rare species given to him by princes in Europe and the East.

Clare's father had spoken somewhat sarcastically of the menagerie of mangy beasts he had seen at the Tower in London and pitied the poor caged animals, but this was entirely different. Though Clare, with her father's outspoken criticism, could still have wished these imprisoned creatures had been left in freedom in their own lands, she could see that none were neglected, that the cages were large and well maintained and the animals probably better fed than many of the Duke's own lowly subjects.

The young page excused himself for a moment,

having caught sight of some acquaintance and Clare remained, gazing with sad, admiring eyes at a strange black and white garishly striped horse, whose soft melancholy gaze looked back at her with equal sympathy, as if it, too, longed for its own familiar terrain. She was intent and did not notice the foppishly clad young nobleman who came to stand beside her. He addressed her in Flemish and she turned immediately and tried to make him understand that she did not understand his words.

He was small and slim, small boned, with a perky, sharp little face and bright, malicious dark eyes. His attire was outrageously modish, a doublet of purple velvet, so short it fully revealed his hips and embarrassingly over-decorated codpiece and he wore shoes with points so long he could hardly trip along in them. He bowed low, sweeping off his low-crowned velvet hat, decorated with an enormous feather, in mock salutation, and repeated his earlier greeting in a fast patter of imcomprehensible Flemish.

Clare was acutely aware that he was very drunk. She stepped back apace but he drew nearer and she smelt the spicy odour of musk, too rich and cloying, made almost offensively intimate by his closeness to her. He was still talking, his black eyes flashing meaningfully and his white, scented hands moving in expressive gestures, so expressive it brought a hot flush to Clare's throat and cheeks. Again she withdrew and looked round huntedly for her page escort, but he was nowhere to be seen.

This part of the garden was deserted at this hour. It was chilly still, despite the brightness of the spring sunshine; the palace denizens preferred to remain within nearness of the cosy warmth of the charcoal braziers and fires inside the palace. She spoke slowly and carefully in French, explaining that she did not speak his language and could not understand him, that she was a stranger to the palace and merely waiting for the departure of three of the Duke's vistors, hoping he would leave her alone, but he laughed shrilly and came on still closer.

Before she was fully aware of his intention, he had placed an arm around her waist and was pulling her towards him. She gave a little hiss of annoyance and pushed at his chest, intent on freeing herself. Again he laughed and, holding her tight against his over-scented person, took her chin within his free hand and bent to kiss her. Furious, Clare struggled but ineffectually, since, though he looked womanly enough, this creature had a man's full strength.

She turned her face aside to avoid the kiss and he laughed again, uttering a spate of further words. She could not now fail to understand his meaning. His actions and expression made his words clear enough. He had found her alone in the garden, a young woman, by her dress not one of the ladies of the Court, and available for the entertainment of any man who came along.

She administered a sharp kick which made contact with his elegantly hosed leg and he spat out what could only be interpreted as a curse and his face darkened with frustrated anger. Once more he bent his head to kiss her and his arm tightened cruelly upon her waist.

Clare felt faint, caught insufferably against this hatefully elegant person, and prepared herself to endure the threatened hot kiss full upon her lips. He was hardly likely to attempt rape in so prominent a place, common sense told her that, but she felt insulted by his impertinent assumption that she was his for the taking.

Abruptly she felt herself freed from her imprisonment as her tormentor was seized from the rear and forced to turn suddenly to face her rescuer. Again the young

Burgundian let out a startled oath and Clare, freed so quickly and unexpectedly, staggered backwards, to collide with the marble rim of one of the ornamental fountains.

Piers Martine had the fop firmly by one shoulder and was shaking him like a terrier with a rat. The man was lifted clear off the ground and the shaking was so energetic that he was unable to do anything but stutter in startled rage.

'*Monsieur*,' Piers said coldly, 'it is perfectly apparent to anyone but a complete fool, as you are, *monsieur*, that the lady does not desire your acquaintance, let alone your attentions. You require a lesson in manners, *mon ami*.'

To Clare's utter astonishment and amusement he conveyed the still struggling nobleman to a nearby lake and neatly dropped him in. Ignoring the man's bellow of fury, Martine turned to Clare and held out his hand.

'*Mademoiselle*, I think it is wise if we return, *maintenant*, to the palace, *n'est ce pas*?'

Clare turned to look at the man struggling to the water's edge, his grimace of distaste for the coldness of the water and concern for the ruin of his finery, comical in the extreme. She found it hard to restrain from laughing outright.

'Oh, Piers,' she said as she took his hand and hastened with him away from the scene lest the man call up servants to revenge themselves upon his attacker, 'thank the Virgin you were so near. I thought you were in the stables.' She was breathless and drew up within sight of the palace rear door and faced him. 'Thank you, oh, thank you but—' here she doubled over in sudden mirth '—how could you? Those clothes must have cost a king's ransom. He will never forgive you and—and he might well be someone of great importance in the household.'

Martine was smiling broadly and he shrugged. 'Dressed with such appalling taste, Mademoiselle Clare? I think not.'

'But—you will have made an enemy.'

His eyes were laughing back at her. '*Mademoiselle*, that is nothing new, *vous comprenez*? And, *naturelle-ment*, I was near. It is my duty to guard you, keep you within my sight, at all times.'

'I should not have ventured out into the gardens. I did have a young page with me, but he wandered off. I'm sorry, I will not stray from either you or Master Skelton again.'

He made her a little bow. 'You do not understand, I think, what a target you are—is that how you say it—for men's too importunate attentions.'

She stared at him blankly. There was something within his gaze now which disturbed her and again she felt herself flush unaccountably. She made to reply when, fortunately for her bewildered state of mind, John Skelton appeared in the doorway still escorted by the majestic-looking major-domo and preceded by his two excited young charges.

'Oh, Mistress Clare.' Richard threw himself at her, clutching at her gown, his face radiant. 'Ned was victorious at a village in Yorkshire called Towton and he has been proclaimed King and we shall all soon be going home.'

She caught him close to her heart and ruffled his dark hair. 'I am so very glad, my lord.'

George was impatiently pulling at John Skelton's hand. 'The Duke says we may feed his wild animals and there are strange mechanical statues in the garden and fountains that cover people with soot, and paths that drop people suddenly into lakes without warning, and. . .'

Despite her recent fright and embarrassment, Clare could not restrain an outright laugh and Piers Martine's mobile lips twitched as he regarded the boys.

'Well then, we must show you some of those wonders, *monseigneur*,' he said smiling. 'I think perhaps Master Skelton and Mistress Clare would prefer to remain by the fire in the hall until we return. *Excusez-moi*?'

He turned questioningly to John Skelton, who nodded. Clare watched as the Frenchman made off into the gardens again, escorted this time by two servants told to accompany them by the major-domo.

Skelton turned to her his expression sober. 'You must rejoice at the news?'

'Indeed.'

'I hope and pray we shall hear further good tidings about Robert very soon now.'

Her lips trembled a trifle but she made no reply.

'There is much to be done yet in England, before the Lord Edward can be crowned, but I shall be thankful to see London again.'

Clare accompanied him back into the hall, her mind busy with the final acceptance of the news so welcome to all Yorkist hearts. But was she now truly Yorkist — and what of her uncle's fortunes now the Lancastrian hopes were in the decline?

It was some days before Clare found herself alone with Piers Martine again. She had just emerged from the kitchen, having given instructions about supper, when the Frenchman came in from the street. He pushed back his hood and gave her a little respectful bow.

Her own answering smile had far more warmth than she had hitherto granted him.

'I haven't had opportunity, Monsieur Martine, to again assure you of my sincere gratitude for your prompt assistance that day in the palace gardens. I trust you have not been charged with any misdemeanour following that embarrassing affair.'

He grinned at her cheerfully. '*Non*, *non*, *mademoiselle*. The man did not know me and so could not press his displeasure against any person and lay a formal charge. I doubt we shall hear any more of the affair. I think,' he said with that twinkle she had formerly found so disturbing and now found entertaining and infectious, 'the fellow will not wish to talk of the matter. He will feel slightly more than foolish, you agree?'

She laughed and nodded. 'Master Devane will be grateful for your attentions when I inform him of your very great care of his betrothed.'

'You intend to tell him?'

The question was sharp and she sobered and regarded him steadily. 'You believe he would be annoyed to hear of my own rashness in being found alone in the garden?'

He shook his head. 'No, *mademoiselle*, that was not my meaning.'

'Then—'

'Messire Robert is bound to be jealous of any undue attention to your person, he would regard the incident as a grave insult—as I would—were you my fiancée.'

She stared at him intently again, puzzled by the intensity of his explanation, then she lowered her eyes and averted her face.

'Then—' she said, a trifle breathlessly '—you are right. It would be wiser if he were not to be informed.'

'*Bien*.'

She turned back to him. He was looking at her steadily, a slight frown between his brows, and, for once, there was no twinkle in his dark eyes, but an unusual longing. His mouth was slightly open as if he wished to say something then—as if she had caught him unaware in some embarrassing act—he grinned again and made to move towards the rear door along the corridor.

She said very softly, 'I shall not speak of this again, but know you have my undying gratitude.'

He swung round immediately and came partly back along the corridor towards her again.

'Mademoiselle Clare, you must know I would give my life to serve you.'

'I—'

There was a strange, bitter little twist to his lips again. 'We both saw you at almost the same moment, Robert and I, watched your so courageous behaviour on the ride and later in the hut. Robert is my friend. He trusts me, but—'

Then it came again, that little cynical shrug and Clare's grey eyes grew warm with amazed understanding.

'*Je t'aime*,' he said simply. 'I should not say those words but—but—now I find that I must.' He hesitated, then, 'If—if in the future he—he does not treat you well—know that I. . .'

'Monsieur Martine,' she said very gently. 'Please, please do not say any more. I—'

'You love him, is that not so?'

She nodded, blinking back sudden tears.

'And he does not know it?'

'I—I think he does not.'

'Ah.' There was a little sigh.

A familiar voice spoke from the open doorway. 'And what do I not know? What have you been up to lately, my rascally friend?'

So intent had they been on each other that neither Clare nor Piers had heard the door open behind them and they sprang almost guiltily apart as Robert Devane breezed into the hall, flinging back his cloak, pushing free his hood, and advancing on them in high good humour.

For a moment Clare stood irresolute. She longed to rush into his arms, she was so thankful to see him safe and so obviously well, but she could do little more than stare at him, bewildered by his sudden appearance and conscious that the intimacy of the moment following Piers Martine's disclosure had placed a barrier between herself and her betrothed. She forced a welcoming smile and went to greet him, hands outstretched.

'Master Devane, how good it is to see you back. We have been hoping and praying for your safe return. I am so relieved that you have found our new lodging. John established us here soon after you left and Lords Richard and George have since been received by Duke Philip and treated with all honour.'

Behind her, she was aware of Piers Martine moving a trifle uncomfortably, but he called out a cheery greeting and, thinking very quickly, answered Robert's question.

'Well, I have been telling Mademoiselle Clare that the devil will not claim his own just yet. We were merely speaking of some foolishness which occurred in the Duke's gardens.'

'Which you are anxious to keep to yourselves. I take it the boys are responsible?'

Martine ignored that remark and smiled as Robert caught Clare to him and kissed her soundly. 'I see you are looking extremely well. I take it this companion of mine has been a faithful guard dog?'

'Very faithful,' she replied, thankful that her hectic flush of embarrassment was hidden from him by her head pressed against the rough frieze of his cloak. 'We are all well. The young lords were overjoyed by the turn of events. And you, Master Devane?' she questioned, freeing herself from his hold and standing back to look at him closely, to follow every lineament of his loved features, to spy out any further limp or awkward use of an arm which might betray injuries he had recently received. She could see evidence of none and her heart swelled with rapture at the knowledge.

Another voice from the doorway gave her tidings of further joy. Silas Whitcome had come into the hall laden with Robert's bags and gear. He was grinning from ear to ear.

'No longer *Master* Devane, Mistress, but Sir Robert Devane, knighted by the King himself before the battle.'

Clare's grey eyes widened as she looked up into Robert's laughing blue ones. 'This is really true?'

He nodded, a faint flush of mixed triumph and embarrassed modesty tinging his cheeks.

'Aye, the king did me the honour of knighting me and he has promised to confirm me in my inheritance, so all is well for us.'

'I am very glad,' she said gravely. 'You have done him rare service and deserve the honour. But come in and greet John Skelton, who will be anxious for the latest news of the king's situation, and I know the boys will be delighted to hear of your good fortune.'

Piers Martine went up to his friend and embraced him in his Gallic way, kissing him heartily on both cheeks, the two laughing and half crying together.

Robert said, 'To answer your question, I am well, save for some bruising which is beginning to subside. I have been very fortunate but—' he hesitated, the brilliant blue of his eyes clouding a little '—I have further news for your ears alone, Clare, which I will tell you when we have leisure to be alone together.'

John Skelton was delighted to greet Robert and

appeared totally unenvious of his new knighthood. Richard hugged him warmly and even George looked flushed with pleasure for his former rescuer and one who had chosen to remain silent concerning his misdemeanours. George had been grateful for that and was determined to demonstrate that by showing Sir Robert a measure of respect not heretofore apparent.

Robert regaled the company with stories of the battles at the ferrybridge and at Towton, glossing over, somewhat, the grim account of the retreat. He made a hasty meal and later requested leave to take Clare into the solar and have private talk with her. Margery accompanied them but remained half-hidden on the cushioned window seat, too far distant to hear all that transpired.

Quietly Robert informed Clare of the death of her uncle, taking her hand within his own as he saw sudden tears spark on her lashes.

She said at last, 'Did you—did *you*—kill him?'

He shook his head. He had not revealed Sir Gilbert Hoyland's part in the ferrybridge disaster in his earlier telling, and he forbore to do so now.

'His body was found near the Cock Beck. He was killed in the retreat along with hundreds of other Lancastrians. He died an honourable death, Clare, you can be sure of that.'

'He—was often very kind to me—even when Peter—was sometimes harsh. . .' She broke off, her lips trembling. Never before had she revealed to Robert the truth about her brother's treatment of her.

He was silent and she said tremulously, 'Now I am alone in the world—and what will happen to his wife and daughters?'

'The children will become wards of the Crown, doubtless, and I am sure Edward will deal generously with them. As for you, my dear, you are my betrothed, and need not concern yourself over your welfare. As I have said, the King will confirm me in my properties and will certainly approve our marriage. Your future is safe.'

She looked away, thinking of Robert's former suspicions regarding Gilbert Hoyland which, despite misgivings, she had been bound to entertain herself. Her inheritance was safe now from any predator of that quarter—safe from all takers, save Robert.

He was watching her carefully, his heart torn by her natural distress, yet relieved that Gilbert Hoyland could no longer prove any threat to her safety. Until their marriage he might have feared an attempt on her life, were she to be near enough to the man to fall into his clutches. The thought jarred that she might well have felt freed from her oath to remain with him now that the boys were safe. He must watch over her more carefully.

He said hastily, 'I could not come before. The King kept the gentlemen of his household with him on his entry into York and wished us to be present at the—proceedings afterwards.'

She looked back at him sharply. 'There were—executions?'

He nodded. 'The Earl of Devon was executed in York and the Earl of Wiltshire condemned and sent to the block in Newcastle. It was not pleasant.'

She sighed. 'So many good men slain, but the King and Queen are still free, you say, and have taken refuge in Scotland?'

'Yes, but it seems unlikely that Margaret can gather a new army, at least in the near future. The country has received Edward with joy. He is set now to enter London in triumph and will be crowned there shortly.'

He smiled. 'He has a new device beside the white rose of York, a sun. It's said that before the battle at

Mortimer's Cross there were freak weather conditions, a kind of mist which revealed three phantom suns visible in the sky at once, which Edward declared a good omen for the House of York.' He chuckled out loud. 'Edward was ever one to seize the advantage of the moment. 'Tis also being said in Yorkshire that this sun is a pagan sign and Edward rejoices in it.'

Clare was scandalised. 'But surely that cannot be true. Surely the Lord Edward is a true son of Mother church?'

A faint crease showed between Robert's brows. 'Perhaps he deems it wise to honour the gods of all his people. Among those close to the soil the old gods and goddesses are still reverenced, if secretly. The Green Man can be seen in many churches and cathedrals peering from behind a screen of leaves and flowers in the tracery. You must have glimpsed his image yourself in some places.'

Her grey eyes were wide but guileless and he hastened to reassure her. 'Edward is a Christian monarch, I do but jest.'

She smiled thinly. This jest, touching on occult matters, had disturbed her, though she could not deny the truth of his allegations. The church itself was content to remain silent on the subject of these traces of the Old Faith, often seen in village festivals.

He was rising to his feet, aware that she would require privacy to grieve for her uncle and she was conscious that there was much she needed to say to him and—at this moment—could not. She watched him go wistfully. He had spoken of their coming marriage as an acknowledged fact, approved by the King himself.

She would become Robert's wife. Indeed, she had no other protector now. She could not fly to her uncle and those Lancastrian friends of his who might have offered her succour. Yes, she would wed Robert, and he had

been kind, sensitive to her sorrow and solicitous for her
welfare — but he had spoken no word to her of love.

Throughout May the exiles waited impatiently for their
recall to London. They were no longer penniless suppli-
cants. Now that Edward IV was safely established on
the English throne, Philip of Burgundy was pleased to
treat the young Yorkist lords as honoured guests.
Frequently they were invited to the magnificent palace
at Hesdin and escorted through Utrecht and Bruges to
view the towns' many treasures of architecture and
other wonders.

Richard was particularly delighted to be taken to visit
the premises of an English merchant who had settled in
Burgundy under the patronage of the Duke, Master
William Caxton, who was printing books almost exclu-
sively for Philip's use. Richard was fascinated by the
huge wooden presses and the ink-smeared apprentice
lads who laid out the blocks of raised letters and rolled
under the long sections of paper and parchment,
instantly reproducing a page a monk might have taken
days, possibly even weeks, to copy.

'We must have such a shop in England,' he said
enthusiastically to John Skelton. 'I shall speak to Ned
about it. Imagine, we could have shelves of such fine
books for a fraction of the time and cost of a hand
written volume.'

George had laughed heartily. 'I think Ned will have
far more important things on his mind than interesting
himself in some merchant,' he said contemptuously,
'and a book copyist, to boot. When did you ever see Ned
read a book?'

Richard said defensively, 'He has had much more
pressing matters to interest him, I know, but Ned is
interested in all things which bring riches to his people.

He has said more than once that it is important for the merchant class to prosper. Duke Philip thinks so and, anyway, I am glad I can write—and read dispatches for myself. It will come in handy one day when I am on campaign.'

Clare had accompanied the boys to the palace, indeed, she found herself separated more and more from Robert these days for he was seldom invited. When their paths crossed he was gravely courteous but, even when they were alone together, he did not refer again to the incident in her chamber which had followed the attack in the alley. She was not sure if the matter still embarrassed him or if he had simply forgotten.

He rarely spoke of their coming marriage and she guessed he was impatient to return to England and take up his life there again, for his own manor needed his attention. She found him staring at her intently sometimes and flushed under the scrutiny. In York and Pontefract on campaign and after the battle, and certainly at Baynards Castle, he must have come into contact with some of the Duchess's ladies, women more beautiful and experienced than she was.

In the privacy of her own chamber she bit her lip in frustration, and even occasionally wept bitterly, unable to come to terms with this delay in their marriage arrangements and finding the uncertainty about her own feelings almost unbearable.

At the beginning of June the call came at last and Duke Philip, knowing that his two protégés would soon return home and speak to the King, their brother, of their reception in Burgundy, planned to fête them within the magnificent Hôtel de Ville in Bruges at a state banquet. This time all members of their household were invited and Clare found herself seated next to Robert at table.

Though she had purchased several gowns during these last weeks while she had been in attendance on the two young lords, she had always previously chosen to wear somewhat sombre ones, mindful of her continued mourning for Peter and, more recently, for her uncle. This evening, one of the Duke's ladies had protested at such drab and modest garb and insisted on lending her a gown more suitable, she said, for this great occasion.

Clare had given way finally and allowed herself to be adorned for this memorable ceremony, aware that her charges must not be shamed by her appearance. The two boys were clad in fine-cut velvet doublets and had been given jewelled chains as parting gifts. Clare sat part way down the long table beside Robert, glowing with pride at the demeanour of her two charges who were on their best behaviour and radiant with excited joy at the prospect of soon returning home.

Robert shared cup and magnificent plate with his betrothed, helping her to the choicest delicacies from the innumerable rich dishes brought for each remove. Throughout the seemingly interminable meal the Duke's musicians played from a gilded and decorated gallery and the guests were entertained by mime shows, acrobatic displays and the amusing, though pathetic, tumbles of the Duke's famed dwarves.

Robert was more than a little bored by the proceedings and found himself gazing intently at his betrothed whose attention was largely upon her charges, some distance from her as protocol demanded, seated at the high table, ranged as honoured guests on either side of the Duke, but whose doings still needed her complete surveillance.

He had been totally taken aback by her magnificence tonight—and her loveliness. The gown she wore was slightly outmoded, having been lent by an older lady, but it merely sufficed to reveal the unusual quality of her beauty. He had noted proudly on several occasions how tall and stately she was; now the heart-shaped headdress with its golden caul, trapping yet showing glimpses of her shining brown hair, enhanced that nobility of carriage he found always so endearing.

Her gown of heavy gold and brown patterned brocade was cinched in tightly with a broad belt of cloth of gold and cloth of gold sleeves, tight to her wrists, showed beneath the jagged-edged trailing oversleeves. Altogether there was a golden shimmer about her tonight. A heavy gold brooch centred her brocaded headdress though she wore no other jewellery. She resembled some beauty he had seen in an illuminated romance, one young Richard had so admired in Master Caxton's workshop.

Robert had never seen her before in Court dress and his heart fluttered within his breast as he thought how far above him she was in station. He was knighted now, it was true, no longer humble Master Devane, and the Devane lands would be his, but in England she would shine even more grandly at Court. She would put aside her mourning and men would look on her as he had seen several of the Duke's courtiers ogle her tonight. She had appeared utterly impervious to their flattery. Most of their utterances she did not understand, he thanked the Virgin.

A young fair-haired fop hastened to her side, offering to escort her to a padded chair after the banquet was over, so she might enjoy in comfort more of the sumptuous entertainment and appreciate the skill of the court musicians, later even, dance.

She turned, a little anxiously, to Robert, who replied courteously that his betrothed was somewhat wearied by the length of the banquet and anxious to retire for a while from the overheated room to find cooler air in the corridor. Thankfully she rose, curtsyed to the aspiring admirer, took Robert's proffered arm and went with him from the banqueting hall.

She stopped in one of the anterooms near an opened casement and drew in the fresher air.

'Thank you,' she said simply. 'I was not sure—how to behave on these occasions. Life at Hoyland has never prepared me for this sophisticated behaviour.'

'Nor me,' he replied frankly.

'But you were one of the Earl of Warwick's squires. You must have been present at many Court gatherings.'

'For these past years Warwick's household has either been at Calais or on the march. I spent a short time at his Wensleydale castle at Middleham but never experienced such splendour as this.' He shrugged. 'Oh, I was trained to serve at table and carve, bend the knee and proffer bowls of scented water and towels, but most of my time was spent in the tiltyard and, lately, on campaign.'

'You were not trained to run the manor either,' she said thoughtfully.

'No,' he confessed with a sigh, 'but I am quick to learn and my steward is faithful.'

'Will you regret leaving the Court? You have been in the King's presence now and you have close friendship with Sir Reyner Astley. Won't you wish to be in attendance at Westminster?'

'I doubt I shall be summoned to Court. Once this is over and the King crowned he'll have no need of my services, nor will my lord of Warwick.'

He felt a further stab of doubt. Clare had tasted the heady excitement of Court life. Would she be bored now at Hoyland? He repressed a deep sigh. He had seen her so many times with the children that he had come to picture her with his, living contentedly as chatelaine of her own household at Hoyland and Devane Manor. Now he was no longer sure.

She was gazing at him, a faint frown between her own brows as if some private thought disturbed her. Impulsively he reached up to cup her chin within his two hands.

'I was so proud of you tonight. You shine gloriously like Edward's new device of the sun in veritable splendour. There was not a man in the hall who did not envy me,' he murmured a trifle hoarsely, and kissed her gently, full upon her lips. Her own parted a little to receive the kiss and he smelt the warm, wine-fumed sweetness of her mouth. The longing to possess her stabbed at his loins and he released her, standing back a little to take in the perfect splendour of her beauty.

CHAPTER NINE

CLARE watched with Robert beside her as King Edward rode triumphantly into his capital. Robert had taken a lodging near the Chepe for himself and his small household, but Clare and Margery had been established temporarily at Baynards Castle amongst the Duchess of York's ladies. Now all of them, Robert, Piers Martine, Margery with Silas Whitcome and the Fletcher brothers behind them, were assembled near the upper chamber window to witness this splendid event.

Cheering crowds received their new young sovereign, wall hangings and tapestries had been torn down and draped over sills to be displayed from windows. The Mayor had had stands entwined with white paper roses erected along the principal route the King would take, and young girls in white dresses waited to strew more artificial roses before the hooves of the riders in the procession. Edward, Robert thought, with a smile, would like that, especially the young golden-haired damsel who waited near Temple bar with a basket of real roses to offer to him.

The noise swelled louder and the first riders came into view on richly caparisoned horses, preceded by men-at-arms in the Yorkist colours of blue and murrey. Clare leaned forward, anxious to get her first view of her two charges who rode behind their brother.

'There they are,' she said delightedly to Margery whose eyes were wet with emotional pride. The two boys sat their ponies rigidly upright, both clad in blue velvet, and Clare saw George doff his hat and wave it at the onlookers who cheered ever more loudly at the sight of the golden-haired young lordling flushed and smiling at his brother's triumph. Beside him Richard looked very slight indeed, and so very young that the sight of his upright carriage in the saddle touched Clare's heart and she found herself crying openly with joy as Margery was.

The King was accompanied by his principal support-ers, among them the Earl of Warwick and William Hastings, a close friend of the King whom people were already prophesying would rise to high honours very soon now. This was Friday, the twenty-sixth day of June, and on Sunday next Edward would be crowned.

Behind the nobles came more men at arms and the Mayor and alderman of the city, dressed in scarlet, followed by many notable citizens dressed in green. Clare leaned yet lower from the casement to watch as the King passed beneath them on his way to the Tower. He too laughed and waved at his jubilant subjects.

Across the road from other upper chamber windows and balconies laughing dames and maids threw flowers and trinkets down to their handsome monarch. It was clear that London was delirious in its heartfelt welcome. The threat of Margaret's vengeful entry into the city was well past and this new sovereign they hoped would bring them a welcome respite from the fear of plunder and more skirmishes.

Yet, Clare thought it was merely a respite, for Margaret, with King Henry and her heir, Edward, were still at large, gathering support north of the Border. Edward would have much to do yet to establish firmly the Yorkist power base here in the capital. At least he had the support of his southern citizens.

They had sailed from Damme just two days following the banquet at the Hôtel de Ville in Bruges and been joyously welcomed by the people of Kent. In

Canterbury, the two young lords had been feasted again and Clare had privately feared for their health after she had seen the rich delicacies constantly being placed before them. Her fears had proved groundless. Both boys weathered both the journey and the excitement of state occasions well.

She had found she had had little time to dwell on the incident in the corridor of the Town Hall in Bruges. Robert's manner had seemed to her strange indeed. He had looked at her that evening as if he had never set eyes on her before. She wondered, regretfully, if he was relieved that she was now living apart from him at Baynards.

The procession had passed now and the noise of acclamation was dying down, lost in the distance. Robert drew Clare back from the window and closed the casement.

'They looked very well, didn't they?' he said. 'Young Richard was handling his mount as if he were born in the saddle and George appeared heartily used to all this adulation.'

Clare nodded. Tonight, she knew, the boys were to endure the ritual bathing and preparation for the Vigil which would precede the ceremony of knighthood to take place on the morrow. She was concerned that all this excitement, too soon, would be far too tiring for Richard in particular.

He had not yet reached his ninth birthday and the thought of him becoming a Knight of the celebrated Order of the Bath, so young, seemed ludicrous, yet she could not help that feeling of maternal pride sweeping through her again as it had when she had seen him ride in the procession. She had not dared to voice her concern to the Duchess of York, whose delight at her eldest son's elevation filled her mind to the exclusion of all other considerations.

Robert said quietly, 'You have become very attached to the boys. You will miss them when you return home to Hoyland. You will wish to do so very soon now, I imagine.'

'Yes.' Clare fiddled uncertainly with the tasselled ends of her silken girdle. She looked very well today in a gown of russet silk and a truncated hennin from which a snowy veil floated to her shoulders. 'There will be much to be done and—and I think I ought to send messages to my aunt in Northamptonshire to enquire if there is anything I can do to—lighten her burden of sorrow.'

A shadow crossed her face as she realised for the first time on this special day that she was beginning to consider herself truly Yorkist and rejoice at this victory. What would her father have thought of her part in this triumph, for she had undoubtedly helped the Yorkist cause by her care for the young heirs?

Peter would have been furious and certainly not backward at slating her for her treachery. Yet she *was* undoubtedly Yorkist now. Robert would soon become her husband and her loyalty must be to him and those he served.

He was gazing from the window, frowning, and she thought, with a sudden pang, was he regretting their betrothal, now all the alarums and excursions were over and he was free to take her to wife?

He said abruptly, 'When the streets are a little clearer I must escort you and Margery to Baynards. Are you to be present at the Tower tomorrow at the Knighting ceremony?'

'Yes, the Duchess has been very kind and has invited me to walk with her ladies in the coronation procession and to be present in the Abbey.'

'I should think she *is* grateful, indeed,' Robert said tersely. 'I, too, am to be present in the Abbey and at the banquet following in Westminster Hall.' His voice carried a strange cold note as he added, 'I have been given instructions to present my betrothed to His Grace the King at the close of the feasting.'

She glanced at him sharply. Had she mistaken that diamond-hard note in the tone? Was he ashamed of her? There would be many noble and more beautiful ladies present on that occasion.

To change the subject she questioned him about the ordeals facing the two boys tonight.

'They will be led into the initiation chamber by two chosen governors and, accompanied by other young squires and singing boys, helped to undress and to step into the ritual bath where the chief knight of the Order will sprinkle water upon their shoulders. Afterwards they will be assisted to dress and led into the chapel, where they will kneel before the altar for the remains of the night.'

'It is too arduous for them to remain so, for so long,' Clare protested, 'and frightening in the chapel during the hours of darkness. They are not grown men, as would normally be facing these ordeals.'

'They won't be alone,' Robert consoled her. 'There will be the two chosen sponsor governors and a priest with them. They'll be buoyed up by the honour of the occasion. Do not fear for them. Richard will come through it bravely enough.'

He added soberly, 'Young though he is, he will have to endure more sombre moments and some hard fighting within the next ten or twelve years. Better he get used to hardships and feats of endurance now and,' he said with a mischievous little smile, 'you must get accustomed to facing the thought of your own sons facing such hardships, my girl, if you are to be the mother of warriors.'

Clare swallowed and made no riposte. She could have said she hoped sincerely the world would have become more settled before such a test of courage faced her, but forebore to do so.

Robert kissed her tenderly when he took his farewell within the hall at Baynards. She lifted her face gladly to meet his kiss but discerned no trace of passion. It was the kiss of a betrothed man to his promised bride, not cold but warm, intimate, in friendship. She was aware that a comradeship had grown up between them during those weeks in exile, a friendship which had totally replaced the spirit of enmity she had believed had first been the barrier between them, but now she longed for more—much more.

Clare rode to the Tower in an open carriage similar to the one which had conveyed her to the Ducal palace at Hesdin. Ahead lumbered the Duchess's vehicle and that lady was received vociferously by the worthy citizens who had risen early and erupted onto the streets to see yet more of the pageantry of these celebrations.

Margery accompanied Clare and was a-twitter with excitement—for she had not expected to be allowed to see her dear young lordlings be made knights—even more so when she was informed that Lord George had personally requested that she be present.

Clare was gratified by his consideration for the dour woman who had given such care to him during the days of his exile. Knowing him, she had thought it likely that he would quickly forget those who had befriended him in his hours of need once that dependence was no longer deemed necessary for his survival. Apparently she had misjudged him and was glad to acknowledge the fact.

She glimpsed Robert amongst the throng of nobles and attendants within the courtyard of the Tower. He acknowledged her presence with a wave and bow. She took her place with the Duchess's other ladies on a stand specially erected for their comfort and looked anxiously towards the door of the royal lodging from which the two young accolytes would emerge.

There was a little stir amongst the watchers as the King emerged to take his position before the stand, bowing to his mother and then turning solemnly to await his brothers.

A marshall of Arms headed the small procession. First George, as the elder, came to stand before his sovereign and then Richard, whose horse was led, like George's, by the marshall. Clare was to discover afterwards that the two horses would be granted to the marshall as a fee. She watched through a blur of tears as the stately ceremony began, first George receiving the accolade then young Richard stepped forward to gaze adoringly upwards into the face of the golden giant, who was his brother and sovereign and receive the command to kneel.

His two sponsors had already fastened the gilded spurs of knighthood to his heels. Edward girded on his brother's sword, one smaller and shorter than normal, specially made for this youthful knight, after he had touched his shoulders first right, then left, then right again with his own sword and commanded the small boy to rise. Clare heard Margery give an emotional sniff as the King's voice floated across the courtyard. He kissed his brother soundly, bending low to do so then admonished him, 'Be thou a good and worthy knight.'

The new made knights returned to the chapel to swear oaths of knightly chivalry before the high altar and to hear from the master Cook, on leaving the chapel, that their spurs could well be hacked from their heels were they to defile their honoured rank by an act of treachery, cruelty or cowardice.

Clare found Robert at her side. She said excitedly, 'Oh, what a colourful cermony it is! Are you not disappointed that you did not receive the accolade in like fashion?'

He shook his head, smiling. 'No, I was glad to take the field before Towton a King's knight and to be spared some of this.' He wrinkled his nose a trifle. 'To be honest, this Court etiquette is beginning to become somewhat wearing and more than a little boring. I shall be glad to be done with it soon.'

Her cool grey eyes regarded him steadily. It was not a comment she had expected. Robert Devane had confessed to her, months ago, that he had wished to serve the Earl of Warwick in order to aid his own preferment. He *had* done so and his part in the King's victory had been recognised. Now he was saying he was already tiring of court life.

She gave a little sigh of agreement. It was good to see her young charges so honoured and she would undoubtedly miss them when the time came to part, yet she, too, was hungry for the rolling hills and gentle pastures of north Leicestershire. Hearing Robert admit his own desire to return home, she had hopes he would stay with her there for longer periods of time than she had anticipated.

The strain of attendance at the coronation took its toll of Clare on the next day, Sunday, June the twenty-eighth. She walked with the Duchess of York's ladies from the Tower to Westminster Abbey and stood in the sweating throng to see the Archbishop of Canterbury place St Edward's crown on the young King's head and hear the joyous acclamation, 'Vivat, Vivat, God save King Edward the Fourth.'

She thought the two young lords who sat within the gallery with their mother, dressed in velvet and ermine-collared robes, must feel the heat abominably, as did she. Like Robert, she was almost sorry she must attend the sumptous feast which would follow in the great hall of Westminster Palace.

Towards the close of the feasting Clare's head pained her so much that she longed to retire to the dormitory at Baynards, which she shared with others of the Duchess's ladies. As Robert had confessed to her earlier, she, too, was tired of the interminable over-rich dishes, remove after remove. She sat some way down the hall with Robert on her right and Reyner Astley on her left. Robert plied her, as usual, with the daintiest titbits, many of which she toyed with for form's sake and others she politely refused.

She could not believe that the simple girl she had been, living so quietly on the manor at Hoyland, could so quickly tire of this continual feasting. There had been the banquets in Bruges and Canterbury and now this, the greatest of them all. The smell of the over-spiced food and wine almost nauseated her and the constant racket of talk and cheering all around her, combined with the excessive heat of this June day, had given her a headache.

She saw the King's champion ride into the hall to challenge all those who might oppose his claim and ride off with his fee, the richly decorated goblet from which the King had drunk thoughout the evening. She had strained her eyes towards the high table, under its tapestried cloth of estate, where the King sat with his mother and his two brothers and older sisters, together with his cousin of Warwick, Will Hastings, now honoured and knighted, and many other friends and nobles who had ridden with him to Towton.

Richard looked tired and somewhat strained, she thought, and should have been put to bed long since. George looked flushed but jubilant. She hoped he had not partaken of too much rich food as he was prone to, or someone would have the unpleasant task of cleaning up after a very sick young new-made knight.

She was faintly amused by the attention she was receiving from many around her. Reyner Astley had scarce taken his eyes from her all evening. She turned a puzzled gaze to Robert who, as he did frequently these days, was staring at her very intently. She flushed under his scrutiny and wondered, as she did so many times a day, just what was passing through his mind. They had had little private time together.

Passionately, she hoped he would soon be excused from Court attendance so that he could take her home at last. He was called away momentarily and some elderly noblewoman was questioning her about her care of the King's brothers in exile. She was finding it hard to hear over the sound of the musicians in the upper gallery and the banter and ribald comments of those around her.

Her shoulder was touched very gently and she turned hastily, expecting Robert to have returned to her side, only to see the Duchess's steward, with his wand of office, waiting behind her seating bench to speak with her.

'Mistress Hoyland,' he said in his stately, dignified way. 'His Grace the King has requested that you be presented to him.'

Flustered, Clare looked huntedly round for Robert to escort her, but he was nowhere to be seen.

Gallantly, Reyner Astley stood up and offered her his arm.

'There is nothing to be concerned about, Mistress Clare. I am sure the King wishes only to thank you personally for your services to his brothers. Allow me to escort you in Robert's absence.'

She went with him gladly, conscious that the eyes of all those who were seated near and had heard the steward's words were fixed upon her in avid curiosity.

Before the high table she curtsied low, almost afraid to lift her eyes to the glittering figure, clad in scarlet and cloth of gold, who lolled at his ease in the chair of state.

A pleasant voice bade her come to his side of the table and Will Hastings stood up to make room for her approach as, timidly, she obeyed the King. The Duchess, on his other side, was smiling down at her graciously as Clare nervously curtsied again.

'Mistress Clare—I may call you that? My brothers have said that is how they have always addressed you. I cannot express properly my gratitude for your care of them and—' his blue eyes twinkled '—I am aware, knowing them, that it could not always have been easy.'

'The Lords George and Richard were always aware of their duty and manners, your grace. It has been a pleasure to serve them. I shall miss them,' she said a little diffidently.

'As they will you. Both must be dispatched soon to their training at arms and you to your home in Leicestershire, I understand, where you hope soon to be wed.'

'Yes, your grace.' Clare hoped her voice was audible as she could hardly hear her own words, so in awe of this smiling giant was she.

He bent and lifted her chin with one finger. 'Sir Robert Devane is a lucky man, as I have told him many times. Had you not been already betrothed, as your guardian, since you are now a ward of Court due to the death of your uncle at Towton, I could have looked very high for you indeed.' He sighed in mock regret, still smiling genially. 'But you are bound by Holy Church.'

She did not reply. There was a little pause, then he said, 'Allow me to give you a token of my gratitude and a reminder of this very special day.'

She looked up, startled, expecting nothing from him. She was standing very close to him now and was more than a little bemused by his physical appeal. He was strikingly handsome and his nick name, Rose of Rouen, was in no way a misnomer. He bent his golden head close to hers and slipped over her head a delicate golden chain on which was suspended a gold pendant in the shape of a sun in full splendour with an enamelled white rose at its heart.

She touched the costly trinket wonderingly and looked up into his face.

'I shall cherish the gift for ever, your grace, but you had no need to. . .'

'It will please me if you will wear it at your wedding,' he said smoothly, and he waved her graciously away. 'Ah, here is Sir Robert to conduct you to your place again. I trust I may see you again before you leave for Leicestershire, perhaps when you take your leave of my brothers.'

She curtsied low again and stepped backwards to find Robert very close at her elbow. She looked at him, her eyes a little blurred with excited and nervous tears, and allowed him to lead her from the King's presence with Reyner Astley slightly behind them.

Robert's lips were pressed tight together and he hardly glanced at his sovereign as he made a somewhat perfunctory bow. Clearly he had heard what had been said and Clare knew he was not pleased, yet how could she have refused the King's gift or contradicted any of his statements? She looked at him pleadingly and the pounding in her head intensified.

He conducted her to her seat, since none could leave the hall before the King. He had not been unaware of the frank admiration of those nobles seated within the hall. Did she know what a charming picture she had made in her quiet and dignified acceptance of the King's gratitude? There had been nothing of the usual fawning flattery in her direct glance, though she had been unaccustomed to such grandeur and taken aback by the mark of open favour shown to her.

Robert ground his teeth and hoped his expression did not reveal too openly the sour feeling in the very pit of his stomach, which he had experienced at the sight of her so close to the amorous young monarch. Edward had obviously found her more than pleasing to the eye, and no wonder. She was wearing tonight a simply cut gown of softest blue silk, cinched in at the waist beneath her high and youthful breasts with a band of cloth of silver matching the modesty vest at the low V of the neck and the same material draped her truncated hennin. Her veil, too, glittered with the sparkling sheen of silver thread.

He could see no trace of that glorious nut-brown hair beneath her hennin, for fashion decreed the waving locks must be closely confined and hidden from male view, but he remembered it as he had seen it in the hall at the Hôtel de Ville in Bruges, enclosed in the gilded net. How proudly she had walked from the King's presence; her curtsy had been as stately as if she had spent all her youth at Court.

His heart ached with overwhelming love for her, yet was he worthy? He had not failed to hear the King's words. He could have found a husband more suitable, to match her in gold and land, yet she was bound to him, Robert Devane, a simple country knight.

Clare was relieved when a pause occurred in the almost frenzied celebrations and she waited quietly at Baynards for Robert to come to her and inform her they would soon be riding north. Margery was fretting for her youthful charges, for she saw little of them now and knew they would soon be lost to her.

Clare attempted to comfort her by talking of their return to Leicestershire and Margery brightened momentarily at the prospect. The women had drawn together over the long weeks in exile; though Margery Lightbody would never be a communicative woman, she had served Clare loyally and Clare considered her now a confidante and friend.

'Sir Robert will be impatient to get back to the manor,' Margery said two days later, as she began to sort out the clothing which both would wish to pack in Clare's travelling chests. 'Autumn will be on us before we know it and there will be the slaughter and salting to be attended to and the harvest to get in safely, of course. It is to be hoped those lazy good-for-nothing servants on both manors have been attending to their duties.'

She was interrupted by a knock upon the door and, grumbling beneath her breath, went to open it and admit one of the Duchess of York's cheeky young pages.

'And what can you be wanting?' she demanded, hands upon her hips. 'Mistress Hoyland has been excused from attendance today and. . .'

'Her Grace the Duchess demands Mistress Hoyland's presence within her private solar,' the boy announced, unimpressed by Margery's brusqueness. 'She will not wish to be kept waiting,' he added, his head flung back impertinently as Margery sniffed her disapproval of his forward manner.

Clare glanced hurriedly at her reflection in the scratched iron mirror mounted on the wall of the dormitory she shared with the other ladies and was glad that, in spite of being freed from Court duties, she was respectably, if sombrely, clad in a wine silk gown and a truncated hennin covered in gold brocade. She motioned the boy to precede her to the Duchess's private apartments.

Was she at last to be excused from Court permanently on Robert's request to return to his home?

She curtsied on entry and was surprised to see no other lady in attendance, but when she rose to move closer to the Duchess, an erect, dignified figure dressed in green brocade seated in her favourite padded arm-chair near the oriel window, she stopped short in astonishment. The King was seated on the padded window seat near his mother, his long legs stretched out comfortably in repose. She dipped into another curtsy and heard the lazy, good-humoured deep tones bidding her rise.

'You are welcome, Mistress Hoyland. Please come and seat yourself. My mother has something of import-ance to say to you.'

Mystified, Clare did as she was commanded and, striving to keep her trembling knees from knocking together, for she was somewhat alarmed by this hasty summons, sank down on a small fald stool near the Duchess's feet.

Cecily Neville smiled down at her reassuringly. 'We wished to see you privately, Clare, but there is no cause for alarm.'

'Your Grace?' Clare turned from first one royal personage to the other anxiously.

The Duchess smoothed down the folds of her elegant brocade gown and looked towards her son who nodded imperceptibly for her to speak first.

'We have been speaking with Robert Devane,' the Duchess said. 'He has confessed to feeling somewhat perturbed. Your er—betrothal was made somewhat hastily, he informs us, and he is not certain that you—er—entered into it entirely of your own will, or, at least,' she amended, 'you were constrained by events—the death of your brother and—and the speed of other happenings which followed. Since you accompanied him to Burgundy, he feels that there has been little opportunity for the two of you to come to terms with the situation.'

Clare stared miserably at the floor, not daring to lift her eyes to the speaker.

The King said smoothly, 'The fact of the matter is, Mistress Clare, Sir Robert feels that you should be free to choose without restraint and be under no compulsion whatever. Therefore he has informed me that he will be perfectly willing to allow you to seek a dispensation from Rome and will in no way stand in your way of obtaining one. I will, naturally, add my voice to such a petition.

'You are an heiress, Mistress Clare, and, as I said earlier in the hall at Westminster, it would be my pleasure and duty to find you a suitable husband. Your services to me have been invaluable; I assure you I will do my very best for you. There are several highly eligible bachelors amongst my entourage who would be delighted to be considered as suitors.'

She could find no words to answer him, found it impossible to frame them. Her chest was tight with repressed fury, so much so that she almost choked on it. She dared not utter one single word, even if she could have found breath to do so.

She heard the Duchess speaking as if from a great distance. There was a rushing in her ears like the sound of the sea within the confines of a shell.

'My dear, I am sure it was very proper for Robert to realise now that you should not be held to such a hasty arrangement. Now we are at peace, and God forefend we should live again through such times of fear and confusion, you should have more time to consider what you wish to do. No one will compel you, I assure you. My son the King wished to tell you of this within my presence so that I might reassure you of that.

'It would seem best if you remain in my service and under my protection here at Baynards until we hear confirmation of the dispensation from Rome. Meanwhile, you will have leisure to look around the Court and consider possible suitors.'

Clare rose and dipped into a deep curtsy. The King grinned at her indulgently. 'I'm sure my lady mother will excuse you service over the next few days. Take your time to adjust to your new sense of freedom. I will arrange for suitable funds to be placed at your disposal so that you will be denied nothing here at Court to make yourself thoroughly presentable. The Lords Richard and George will be glad that you will be staying longer with us, I know.'

She was being courteously dismissed, she understood. She swallowed what appeared to be a great lump in her throat, murmured some almost incomprehensible words of gratitude for the marks of the King's favour and moved out of the chamber.

She stood outside the door with her back to it, thankful no other person was present in the corridor, her back hard pressed to the sturdy oak of its panels, her knuckles thrust tight against her mouth to prevent herself from crying out in grief and impotent fury.

How long she stood there, she could not, afterwards, have said, but the sound of approaching footsteps warned her of possible discovery and she thrust herself up, rigidly stiffening her spine to force her unwilling limbs to obey her and began to move slowly, painfully, like an old woman, towards her own dormitory.

To her immense relief she found only Margery still present, occupying herself with the heap of garments spread across the truckle bed where Clare slept. She turned, her eyebrows raised, to hear what she expected, the news of their impending departure and was shocked and horrified by the picture Clare presented, her face pale as death, her mouth hard drawn in a silent cry of anguish.

Instantly she drew her young mistress down upon the bed. 'Oh, my dear, what is it? You have not been told ill news? Nothing has happened to Master Rob?'

At the mention of that name Clare dissolved at last into a storm of relief-giving tears. Margery held her close and rocked her against her angular form. Margery's childless state constantly demanded that she give maternal love and she had grown increasingly fond of her mistress. Hardships and dangers had strengthened the bond between them. She did not press Clare to divulge the source of her terrible unhappiness but simply remained, holding her very close.

At last Clare checked and stared upwards, pushing Margery gently but firmly away. There was a glassy light in those usually warm grey eyes and Margery knew she had sustained a hard shock. She had known too many cruel knocks in her own life not to understand now. She simply waited impassively to be informed of what was so dreadfully wrong.

Clare drew a hard breath. Still her chest seemed tight and every breath was painful. 'Sir Robert has decided to hold no opposition to my seeking a dispensation from our betrothal,' she said at last. 'It would seem that he no longer wishes to wed me. He will go north soon, I think, and you will wish to go with him. I am to remain here at Baynards, a ward of Court, until—until the King makes his wishes known concerning my marriage.'

Margery gave a great indignant snort. Clare was never to know if that was to indicate anger against Robert for repudiating Clare or anger against the King whom she thought responsible for this hurried change of plan for, at that moment, Lord Richard rushed impetuously into the dormitory.

'Mistress Clare, Thomas, my mother's page, told me I would find you here and. . .'

He stopped instantly, sensing, by Clare's rigidity of pose and drawn expression, that something was very wrong.

'Margery,' he said quickly and Clare recognised the slightly haughty tone which he sometimes used when faced with some problem and one which brooked no argument, 'George is in the tilt yard riding at the quintain. I'm sure he would love you to see how good he is.'

Margery turned hurriedly towards Clare, not wishing to leave her, but Clare slowly shook her head. Margery frowned at the imperious young lord who was standing impatiently near the door waiting for her to leave, then she shrugged helplessly and hastened out, ruffling his dark hair as she passed as a sign that she did not acknowledge entirely his commanding manner. At any other time Clare would have felt the inclination to laugh. She faced Lord Richard, striving to regain her composure.

'Why, my lord,' she questioned lightly, 'are you not with Lord George? I thought you were very anxious to practise your skill at arms.'

He ignored her attempt to evade answering any direct question he might pose and firmly latched the dormitory door and came towards her. How very regal he appeared at these moments, she thought, almost more authoritative than his elder brother, the King.

'What is the matter, Clare?' he said soberly. 'I can see that you have been crying. Has my brother the King said something to upset you? I'm sure he would not mean to do so.'

'No, no, ' she said hastily. 'The King has been very kind.'

'Then who has hurt you? Robert?' It was very direct and she gave a little gasp.

'Not exactly,' she said as evenly as she could. 'Sir Robert has informed the King that he no longer wishes to marry me. I was taken by surprise. That is all.'

'Not marry you?' His high tone revealed that he was quite scandalised. 'But you are betrothed, bound by Holy Church vows.'

'Yes,' she agreed, 'but the King will apply for a dispensation and then—then I shall be free to marry someone of the King's choosing and. . .'

'But, Clare, you love Robert.'

She turned from him, tears beginning to fall again. 'Yes, my lord,' she said brokenly, 'but it seems he does not wish to marry me and—and he must have his freedom if that is what he wants.'

'I don't understand. I know you love him. I saw it in the alley when you were ready to die—and—and many other times. Will you let him go like that?'

She turned and, kneeling before him, took him gently by the shoulders, looking earnestly up into his face.

'My Lord Richard, you must never tell him that I love him. Promise me that you will not.'

He frowned and she saw that he was bewildered. 'But you do not wish to marry someone else, however noble, do you?'

She shook her head, tears sparking on her lashes. 'No,' she whispered.

Again he murmured, 'I do not understand. You were betrothed and I thought. . .'

She gave a little gulp. 'There were reasons, my lord, reasons which no longer apply. I have to accept that Robert does not love me.'

His young features assumed a mulish expression. His lips tightened. 'I cannot believe that. You love him and. . .'

'When you are older, Lord Dickon, you will realise that we cannot help it if the one we love fails to return that love. You would not wish Sir Robert to be unhappy, would you?'

'I love you both,' he said in a more childish rush of candour, 'and I want you to be happy together.'

Her lips were trembling as she forced a smile. 'We shall both find happiness, you will see, and so will you, now that your brother is safe on the throne. I shall be quite safe. The King's Grace will see to that. You must not be unhappy because—because I am—just at this moment.'

He stood regarding her gravely, still frowning, then he gave a little nod.

'I think you want me to leave you alone.'

'Yes,' she said shakily, 'if you will, just—just for a little while.'

She stood up, releasing her hold on his thin shoulders.

His lips tightened again and he gave her his little formal bow then turned and went to the door.

'Lord Dickon?'

He turned to face her.

'You will remember your promise?'

His face was shadowed with doubt then, again, he gave a little nod and unlatched the door and left her.

Richard knew he would find little peace in the apartment he shared with his brother, nor in the tilt yard. He needed to think. He sought refuge in his mother's private chapel where he spent some time before the altar in private prayer. Later, the King found him, sitting disconsolately on the step outside, his chin cupped in his hands, elbows resting upon his raised knees.

'Dickon?'

He looked up instantly at the sound of the well-loved voice.

'What is it? Why aren't you in the tilt yard? You aren't concerned for your pony, are you? I told you I would see to it that the Lord Marshall would have another mount and you could have yours back.'

Richard shook his head and King Edward sank down on the step beside him.

'Has Mother scolded you?'

'No, Ned.'

'Have you quarrelled with George?'

'No.' Richard kicked at a small stone with his foot. 'I am not in trouble, Ned, I was just—considering.'

The King laughed. 'It must be important enough to affect the state of the realm, the way it is preying on your mind. Can I help?'

Richard pursed his lips doubtfully. 'Ned, it is not honourable or knightly to break a promise, is it?'

The King's amusement faded as he realised his young

brother must not be laughed at. This matter was too important to him.

'You made a promise to someone and now wish to break it? Is that it? There must be a very special reason.'

Richard sighed. 'I promised—this person—that I would not tell a secret entrusted to me—to another—person.'

'I see.' The King considered. 'And you think you should—break this promise?'

'I don't know what is right,' he said unhappily, 'but—if I keep the promise—then—the first person is going to go on being unhappy—and—I don't want that and I think—well, I think I do—that if the second person knows—he will, well, behave differently.'

'Is this first person a woman?'

Richard gave a little birdlike nod. He avoided his brother's eye.

'And you are deeply fond of this person?'

Again there was a little nod accompanied by a troubled expression.

The King drew a breath. 'Sometimes, Dickon,' he said very softly, 'if you are in a position of power you have to consider carefully, for the good of the realm, that is, if it is proper—and necessary—to break a knightly oath, if you truly think that broken oath justifies the need, for the good of all parties, not just for your own happiness, of course.'

The dark eyes of the boy looked gravely up into his brother's blue ones.

'So,' the King said slowly, 'you have to decide if it is more necessary—for the good of both parties, that you break your word to one. Do you understand?'

There was a little pause and then came another nod.

'Have I been of help?'

That glorious smile, so rarely seen on that narrow,

over-thoughtful young face, flashed out suddenly and Richard scrambled up. 'Will you excuse me, your grace?'

'Of course.'

The King watched good-humouredly as his younger brother dashed off towards the courtyard.

Clare sat dejectedly upon her bed in the dormitory. Margery had not returned and she wished, profoundly, she had not had to worry young Lord Richard with her tale of unhappiness. It had been most unfortunate that he had seen her so distressed. Everything was going well for all of them now—the King seemingly firmly established upon his throne, Robert in favour. More than likely the King would reward him well for his part in the care of the young lords and his support at Towton.

Wretchedly she reviewed her own situation. Many women in her position would have considered themselves fortunate to have the sovereign occupy himself, especially at this time, when he was busied most about State affairs, in promising to find her a husband. From her point of view it was disastrous. She wanted Robert Devane and would go to her grave loving him.

The door was unceremoniously jerked open. Clare turned instantly, thinking Margery had returned, yet even Margery did not enter a room in so presumptuous a fashion.

Robert Devane stood with his back to the door facing her. His breath was coming raggedly as if he had taken the stairs at a run.

She stared at him for some moments, speechless, as if she could not believe he would have the effrontery to present himself. Then she rose and advanced upon him in a sudden fury.

'How dare you break in upon me and without my

maid present? Go away. We have nothing to say to each other.'

He put up a hand as if to deflect a blow, but before he could give her a reason for entering her chamber without knocking or sending a page to announce himself, she faced him squarely, grey eyes blazing, bright colour mounting to her olive-tinted cheeks, her breast rising and falling in the heat of her blinding anger.

'I understand,' she said cuttingly, 'that now you have abducted me, abused me, compromised me, you have decided that I am no longer of use to you. The King will find you richer pickings and a bride more beautiful and accomplished than I. You are now *Sir* Robert Devane and doubtless will be provided with the funds needed to restore your manor. I thought you would, at least, have had the courage, *Sir* Robert Devane, to have the courtesy to tell me to my face why you choose to repudiate me, but I suppose it is all a part of your usual high-handed treatment of women: use them and discard them. I am simply the last of a long line.'

She paused to take breath and he stepped forward and seized one arm she held rigidly to her side to prevent herself from striking him across his handsome face.

'Whoa, whoa,' he said loudly, loud enough to stop her in her tracks, 'just hold this a moment. I have had to endure a great deal of abuse of this kind from young Lord Richard and stand, if you please, and take it, without responding, and all that from an eight-year-old boy. I will not hear it all from you again, mistress, and without giving me opportunity to defend myself.'

She cast him a contemptuous look. 'What defence have you, sir? Do you deny that you have used me abominably?'

'No, I cannot,' he protested, 'but. . .'

'You have ruined me and now wish to abandon me. I know I have no beauty nor the grace and charm of an accomplished Court lady but. . .'

He threw back his handsome head and laughed. 'What in the name of all the Saints are you talking about? Beauty? Grace? Charms? Clare Hoyland, there is no high-born lady in all this Court who is a match for you. Don't you think King Edward himself is aware of that? And, I assure you, he has an eye for pretty women, he is an expert in the lists of love. Didn't I see him with my own eyes, at the Coronation feast, admiring you, ogling you almost? If his mother's eagle gaze had not been upon him he would have declared himself readily enough, I wager.'

She tried to draw back from him, her lips trembling. 'I do not understand. . .?'

'Understand? You don't understand that Reyner Astley can hardly control himself in your presence, to say nothing of Piers Martine, who is hopelessly besotted with you. I know it and pity him, but cannot help it.'

'But you are not,' she said bitterly.

'I?' His lips twisted wryly. 'I love you with every beat of my heart, every breath I take; every thought I have from waking to sleeping is of you.'

She drew a hard breath, tears beginning to form on her lovely eyelashes. 'Love me?' she whispered brokenly. 'You say you love me — then why. . .'

'Why?' He took her two hands within his own. 'Because I know I'm not worthy, my beautiful, brave, wonderful Clare. I have not a quarter of your fortune and, despite your avowal concerning the King's favour, I am never likely to have. I cannot match you. The King could find you a nobleman — an earl, perhaps? Can I deny you such a fine future by holding you to a promise I forced you to make, aye, most dishonourably, by threatening you with rape? You needed your freedom, my Clare, to wed with one who can give you a future fit for you.

'It breaks my heart, but I have no right to constrain you. I was wrong to blame you for the harm your uncle and brother did to me and mine. That was never your fault. When I saw you that first time on the road to Coventry I abused you, I confess it. The revenge I sought from your uncle I took out on you. It was unknightly and I am now seeking to undo that wrong by freeing you. The King will do well by you, even if only because he will gain by arranging an advantageous marriage for you. He will allow no hint of scandal to sully your name.'

She was weeping freely now and he caught her close in his arms.

'Do not weep, my Clare; it fair breaks my heart. Tell me you forgive me and that we can part friends.'

In a sudden rage she beat impotent fists at his muscular chest.

'You fool,' she snapped. 'Idiot. Do you think I wish us to part friends? Do you think I wish us to part at all? I want *you*, Robert Devane, not some fine Court fop of the King's choosing. Did Lord Richard not tell you I had confessed to him that I love you, you great oaf, and will till I die?'

He gently stood her at arm's length, bending to stare intently into her tear-filled eyes.

'You would wed with me, freely, of your own will?'

'I thought—thought,' she said brokenly, 'that you wished to discard me for a more beautiful. . .'

'Do not start that again,' he said, bewildered. 'Whoever convinced you that you were plain must have been half-blind at the very least and half-witted not to recognise your other qualities. I adore you, my sweet, have done from the moment on the carrack, aye, even before that. How many other women would have partnered me so bravely through these hard months? And when I saw you in dire peril in that alley...' His blue eyes narrowed and flashed with such a steely glint that she caught her breath at the wealth of menace in them for those who had dared to threaten harm to her.

He drew her close again and cupped her chin in his two hands. 'Are you sure? Do you wish to spend your days in humble retirement from Court managing our two manors in Leicestershire? You could have so much more, my darling.'

'Kiss me,' she demanded, 'properly, oh, Robert, kiss me, as I want to be kissed, as your betrothed wife has a right to be kissed.'

He pulled her into his arms, hoarsely murmuring words of endearment. His kiss was hungry, demanding, dominating, and she revelled in it, opening her lips to receive his, her arms, hungry as his own, reaching up and pulling his head nearer and nearer to her. She had removed her hennin after Lord Richard had left her, since her head was paining her—the result of all those tears—and her luxuriant hair fell in a glory of chestnut brown about him.

He could smell the scent of lavender and rosemary in the water she had recently washed it in and the sweet cleanliness of it almost maddened his senses. He had expected her to be afraid and, after the first desperate embrace, began to temper his passion so as to reassure her, but she clung to him wildly and he realised, at last, the depth of her need for him. His eager hands fumbled against the firm hard breasts, straining the silk of her gown and she gave a little moan of desire.

He whispered against her ear, 'Even now the King may be making plans for your marriage. You are my betrothed. It would be no sin. Will you let me bed you, so no one will ever be able to part us?'

She lifted her flushed face to his, her eyes shining with longing.

'Please, yes, very soon, my love?'

'Now?' His lips were nuzzling her hair.

'Here?' Her eyes widened in desire, tempered with doubt. 'If Margery should come?'

He chuckled. 'If she does she will have more sense than to insist on entering.'

'But someone else might come. I—share this place...' Her voice trailed off breathlessly as he left her for a moment and hastily locked the door. 'Robert!' It was a little cry of half-amused alarm.

He came back to her, laughing. 'My heart, ladies in waiting do this sort of thing all the time and their companions are discreet. Do you know nothing of Court life?'

She was laughing back at him, totally unafraid, and he swept her up, after first demanding to know which was her bed, and carried her to it.

'Sit up, my love, while I struggle with the lacings of this gown. I must be tiring-maid this afternoon.'

Afterwards she could not imagine how she could have been so wanton or reckless of her reputation. She only knew that she wanted Robert Devane more than anything in life and wanted him now, at this moment, before anything could part them. She found herself laughing delightedly as the two of them struggled with refractory hooks and laces on garments until finally she lay in his arms on the narrow truckle bed and he leaned down to stare at her beauty.

She was all that he had believed; a tall, slim, finely boned young body, buttocks and breasts rounding with a promise of maturing womanhood. The June sunlight streamed through the dormer window and tinted her silky skin golden. Her hair tumbled about her and, as if understanding suddenly what they were about, she tried to cover her naked breasts, rosy-tipped and hardened with desire. He bent his head and gently removed her hands, kissing the nipples so that she cried out in sudden excited delight.

'I will not hurt you, my sweet,' he assured her gently, 'at least as little as possible. I shall wait until you are ready for me. Do not be afraid.'

Surprisingly she was not afraid, even when she felt the weight of his hard, soldier's body full upon her.

He was an experienced lover and wooed her with skill so that she thought she would faint with eagerness for the consummation. When he entered her, she cried out once and he covered her lips with his own. Her body arched to meet his and he heard her give the faintest little cries of fulfilment. She had longed for him so long.

She had never doubted for one moment how it would be for her and was not disappointed. There was momentary pain certainly, but the ecstasy which followed made up for that a hundredfold. She wanted him to possess her utterly, fill her to the very brim of her being with total joy. She gloried in his loving and did not even fear they would be interrupted. She was beyond caring. She rose with him to the heights of passion, so that her very world seemed to tilt and seem remote from her. As if from a distance she heard her own voice murmur his name over and over, 'Robert, Robert.'

He laid her back on the truckle bed at last, leaning over her, on his two arms, spent and smiling, one eyebrow raised as if to hear her assess his own skill.

She shook back her hair and for the first time looked enquiringly towards the door.

He chuckled, deep in his throat, 'It is far too late to

concern yourself about your reputation now, my sweet. You are mine and not the King, nor the Pope nor the devil himself can part us.'

Her lips were trembling as she shakily whispered, 'I pray that is so, but, oh, Robert what have we done? If we have angered the King. . .'

He stood up and reached for the linen sheet to cover her naked loveliness.

'We are betrothed. No one has the right to censor us, but, as you say, we may well find ourself under royal displeasure.'

Clutching the sheet to her chin, she said fearfully, 'You could be in danger.'

'I think not, but it might be wise to take precautions. I think flight might be the best policy.'

'Today?' she mouthed the word doubtfully.

He nodded. 'Aye, today. I have already received permission to withdraw from Court attendance but the Duchess could be annoyed, if not downright angered, should you absent yourself without being formally excused. Are you willing to take that risk?'

'Yes, oh, yes. Where shall we go?'

'To our own estates, to Hoyland Manor, since it is in better shape than my house.'

'Shall we be safe there?'

He frowned slightly as he bent to pick up his discarded hose. 'Edward will understand. He *should* do. He is not unfamiliar with the needs of love. Naturally I shall leave a message informing him of our desire to forgo a dispensation after all and petitioning him to accept our hasty marriage. I shall find us a priest without delay.' He was dressing hurriedly and his lips curved into a smile again as he turned to face her. 'If I find myself a recipient of royal rage I shall call on Lord Richard to defend me.'

She gave a little crow of laughter. 'He is, indeed, the one who brought us together at last.'

'Aye, the little blind son of the goddess of love. What was he called?'

'Cupid,' she answered, reaching up to trace the line of his jaw.

'And an interfering young god,' he muttered drily. 'I'll find Margery and send her to you. Then I'll go to the stable and order the grooms to prepare your mount. Mine is already in the courtyard. Piers will ride with us and the Fletchers and Silas, if I can find them quickly enough; if not, they must follow at their own speed. I'll leave my petition with Reyner who will deliver it to the King and make your humble excuses to the Duchess.'

He bent and delivered a little slap upon her rump. 'Rouse yourself, my lovely, and find more suitable riding apparel. I'll not suffer any delay. Remember I have the right to chastise a slothful wife, now she is mine.'

She reached up her arms for a tender embrace before, having completed dressing, he unlocked the dormitory door and prepared to leave her.

She lay back on the narrow cot, luxuriously stretching as he put his head round the door. 'I shall be ready for you in an hour. Come with Margery to the gatehouse. Do not delay to gather all your gowns. We'll buy more sober and practical ones for country living in Leicester.'

Clare was emerging from the dairy after supervising the girls there when she saw Robert coming towards her across the courtyard. Her pleasant mood was suddenly shadowed as she glimpsed his set expression.

It was getting to be late in October and all around them she could hear sounds of the frenzied activities the autumn demanded. The late slaughter was finished and the salting down of carcasses in progress, as well as the gathering-in of sufficient wood for the long winter months ahead. Hoyland was well prepared. She was satisfied and the thatchers and builders were still at work on the Devane Manor, making sure the house would be protected from winds and winter rains and snow.

There had been so much to do there. The place had been thoroughly gutted and Robert's depleted household had only been able to begin the work, short of ready gold as they had been, and, until now, bereft of the orders of their master. Clare herself had supervised the making of candles and rushlights and the last-minute repairs to arras and tapestries to keep them snug from winter drafts.

They had been married at Reyner Astley's manor near St Albans by the same priest who had betrothed her to Robert so unwillingly only five short months before. Reyner Astley had insisted upon accompanying them and standing witness to the ceremony before himself presenting proof to King Edward of what was now a *fait accompli*. Clare had protested that Reyner himself might be involved in what could be termed their disobedience but he had laughed it off and declared they needed an irrefutable witness so there could be no doubt in the King's mind.

So Clare had stood there in the hall before a hastily constructed altar, still in her riding dress, with only Margery to attend her and Silas Whitcome and the Fletchers, scrubbed and looking delighted, but embarrassed, behind. Reyner Astley had conducted her into the hall and given her to her husband and Piers Martine had stood beside Robert, a saturnine, unsmiling groomsman. Afterwards he had kissed Clare soundly and wished her all happiness, and seemed sincere enough, though she had glimpsed a trace of sadness in his fierce dark eyes and a line of suffering round the mobile mouth.

She had lain in Robert's arms in a state of blissful contentment in the number of small inns along the way where Robert had demanded, and got, a private chamber for them.

Margery, for once quite garrulous, had declared herself overjoyed, and only once or twice upon the journey had Clare found her maid in tears and knew she had been sorely missing her two young lordling charges.

There had been no censure from Westminster and Reyner's couriers had brought only news of Court activities and hearty wishes for Robert's continued happiness with his young bride. Clare had thought she could never have experienced such fulfilment. Robert had shown himself a demanding but competent lord of the manor and though both her men and his had grumbled secretly at the amount of work he had insisted must be completed before winter, they had seen the need and worked with a will.

Now, as Robert came towards her frowning, and she saw he was holding a slip of parchment in his hand, her heart contracted.

He nodded. 'A courier has just arrived from Westminster. This missive commands our presence at Court for the feast of All Hallows.'

Clare paled and caught at his hand. 'Must we go?'

'It is the King's express command—and he has insisted upon your presence too. I would have preferred to leave you safe here, just in case. . .'

'But it has been almost four months. Surely King Edward cannot hold a grudge for so long.'

Robert raised one eybrow doubtfully. 'I don't know about that but there is no possibility of an annulment.'

His lips curved into a wry smile. 'We have made very sure of that.'

She gave a nervous answering smile. That was certainly true. She was Robert's wife indeed and no papal pronouncement could change that and yet—there was one decisive way—the King could make her a widow.

She reached up to kiss Robert's cheek. 'At least all is well in hand now and—I am going with you.'

'I wish I could defy Edward in that.'

She shook her head decisively. 'I am going with you and will remain by your side—whatever the King has in store for us.'

The weather throughout the journey south turned appallingly bad. It rained almost continually and the fierce wind pierced through them. Mud bogged them down and it was late on All Hallows' Eve when the little party arrived at Westminster Palace and was conducted to an apartment prepared for them.

Clare was disappointed that it was too dark for her to see properly the famed palace as they were hurried along through courtyards and down innumerable corridors, following servants lighting their way with flaming brands, but she got the impression that the place was a warren of interconnecting buildings and less impressive than she imagined, certainly less intimidating than the fortress of Baynards.

Servants provided them with food, cold but palatable, and Margery, who had grumbled constantly throughout what she had termed the interminable journey, was mollified to find sheets well aired and even warmed bricks placed in the beds. She had watched Clare like a dragon during the early months of the marriage, looking for signs of pregnancy.

Clare, smiling faintly tonight, as Margery helped her

to undress, rather thought that soon her vigilance would be rewarded. She had not told Robert yet. She was not sure, and he might have forbidden her to make this journey had he dreamt she might be carrying his child. Nothing, she decided, was going to part her from her love, especially at this time, when they both secretly feared the King's displeasure.

'Well,' Robert murmured, after Margery had undressed her mistress and retired to the small room adjoining, where a truckle had been provided for her, 'at least we were expected and suitably provided for. When you are better acquainted with courts, my love, you will find accommodation for courtiers, even the noblest in the land, is often very cramped and far less commodious than these quarters.'

Clare agreed with him, hoping this sign intimated that they had not been summoned for due punishment at the King's hand, but she clung to him fearfully throughout the night and slept little.

They were summoned very early to the King's chamber of presence, so early that Clare had had no time to attend early mass on this special Holy day of All Saints, and doubted the King had been able to attend either. He bustled cheerfully into the chamber only moments after she and Robert had been conducted into the antechamber and called for them to be brought to him.

Edward looked as he had done on the day of his Coronation, alert, cheerful and flushed with his delight at his elevation to the throne. His expression revealed no hint of petulance, let alone anger.

Clare sank into a deep curtsy. Both she and Robert had attired themselves fittingly for their appearance before their sovereign, Clare in amber-coloured cut velvet and Robert in his finest fashionable doublet of padded blue silk. Robert had dropped to one knee but the King bade them both to rise and come to his chair.

He rose and bent to kiss Clare's hand and then soundly kissed her upon both cheeks. 'I am delighted to see you again, Lady Devane. Robert, you are a lucky dog. I can see for myself that both of you have no regrets for your decision to go ahead with your marriage.'

For once Robert appeared somewhat tongue-tied. 'Your Grace,' he said at last, 'it seemed that — we found we could not bear to part and. . .'

The King laughed delightedly. 'No need for explanations. Your offer to free the lady was indeed admirable and honourable, but I have it on the finest authority that both of you were too proud to confess that you loved each other. Now you have discovered it, I can only congratulate you on your decision.' His blue eyes twinkled. 'I hope I may be able to congratulate you on the birth of an heir in the very near future, eh, my lady?'

Clare blushed hotly and could only nod in reply.

'Well, I imagine you are puzzled as to why I summoned you to travel at such an untimely month of the year, for I conclude you had an uncomfortable journey. You can blame my young cub of a brother. He has pleaded, nay, demanded, you be present at his investiture.'

Clare gave a little gasp and the King smiled more broadly. 'Today I shall invest Richard with the Dukedom of Gloucester. You probably know George was made Duke of Clarence some months past, but I thought it advisable for Richard to wait until he had celebrated his ninth birthday, which he did on October the second, and this Holy day seemed most fitting for the occasion.'

Clare cried impulsively, 'Oh, your grace, this is so

great a pleasure and honour. I have great affection for
Lord Richard.'

'And he for you, as I have especial gratitude for you,
Sir Robert.' The King reached behind him and took up
a scroll of parchment which lay on a table close at hand.
'You left in so great a hurry you gave me no opportunity
to fittingly reward you for your services in Burgundy
and at Towton.'

'Your Grace honoured me with knighthood on that
field. . .'

'That, man, was your natural desert. This is to show
my personal appreciation. It is the gift of a small manor
not ten miles from your own on the border of
Northamptonshire. The late tenant was killed at Towton
and had no heir. Gladly I gift it to you, Robert, and may
it go some way to compensate you for your other
troubles.'

Robert knelt gracefully and took the scroll from the
King. Again Clare saw that he was so overcome he had
difficulty in finding words to express his gratitude.

'Sir Robert, I have one final favour to ask of you.'

'Your Grace?'

'There has been some signs of discontent on the
Northern Border and I have appointed my cousin of
Warwick, with his brother, Montagu, and the Dukes of
Clarence and Gloucester, to call out the Northern levies
on my behalf. George will remain here in London. He is
too young to do more than add his title to the commission, and I intend sending Richard north to my cousin's
stronghold of Middleham in Wensleydale to begin his
training at arms. I would be grateful if you would
accompany his escort and see him safely there. Warwick
will have more than enough on his hands to be able to
give full attention to a nine-year-old boy, but I know

Richard would appreciate your guardianship on the journey.'

'May I accompany my husband, your grace? I shall find great pleasure in being with Lord Richard again.'

'As he will be in your company, Lady Devane. He never ceases to speak of your time together in Burgundy.'

Later that day Clare sat with Robert in the great hall and watched as the King solemnly placed the cap of estate upon his younger brother's head and pronounced him Duke of Gloucester. Her heart swelled with maternal pride as great as that of his mother, the Duchess of York, who sat there in state. How small Richard looked in his ducal robes, trimmed with ermine, and how proudly and bravely he spoke his words of fealty as he placed his two hands between those of his brother the King and made his oath of allegiance.

On the journey north, several days later, Richard sat his pony with expert skill as he rode beside her.

He cast her one anxious glance when they were, for the moment, out of earshot of the other members of the escort.

'You are truly happy, Clare?'

'Your Grace, Robert and I are blissfully happy, but when we rode south we were afraid we had angered the King.'

He looked puzzled. 'Why?'

'Because Robert had requested a dispensation and I feared the King might already have made grander plans for my marriage to someone else.'

'But I know he was aware of how much you loved each other.'

'You told him, Lord Richard?'

He looked suitably chastened. 'Oh no, that is—I think he guessed when he saw how worried I was about...' He was silent for a moment then he said, 'I—I broke my knightly oath to you, Clare. I told Robert that you loved him. Did I do wrong?'

She turned her head and he saw the glory of her happiness shine in her eyes. 'Oh, Lord Richard, if you had not done so, I might never have experienced such delight as Robert and I find in each other. I'm sure you will be forgiven for the breaking of that oath. I shall pray always that you will be—and for your happiness and future prosperity, my lord of Gloucester.'

He smiled at her sunnily. 'Then I am content. I have chosen a white boar as my personal device, for the first letters of the Latin name for York, Eboracum. Don't you think that appropriate? And my motto will be 'Loyalty Binds Me', for I shall serve my brother, Ned, loyally, for ever.'

'Boar,' she repeated the word and the letters thoughtfully. 'That is an excellent choice. Your father would be proud of you.'

He gave a little boyish laugh. 'When I was little, my nurse told me tales of a magical white boar which came to help the people in a stricken village in Yorkshire. She came from the north with my mother. I loved those stories, so that was another reason why I chose the boar when the heralds asked me to decide.'

Clare told Robert that night as they stayed in a priory near Nottingham of Richard's choice. 'And he was concerned that he broke his promise to me. Oh, Robert, how should we have lived, if he had not done so? I told him he was bound to be forgiven.'

Robert took her in his arms and kissed her gently.

'Margery is a little worried that this journey is tiring you. There is no special reason for her concern, is there?'

Clare sighed. 'I didn't want to tell you yet—till we are sure. . .'

'A child?' His face was radiant.

'I think so. Margery is very careful of my health just now.'

'Surely it was unwise for you to come on this long journey?'

'Margery says there is no danger yet and the weather has improved so I am enjoying the air and the freedom from all the responsibilities of work on the manor. Your new holdings will be so great a help to our prospects. The King has been truly generous. Do you think Richard helped to persuade him?'

Robert grinned. 'More than likely. He is determined to control our lives.' He flung back his head and laughed outright. 'I wonder if he will be as haughty and prickly as we know he can be, at Middleham?'

'Oh, I am sure he will behave. He is so anxious to begin his knightly training.'

'Are you? I am not.' Robert was still chuckling. 'He will meet his match in Jehan Treves, who trains the donzels. Duke of Gloucester, or no, Richard will earn a box on the ears for his pains if he disobeys instructions or tries to order his companions.'

Clare's first sight of Middleham Castle, set in the beautiful Wensleydale, was coloured by Robert's affection for it. Its stolid grey walls gave the same impression of serene security that Baynards had. She loved the small town with its market place and cobbled streets as they entered the castle through the gatehouse, and she saw Richard gazing about him with some curiosity and delight. Here he would achieve his ambition of becoming a famed soldier like his brother, Ned.

They dismounted in the courtyard and, from the steps leading down from the keep, the Countess of Warwick came with her two small daughters, Isabel and Anne. She advanced to the small boy who was to be her charge and kissed him soundly.

'Welcome to Middleham, my lord of Gloucester, or shall I call you Dickon, for I hope I may, cousin?'

He received her kiss, his cheeks glowing with the exhilaration of the ride and his pleasure at the warmth of his welcome.

'My lady, of course I shall want you to call me Dickon.'

He looked round, taking in the stately keep and gatehouse, the chapel with its fine glazed windows, and the cluster of outbuildings, kitchens, dairies, buttery.

'I know I shall be happy here.'

The two little Warwick heiresses had stopped a little behind their mother, shyly. The younger must be scarce more than six, Clare thought.

Suddenly a hound puppy raced across the courtyard, barking furiously, and the younger child, Anne, tried to stop it tearing excitedly towards their newly arrived guest too roughly. The puppy impetuously dashed across her path and she stumbled and fell.

Instantly Richard ran towards her and helped her to her feet, asking anxiously if she had hurt herself badly.

The little girl smiled up at him trustingly, shook her golden brown head and came, hand in hand with him, back to her mother.

Robert looked sardonically across at his young lord and whispered to Clare, 'I wonder if, now that he appears to have found a lady of his own, he will stop interfering in my affairs?'

Clare put her hand in his and lifted her face to her husband as Anne had done to Richard.

'If he finds a love as great as ours, he will be fortunate indeed, my heart,' she said.

$\mathcal{H}istorical$ $\mathcal{R}omance$™

Coming next month

THE KNIGHT, THE KNAVE AND THE LADY
Juliet Landon

NORTH YORKSHIRE, 1350s

Marietta Wardle *never* wanted to get married—but her stance proved no hindrance to the desires of Lord Alain of Thorsgeld! He wanted her and had no scruples about compromising her into marriage. Their nights were ecstatic, and Thorsgeld Castle provided her with plenty of work. Marietta began to love her role, and her husband, until she realised that she was playing second best to his dead wife—a position that would lead her into danger…

A HIGHLY IRREGULAR FOOTMAN
Sarah Westleigh

KENT/LONDON 1803

Jack Hamilton was the new footman at Stonar Hall, and housekeeper Thalia Marsh could sense that he was trouble! He was so charming, smooth and friendly, spoke a little too well and liked to take charge—even though she was his superior! He was surely no footman and Thalia was determined to discover his true identity even if this risked the exposure of *her* darkest secrets. But Thalia soon succumbed to his charms—and fell in love! But *who* had Thalia fallen in love with—the footman
…or someone else?

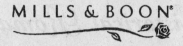

FREE!

FOUR FREE
specially selected
Historical Romance™ novels
PLUS a Mystery Gift
when you return this card...

Return this coupon and we'll send you 4 Historical Romance novels and a mystery gift absolutely FREE! We'll even pay the postage and packing for you.

We're making you this offer to introduce you to the benefits of the Reader Service™– FREE home delivery of brand-new Historical Romance novels, at least a month before they are available in the shops, FREE gifts and a monthly Newsletter packed with information.

Accepting these FREE books and gift places you under no obligation to buy, you may cancel at any time, even after receiving just your free shipment. Simply complete the coupon below and send it to:

MILLS & BOON READER SERVICE, FREEPOST, CROYDON, SURREY, CR9 3WZ.

No stamp needed

Yes, please send me 4 free Historical Romance novels and a mystery gift. I understand that unless you hear from me, I will receive 4 superb new titles every month for just £2.99* each, postage and packing free. I am under no obligation to purchase any books and I may cancel or suspend my subscription at any time, but the free books and gift will be mine to keep in any case. (I am over 18 years of age)

H7XE

Ms/Mrs/Miss/Mr _____

Address _____

_____

_____ Postcode _____